Sif grinned as she closed th
between her and her quarry. Whatever the mountain giants thought they would accomplish here today, there was nothing in their future but ignominious death. Tightening her fingers around her sword hilt she leaped, high and far, shield up and sword out. The giant had seen her coming, and despite being almost four times Sif's size, he was quick.

The club he swung with deadly precision was the trunk of a young tree. It hummed horizontally through the air, but Sif's timing was impeccable. She hit the giant's chest an instant before the club carved through the air where she'd been. She let go of her shield's handle to grab onto his ragged chest armor and hacked down at the juncture of his neck and shoulder. The steel was sharper than Hela's temper, and the blade bit deep into a neck wider than Sif's torso.

ALSO AVAILABLE

Marvel Heroines

Domino: Strays by Tristan Palmgren
Rogue: Untouched by Alisa Kwitney
Elsa Bloodstone: Bequest by Cath Lauria

Legends of Asgard

The Head of Mimir by Richard Lee Byers
The Sword of Surtur by C L Werner
The Serpent and the Dead by Anna Stephens

Marvel Untold

The Harrowing of Doom by David Annandale

Xavier's Institute

Liberty & Justice for All by Carrie Harris
First Team by Robbie MacNiven
Triptych by Jaleigh Johnson

MARVEL LEGENDS OF ASGARD

The SERPENT *and the* DEAD

ANNA STEPHENS

FOR MARVEL PUBLISHING

VP Production & Special Projects: Jeff Youngquist
Associate Editor, Special Projects: Caitlin O'Connell
Manager, Licensed Publishing: Jeremy West
VP, Licensed Publishing: Sven Larsen
SVP Print, Sales & Marketing: David Gabriel
Editor in Chief: C B Cebulski

Special Thanks to Wil Moss

First published by Aconyte Books in 2021
ISBN 978 1 83908 068 5
Ebook ISBN 978 1 83908 069 2

Cover art by Massimiliano Haematinon Nigro

Distributed in North America by Simon & Schuster Inc, New York, USA
Printed in the United States of America
9 8 7 6 5 4 3 2 1

ACONYTE BOOKS

An imprint of Asmodee Entertainment Ltd

Mercury House, Shipstones Business Centre

North Gate, Nottingham NG7 7FN, UK

aconytebooks.com // twitter.com/aconytebooks

Girls (of all sorts):
be your own heroes.

ONE
LADY SIF

Lady Sif braced herself beneath the protective arc of her shield, grunting as the boulder's impact drove her back a step. Across the battlefield, the mountain giant who'd thrown it roared his fury and lumbered forward. His magic scooped a great trench in the earth and fashioned the soil into a wave that would bury the shield-maiden beneath its crushing weight.

Sif snarled and slashed her sword through the dirt wall threatening to engulf her, severing the magic. The soil collapsed back on itself, and she leaped over it and charged. There were almost a hundred mountain giants fouling the plains east of Asgardia, and Sif knew – all the warriors knew – why they'd come now: Odin was in Vanaheim, trying once more to shore up the peace with the Vanir they had fought so hard to win. In the All-Father's absence, it hadn't been so much whether an attack would come as from who, and how many.

And why.

Sif didn't concern herself with the why, at least not now. Her brother, Heimdall the Farseeing, had sent warning to Thor of the giants' arrival in Asgard, adding that they might be the vanguard of a larger invasion. Sif had begged command of the defenders, and Thor had granted it so he could remain in Asgardia and plan a counterattack against further incursions.

Sif grinned as she closed the last of the distance between her and her quarry. Boulders rained down and dirt was kicked up all around her and her three hundred warriors. Whatever the mountain giants thought they would accomplish here today, there was nothing in their future but ignominious death. Tightening her fingers around her sword hilt she leaped, high and far, shield up and sword out. The giant had seen her coming, and despite being almost four times Sif's size, he was quick. The club he swung with deadly precision was the trunk of a young tree, trimmed and polished until the bright Asgardian sun gleamed across its knotted surface. It hummed horizontally through the air, but Sif's timing was impeccable. She hit the giant's chest an instant before the club carved through the air where she'd been. She let go of her shield's handle to grab onto his ragged chest armor and hacked down at the juncture of his neck and shoulder. The steel was sharper than Hela's temper, and the blade bit deep into a neck wider than Sif's torso. She kicked free as her enemy staggered, somersaulting backwards as he made a wild grab for her.

The warriors of Asgardia's first shieldwall had quickly surrounded the mountain giants in threes, one always attacking from its blind side or from behind. Now, as Sif landed in a spray of dirt and torn grass, her friend Gyda leaped onto the giant's back, the long daggers in each of her hands ripping through leather armor. The giant arched and screeched, scrabbling over his shoulders to try and reach her. When he couldn't, he gestured, and there was an explosion of dirt from every side.

"Gyda!" Sif shouted. She was already running when the earth around her fountained upwards. On instinct, she closed her eyes and covered her face with her shield as dirt and sharp stones flew at her. The giant's club slammed into her ribs and flung her twenty yards across the battlefield. Sif's armor held and she rolled as she hit the ground.

Even from here, even over the clash and roar of battle, she heard Gyda shout her name in turn. Sif took a deep breath and felt a flare of hurt through her flank, but no bones were broken, and she was back up on her feet a heartbeat later. She raised her arm to show she was all right and heard her friend whoop even as she stabbed with her dagger again, distracting the giant once more. "We've got this one, my friend. On your right!"

Sif was blinking grit from her stinging eyes, but she didn't hesitate when Gyda yelled her warning and dodged sideways. She wasn't quite fast enough as the giant – this one female, slightly smaller in stature but no less formidable – hurled a boulder with a furious grunt.

The rock slammed into Sif's lower leg, turning her tumble into a graceless sprawl. A shout of pain burst past her teeth. The rock bounced on, mercifully not pinning her, but she would almost have preferred that, for in the next breath the giant who'd thrown it wrapped her immense hand around Sif's face and throat and lifted her bodily off the ground.

It was easy to single out Sif on the battlefield, for her to become the focal point of an enemy's attention. Her hair was blacker than a raven's wing amid a sea of golds, a banner of night that drew all eyes, all ire. When the first enemies fell to her blade, Sif could always guarantee that there would be more coming to avenge their dead kin. She welcomed it.

Now, the pressure from the giant's huge palm cut off her breath and obscured her vision as she was wrenched up into the sky. Fortunately, she didn't need to breathe or see in order to strike. Letting her shield hang by the strap around her forearm, Sif grabbed the giant's wrist and then hacked into it, feeling the edge bite deep, sword hilt jolting in her palm.

The giant's hand flexed, loosening just enough for her to suck in air, and then tightened once more. She cut again and again, kept cutting even when the giant's other hand grabbed her ankle and tried to pull her in half. Sif's hands, arms and armor were sticky with hot, viscous giant blood and her spine was beginning to stretch almost to snapping before the giant finally threw her down, howling in pain.

Sif bounced once as she struck the torn and ravaged earth, limbs and sword flailing. She rolled away as the giant fell to her knees and then toppled sideways, slamming into the ground where she'd just been. There were three spears protruding from her neck.

"My lady!" a warrior bellowed as Sif got her feet under her. "Behind!"

Sif dove forwards, over her shield and her shoulder, a

forward tumble up into a hop and a leap over the giant's body. She ripped a spear out of its neck and spun, sighting along its bloody length. The other giant she'd been fighting, with Gyda and the third warrior, was one of the last still alive on the field. Sif's initial bloom of relief – it was almost over – was replaced with horror when the giant raised a huge, armored foot and prepared to stamp it down onto something – someone – lying helpless beneath him.

Sif let the spear fly, hard and fast and true. It pierced the giant's thigh, ripping a great gash along the inside, and he wobbled, and she thought she'd done it, but then his balance steadied. He made eye contact with her, his lip curling in a cruel smile, and *stomped.*

Sif recognized the vambraces adorning the arms of the warrior as they were raised in a final, pitiful attempt at defense: it was Gyda. Gyda the shield-maiden, who had been Sif's companion through a score of battles and ten times as many feasts and celebrations. Gyda: her friend.

"*No!*" Sif shrieked, tearing another spear out of the dead giant's neck and hurling that as well. She raced after it, her feet barely touching the ripped-up earth, and then leaped high, sunlight flashing from the face of her shield and sword angled to hack beneath her enemy's chin. She was fast, and she was deadly, and now she was *angry*. The wickedly sharp tip of her sword went into soft, unprotected flesh, all her weight and fury behind it. It punched through meat and cartilage, opening his windpipe and exiting through the back of his neck.

Sif braced her feet against the massive chest and wrenched the blade sideways, seeking – and finding – the main veins and arteries. The giant crumpled, first to his knees and then to his side, his enormous heart pumping a river of blood out of his neck to soak her sleeves and run down the inside of her breastplate in a hot flood.

The shield-maiden paid it no heed. She jumped free, landing lighter than a cat, and bounded towards Gyda. A shimmer was rising from her body, and Sif slowed, a lump in her throat and tears in her eyes, waiting for the Valkyrie to shepherd her in peace to Valhalla. There were a few Choosers of the Slain dotted across the battlefield tending to the dying, but though she waited, none arrived for Gyda.

Sif drifted closer, for perhaps her injuries weren't so severe if the Valkyrior were not attending her. She heard her friend's ragged inhalation and the shimmer of light rising from her increased, and then – nothing. The light winked out and Gyda fell still.

Sif's lips parted in shock. What had just happened? Was she unconscious? Was she dead? She scanned the battlefield again, but no demi-goddess was approaching, so she ran the last few strides and flung herself on her knees at Gyda's side, fingers going to her throat, looking desperately into her face for signs of life. There was nothing.

"Gyda? Gyda, look at me. Answer me!"

She dragged Gyda's unresponsive form into her arms, into her lap, holding her tight. The warrior didn't move. Didn't breathe. Her breastplate was crushed, testament to the state of her chest within it.

"No," Sif whispered into her slack face. "No, that's not right. That can't be right. You… where are you, Gyda? *Where did you go?*"

"Lady Sif? Let us honor her now, my lady."

Sif turned wild, horrified eyes to the voice. "Brunnhilde? How could you? How could you take her before her time? She wasn't dead! She was still breathing; I saw her breathe in, and then you took her. She wasn't ready." Her voice cracked on a sob and a dangerous fury filled her. "How could you steal her away before her time?"

Brunnhilde, the leader of the Valkyrior and one of only a handful of warriors to beat Sif in combat – and then barely – squatted next to her and put a sympathetic hand on her bloody, dented armor, patting gently. "I'm sorry, Sif, but there's nothing I can do for her. I know you were close, but she's on her way to Valhalla with one of my sisters now. She was glorious in life and glorious in her death – and she'll wait for you, I'm sure."

Sif shook her hand away. "You're not listening," she insisted, her voice harsh. Brunnhilde's eyes narrowed. They'd been friends for longer than either of them cared to remember, but here, at the end of a battle, they were in Brunnhilde's domain. Sif owed her respect. She didn't care.

"She wasn't Chosen," she insisted. "None of yours came to take her, but she's gone. She was still breathing!" She could hear the desperation in her own voice, but she was grateful for it when the Valkyrie frowned and leant closer.

"Say that again. Tell me everything you saw."

The memory was both seared into Sif's mind and clouded by grief, but this was important. She took a breath to compose herself. "There was a… a shimmer over her body. I heard her breathe in, ragged and bubbling–" she stopped again to clear her throat of sobs"–and then nothing. As if she just never breathed back out. The shimmer vanished. You took her before her time. She might have… I might have been able to say goodbye." She couldn't keep the accusation from her tone.

"Put her down." The Valkyrie snapped the words, a crack of command that Sif obeyed without thought. She shifted on her knees to give them space. Brunnhilde leant over Gyda and unstrapped her breastplate with difficulty, easing it off of her shattered body. She slid one hand gently under the damaged armor onto broken flesh and bone and put her other palm on Gyda's brow. She closed her eyes, and Sif felt the tingle of magic brush across her skin.

Brunnhilde knelt there in silence for endless, torturous moments, and Sif sat in clench-fisted misery until the other woman opened her eyes and sat back. "Odin's eye," she swore. "She's gone."

"That's what I said," Sif pointed out through gritted teeth. Her gaze fell on her sword, abandoned in the mud beside her, and for one moment of utter madness she wanted nothing more than to swing at the Chooser, consequences be damned. Something of her thoughts must have shown on her face, because Brunnhilde watched her with calm intent until she took in a deep breath and packed her emotions back inside. She nodded, and the Valkyrie nodded back.

"You don't understand," she said softly. "The deathglow is here – she was dying, Sif, and nothing could have stopped it – but then she didn't actually die."

Sif stared at her, blank. "She didn't die? Then what, *where,* is she?" The shield-maiden leant forward again, ebony braids tumbling across her shoulders, and stared into Gyda's blood-spattered face. Her skin had taken on the waxy sheen of death; no breath stirred in her lungs; no recognition in her eyes. "How can… she looks…" she couldn't finish the sentence, gripped by a sudden, awful conviction that Gyda might hear her.

"I know, my friend," Brunnhilde said gently. "I don't understand what's happened here, but I promise you I'm going to find out." The Valkyrie gestured vaguely, as if she couldn't put what she knew into words. "Something was done to her, in the instant before she was fated to die. The… the soul leaves an echo of itself in a body after death. Gyda's is wrong. The shape of the echo of her soul is distorted. And more than that: Gyda's last breath is missing. The breath that the soul escapes upon as a person dies has a particular aura, a certain resonance. It's very obvious to a Valkyrie and it helps lead us to those who need shepherding to Valhalla. Gyda's breath is gone. Or, rather, she never breathed it out at all."

Sif swayed on her knees, suddenly dizzy with all that Brunnhilde had said. "So, she was dying but she's not dead. She breathed in but not out, and her soul didn't escape on that breath, correct?" The Valkyrie nodded. "Is she dead, then? Her body's dead, but her breath isn't? Her soul isn't? I don't understand."

Brunnhilde's brow was furrowed, but she reached out to brush back Gyda's bloodstained hair, her fingers gentle. The motion brought a lump to Sif's throat again, and no amount of swallowing could force it away.

"Can you wait with her?" Brunnhilde asked. "I need to go to Valhalla, and I should check in with the other Valkyrior as well. Gyda may already be there, or on her way in the company of one of my sisters. It may be that in the chaos of the battle, you didn't see what you think you saw. Just… stay with her. Please?"

Sif nodded, mute, pulling Gyda back into her arms. At any other time, she would find someone questioning her word infuriating, but now she clung desperately to the hope that she had been mistaken, that they were both mistaken. Gyda was in Valhalla already, and what she'd seen was something else. *Please, Frigga, please let me be wrong. Please.*

Grief was piling in behind the confusion and rage now, filling her up inside until it overflowed from her eyes. And under that storm, a bone-deep anxiety was building. Brunnhilde was worried. Not once in the long years since the All-Father had chosen her for this task had she failed in it. The souls of warriors who had become einherjar were honored and kept safe; it was impossible to imagine it could be any other way. Until now.

Brunnhilde had never been anything but bittersweet in the discharge of her duty, sorrowful that the warriors were dead, but joyful that she was able to escort them on to Valhalla. Seeing her now, brow creased and gnawing on her lip, filled Sif's stomach with a cold, slick writhing.

Aragorn, Brunnhilde's winged steed, picked his way delicately among the corpses of the battlefield and, after a last squeeze of Sif's hand, the Valkyrie stood and swung into the saddle. "Just hang on," she said, and didn't wait for Sif to agree. She wheeled the animal and urged him into the sky, and seconds later they vanished into the aching blue expanse. Other Valkyrior were flickering in and out of the air, moving the glorious dead to their new home in Valhalla.

The raven-haired shield-maiden held Gyda close, her friend's delicate features stained with dirt and blood and slack in death. Or not-death. *Please, Odin and Frigga, please let her not be dead. Let her soul return to us and to her body. Or if not her body, at least Valhalla. Let my friend rest in Odin's Hall until the Last Battle calls her forth. Let her be peaceful, and joyous, and not lost.*

Let us all not be lost.

Sif knelt in the churned-up earth, her skin drying tight and sticky with the blood of enemies and of allies, and let her tears clean the filth from her cheeks.

Two

Chooser of the Slain

Brunnhilde urged Aragorn ever faster as they made the journey to Valhalla, flashing past her sisters and the souls they shepherded so carefully, with love and honor for their courage, their sacrifice. Some moved reluctantly, as if dazed by the knowledge that they'd been ripped from their bodies and from life. Others, generally older, moved eagerly, excited to reach the Hall and the feast and the comrades and friends who'd fallen before them. The chance to reunite with the honored dead was a balm to many who would otherwise grieve for those they left behind in life. A few, and there were always a few, wept for the loss of their bodies and their lives under Asgard's bright sky, and the Valkyrior held them gently and spoke in the low, soothing tones a parent would use for a bewildered child.

Not one of them begrudged each soul the time or comfort they needed. To be Valkyrie was to be blessed with the highest honor in all the Nine Realms, not just rejoicing in the courage and sacrifice that led the souls to them, but the privilege, deep and painful and wondrous, of being the last sight the dying would ever behold as they slipped from their suffering bodies on the whispered edge of an exhalation. It never failed to move Brunnhilde to the very depths of her own soul. Today, now, she flashed past the dead without a second glance.

Aragorn sensed her anxiety and beat his wings faster, galloping through the sky and into the Realm of the Dead, his great muscles bunching beneath gleaming satin skin as he pounded down towards the edge of the lake and the perfect grassy sward where Odin's great Hall sat in splendor. The Valkyrie leaped from her mount's back before he'd even come to a stop, flinging herself towards the doors with no regard for appearances. This was too important for even Brunnhilde's dignity.

She pushed in through the tall doors, for once not pausing to admire the exquisite carvings inlaid into the surface, of battles fought and enemies slain and Asgard triumphant. Never before had she failed to heed the hails of her sisters or the souls gathered together. Brunnhilde always had time to raise a flagon with the glorious dead. Now, though, she could have been pushing in through the door of a farmhouse peopled by strangers for all the care and attention she paid her surroundings.

Brunnhilde knew, roughly, the shape and taste of Gyda's soul, and could picture the features she'd last seen relaxed in death, infused with all the bursting emotions of a living woman. She stood on the threshold and scanned the faces around the edges of the vast hall. The newly dead rarely joined immediately into the feasting or gambling within, or the wrestling and weapons-play in the fields without. There was a period of adjustment, of grief and acceptance and, often, bitterness and regret, before the einherjar could come to terms with the knowledge that their mortal lives had ended – heroically, yes, but ended, nonetheless.

Now, everywhere she looked, Valkyrior were talking quietly with their charges or smiling softly, hands resting on arms and shoulders as they grounded them and gave them time. Others were waving over warriors who would act as guides and mentors through the first days of their afterlife.

The hall was busy with life and color; bright-painted shields hung on the walls with brighter weapons – swords, spears and axes – alongside them. Brunnhilde's hand dropped to the hilt of her own sword, Dragonfang, and she took comfort from its weight on her hip. The sword reminded her that her loyalty and dedication had been what led the All-Father to select her to lead the Choosers of the Slain; that his faith in her had never wavered, and she had never disappointed him.

And I will not disappoint him now, either. I swear it on my own soul, and my own hope of standing by Thor's side to endure and defeat Ragnarok.

Despite the promise that was also a prayer, none of the new denizens of Valhalla was Gyda, as far as she could tell. She questioned four Valkyrior who, their duty done, bowed to the warriors they were leaving here and made their way out. She gifted them with the shape of Gyda's soul, but none of them recognized it. Brunnhilde nodded and let them go – there were scores more Valkyrior to check with before she would acknowledge the panic that simmered in her belly.

Einherjar were beginning to turn to her, concern and curiosity creasing their faces at her silent, unmoving presence, and Brunnhilde managed a smile and a nod for them before slipping back out through the doors into the sweet, warm air of the Realm of the Dead. She walked around the hall to the training fields and repeated her inspection, then moved to the water's edge and scanned the few boats gliding across the fjord, a prospect even less likely than the sparring matches. But she had to be thorough. She had to exhaust every possibility here in Valhalla before she returned to Sif and the field and had to tell her that her friend was gone. Truly gone. Perhaps forever.

Eventually, Brunnhilde strode back to Aragorn. The winged horse was cropping the grass, but he lifted his head and nickered at her approach, shoving his nose into her chest, his sweet warm breath wreathing her in animal musk. She swung up into the saddle and urged him deeper into Valhalla. They moved into a swift, tireless canter towards the Hall of Records, where the name of every dead warrior was listed. As she rode, Brunnhilde reached out telepathically to all her Valkyrior, asking that they confirm that every soul they had escorted from the battlefield that day had arrived in Valhalla.

The instruction was unusual enough that a few of her sisters questioned it, their voices clamoring in her head, but Brunnhilde injected her response with fire and command, and they quickly acquiesced.

Even with such confirmation, she couldn't be sure. The

Valkyrior could only confirm the souls they themselves had collected were in Valhalla and that none had been lost in transport. If no one had been there to escort Gyda in the first place, then her absence wouldn't be noted. She needed the list from the Hall of Records that would detail every life ending on the plain outside Asgardia. With it, she could double-check what Odin's Choosers reported.

Not everyone who died in Asgard was rewarded with a place in Valhalla, but the Record-Keeper wrote their name regardless. Was it possible that the shield-maiden had been claimed by Hel? Brunnhilde winced at the mere idea of having to break that news to Sif. She'd trained with and fought against – and with – the warrior for most of their lives, growing up as companions of Thor and Loki and the Warriors Three, and in all that time, Sif's loyalty and her stubbornness had weighed evenly in the scales. The Valkyrie wouldn't put it past her to march to Hel and demand Gyda's soul back if she was indeed in that Realm. But it wasn't just the long years of their friendship that made her so keen to discover the whereabouts of Gyda's soul. She was a Valkyrie; she was made to protect the dead.

Brunnhilde pushed Aragorn from a canter to a gallop.

The Hall of Records was a vast, stone-built structure of soaring windows and imposing relief carvings of gods and legends. It had more levels, rooms and corridors than seemed possible when viewed from the outside, and Brunnhilde knew from experience that the swiftest and safest way to find what she needed was to ask the Record-Keeper direct. She might be lost for days among the shelves otherwise.

She pulled Aragorn to a halt and dismounted. Her steed sidestepped just as she put her foot down in the way of recalcitrant pack animals everywhere across the Nine Realms. The Valkyrie adjusted her feet and her grip and gave him a firm pat on the neck – part affection, part warning. His snort stirred the fine golden hairs that had escaped her thick braid as she passed him, but she put him out of her mind and approached the entrance to the Hall of Records.

Brunnhilde's hand fell to Dragonfang's hilt again as she took a deep breath before pushing through the enormous wooden door. The Record-Keeper was… disconcerting. They had held the position long before Brunnhilde had become Odin's representative, and the story went that they had been imprisoned here by the All-Father himself, back when he had been a boy vying with his brothers, Vili and Ve, for fame and glory.

The Record-Keeper was a troll, bound by Odin's strength and magic to do his will for eternity. Their name and past were unknown; their crime, their reasons and their hopes lost to history. All the Valkyrior knew was that the Record-Keeper had the ability to sense the death of every Asgardian and was compelled by Odin's hold over them to record it. None of that made Brunnhilde any less wary when she walked through the doors of the Hall of Records. She had utter faith in Odin's control over the Record-Keeper, but it was still a troll, and she'd fought too many over the years to trust even this one.

Her boot heels echoed on the stone as she strode in, not even trying to hide the hand resting on her sword hilt. The Record-Keeper looked up from the desk and the enormous, leather-bound book they were writing in. A dark hood concealed their features, though the shapeless robe couldn't hide their size or twisted, hunched back. The hand holding the quill was leathery, fingernails cracked and yellowing and far too long. Too sharp. Talons was a better word.

There was a sharp hiss of breath. "Valkyrie."

Brunnhilde inclined her head a bare fraction. "Record-Keeper. Gyda Horunsdottir." She got the impression the troll was waiting for more, but she had neither the time nor the inclination to pander to their wishes. "Now."

Long, clawed fingers shuffled back a page. "Yes. Today, less than two hours ago." There was curiosity and cool amusement in the rasping voice. "Why? Have you lost her, little Valkyrie? Do you wish to know the tally of her life, and where the fates decreed she should go?"

It was impossible the troll could know whether Gyda was destined for Valhalla or Hel; they recorded the deaths only, and to claim to have knowledge given only to the Norn was tantamount to heresy.

Dragonfang was out of her scabbard and at the Record-Keeper's throat before the words had stopped echoing. "What do you know?" Brunnhilde snarled. The troll didn't move, and despite her proximity, she still couldn't quite see through the shadows of the hood. She could feel their gaze, though, locked with hers. Matching wills. Wondering if she had the courage to push the blade's point into their throat. How little the troll knew her to even speculate on such a thing. "Speak," she snapped.

The Record-Keeper leant back very slowly, and Brunnhilde let Dragonfang's steel part company with the thick robe and the flesh beneath. "I know many things, Valkyrie. More things than you might expect. But not this. If you have truly misplaced the soul of a warrior, there is nothing I can do about that. Gyda Horunsdottir is dead. Her name is in the book and that cannot be altered. The fate of her soul is not my concern."

"What did you feel when she died?" Brunnhilde asked.

"Fear, pain, confusion," the troll replied, even more amused now, as though the answer was obvious. They paused, and then added, reluctantly, "Alarm. A sense of wrongness. An almost purple sort of fear."

Brunnhilde's brow furrowed. "Purple?"

"The emotions of the dying are so strong they come to me in colors, or scents, or sounds even. Gyda's fear was purple and a lonely bone flute playing an aria of regret."

"And what does that mean?"

The troll was silent for a few seconds, tapping their long talons on the edge of the desk, a rhythmic *tick, tick, tick* that set the Valkyrie's teeth on edge. "It means she felt the absolute extremity of fear before she died. It means she knew something was wrong, over and above the ending of her mortal life. Gyda Horunsdottir *died screaming*."

The mirth in the troll's voice was so palpable now that Dragonfang sang its song of violence in her blood and Brunnhilde had to physically prevent herself from stabbing the monstrosity until they were nothing but pummeled meat.

"I see," she managed, and marveled at the steadiness of her voice. "And have you felt this wrongness, this color and sound, before?" She made a promise, then and there, that

Sif would never know this particular piece of information. What was important was that Gyda had known something was wrong as she died; Brunnhilde might be able to use that somehow.

"I feel many, many things when Asgardians die, Chooser. Wrongness and alarm are not uncommon. But yes, this particular, ah, flavor of wrongness, I have felt before."

"How many times? When, where? Who were the souls?" Cautious excitement stirred in Brunnhilde's belly, trying to swamp the anxiety that lingered there, sharp as glass.

"It will take time to find," the Record-Keeper said, "and the dead do not stop dying at your word. The battle may be over, but I still have many names to write. Come back in a few days."

Brunnhilde gritted her teeth, but there was little more she could do. The troll was the only one with the ability – and permission – to record the dead, and the only one who had sensed this wrongness of which they spoke. She could not hurry the answer, but her presence here could definitely delay it.

"I will return – or send one of my sisters – in two days."

The troll waved her away and bent over the book, dipping their quill in ink and beginning, laboriously, precisely, to write once more. The names of the dead and the manner of their deaths, whether glorious or humble.

Brunnhilde would get nothing more from the Record-Keeper and find no further answers in Valhalla. There was a hint of something here, a promise that could see Gyda's soul returned, along with any others that had vanished. She shivered at that thought. For how long had the Valkyrior been failing, all unknowing? What foul magic could have stolen a soul and its last breath and leave the very Choosers of the Slain ignorant of the theft?

And most importantly: why?

THREE
GRIEF

Sif was almost gnawing through her shield with worry and frustration as the minutes trickled by as slowly as tree sap, and Brunnhilde didn't return.

Gyda's body had cooled and was beginning to stiffen. Other warriors had come to collect the corpse for the death rites, and she'd snarled them all away, baring her teeth like an animal. She couldn't tell them what was happening, she knew that much instinctively. Valhalla was the promise that strengthened their courage in battle; to know that there was a possibility of not reaching it upon death could have devastating consequences, and in Odin's absence, that revelation would leave them vulnerable. It was possible not even the God of Thunder would be able to stiffen their spines if news got out that souls were vanishing and then the giants launched another attack.

Time passed, an unknowable amount, and Sif stared without seeing, across blood-spattered grass and torn earth, at abandoned weapons and the furrows left by feet as giant corpses were dragged away to be burned. The view was cut off by a pair of legs in soft, calf-high boots and fine blue trousers. She glanced up without much interest; Thor looked back down at her, his face a mix of anger and concern.

"Sif. What are you doing?" Mjolnir hung from his hand as if he expected to find her still embroiled in a fight. "Why didn't you come back with the rest of the shieldwall? You were supposed to debrief me after the battle."

She looked up at him, backlit against the afternoon light so that his flaxen hair glowed around his head. Despite the shadow, she could see the tension in his jaw as he examined her kneeling in the dirt with a corpse in her lap. "Gyda," she said needlessly, her voice breaking on the name.

Thor sighed and squatted next to her. "I'm sorry, Sif. I know you were friends. But it's time to let her go now." He brushed Sif's loosened hair back over her shoulders and then squeezed her arm. "Let her be taken care of."

"Not yet," she murmured and glanced around to ensure they were alone. "There's something I need to tell you." In a low voice, she related everything she'd seen and everything Brunnhilde had said and sensed, including the fact they hadn't yet told anyone else. The God of Thunder went very still while, above them, clouds began to gather with unnatural speed. He smelt of lightning and rain. Danger prickled along her skin.

"Hel's teeth," he swore when she was finished. The sky rumbled above them, and, with effort, Thor suppressed the lightning beneath his skin.

"You've done well to keep this quiet, at least for now. I will have to send word to the All-Father, but not until we have some answers. The peace with the Vanir hasn't completely shattered yet, and he needs to focus on that. Whatever this attack was – and whatever has happened to Gyda – we can't let it distract him from the peace negotiations." He paused. "Unless this was orchestrated by the Vanir themselves."

Despite everything, Sif snorted. "You really think they would do something like this? A surprise attack while the All-Father is in their very own Realm? You believe the Vanir would use *giants* and invent some obscene magic to steal souls from Asgardian warriors? My lord, we all know exactly who this sounds like."

Thor heaved a sigh, but he didn't contradict her, and that was something. "Father will be in Vanaheim for some weeks yet. We need to have this resolved before he gets back – whoever might be behind it."

Sif pulled Gyda further into her lap. "I'm going to find her," she said fiercely. "Trust me, my lord. I'll find Gyda and make sure she's safe and I'll bring the perpetrator to justice."

Thor tapped his chin with his hammer. "Very well. I must return to the city. Your brother is still watching for further attacks. Don't do anything reckless, Sif."

Sif curled her lip. "I won't."

The God of Thunder looked skeptical. "You forget how long I've known you," he pointed out. "Don't just charge off in pursuit, either. I want a full report of what Brunnhilde learns and then I want a solid plan laid out before I'll consider letting you take action." He held up a hand and then stood before she could reply. "That's not a request. I can and will send someone in your place if I need to."

Sif swallowed her frustration quickly. "I promise, my lord."

"I really am sorry about your friend," he added quietly, and bowed his head briefly in honor of Gyda's sacrifice before walking away and leaving Sif with the silence of an empty battlefield and the missing dead.

They were the only ones left on the field, but the shield-maiden didn't have to sit in her solitary vigil for too much longer before Brunnhilde finally returned. Aragorn's flashing hooves alighted with a soft thump, and the breeze from his massive pinions stirred strands of her black hair.

"What news?" Sif demanded as soon as the Valkyrie had dismounted. "Thor was here. He's given me permission to go after Gyda's soul once we know where Loki has hidden it. Tell me what you know."

Brunnhilde's mouth thinned. "We don't know it's Loki," she said, and Sif rolled her eyes.

"*It's always Loki,*" she hissed in a venomous whisper. "Who else would do something like this?" She took a second to breathe through the grief and smoothed Gyda's hair back again. "I'm going to find you and make sure you reach Valhalla, my friend," she murmured before meeting the other woman's gaze with a steely one of her own. "Please, Brunnhilde, what did you learn?"

"Gyda is not in Valhalla. The Record-Keeper said that they felt a wrongness from her just before she died, separate to the expected emotions when she knew it was the end. And they said they'd felt it before, more than once. I'll have a list of who and when and how those people died in two days."

Sif finally laid Gyda on the ground and then stood, stretching limbs stiff with battle and with kneeling for so long. "Two days," she said, and could hear the flat incredulity in her own voice. "You expect me to sit and do nothing for two days while my friend is who knows where, under that, that *Jotunn's* power? Absolutely not. You must have more than that."

Brunnhilde's fingers tapped Dragonfang's hilt, the blade shimmering into existence at her hip as she made contact. "This is an issue for the Valkyrior," she began. "I know Gyda was your friend and you mourn for her, but that's exactly the reason you shouldn't be involved in this. You're too close to it, caught up in your grief and anger. You're liable to be reckless, Sif. It wouldn't be–"

"Don't you start. Thor said the same thing to me less than an hour ago. This is a far bigger issue than something only Valkyrior should handle. The shieldwalls need to know that one of their own is looking into this. Forgive me, Brunnhilde, but why would they trust you when it's the Choosers of the Slain who have allowed this to happen in the first place?"

Fury flashed across Brunnhilde's face, as quick as Thor's lightning, there and then gone as she suppressed her instinctive response out of respect for Gyda. The Valkyrior dealt with grieving warriors and families every day; she wouldn't let Sif's anger affect her.

Her calm countenance only infuriated Sif further. Gyda deserved to be mourned and no one was going to stop her looking for her friend, especially not when Thor himself had given her permission. She told the Valkyrie as much.

"Then I'll come with you," Brunnhilde said. "You have no idea where to look or what you might find. Whether or not it's Loki, it's a being of immense power to overcome a soul's desire to reach Valhalla, to steal it and its last breath."

Sif's fingers clenched on her own sword hilt. "I can handle it," she grated out.

"I agree," Brunnhilde said, stealing much of the shield-maiden's ire. "I'm saying you don't need to handle it alone."

"You should concentrate on protecting the living, you and all Valkyrior. Make sure this can't happen again. It is time for Loki to pay for his myriad crimes. He will not escape me again. I will no longer tolerate his presence in the Nine Realms."

"You are already being reckless, my lady," Brunnhilde said, sharp as a blade. "You are letting your hate of him cloud your judgment. You think Thor wants you to go to war with his brother? You think yourself qualified to be his judge and his executioner? He is a god far higher than you."

"Yes," Sif snarled, "I do think myself qualified. And capable." If not for the body between them, she might have stepped forwards and shown the Valkyrie just how qualified she was. Grief and rage burned white-hot, and now that she had a target for both, she was desperate to use them before they cooled into hurt, heavy and slow and stifling. Anger she could embrace; loss she could not.

"Thor will have to approve any action you take," Brunnhilde pointed out, infuriatingly calm, as if violence didn't crackle in the air between them. It had been years since they'd tested each other in anything other than a friendly fight, and Sif was ready to put the Valkyrie on her back in the mud. Her blood craved it.

Sif gasped in outrage. "You will use him against me?"

The Valkyrie groaned and looked to the sky. "Why do you think everyone is against you, Sif? This is not some grand conspiracy. I am worried about you! Worried that your anger and recklessness will lead you into foolish action. Worried that, if it is Loki – and there is no evidence to suggest it is, no matter your own conviction – you will be too consumed with the need for vengeance to properly care for Gyda's soul, and any other einherjar that may have been stolen."

She was right, and Sif hated it. Instead of answering, she sheathed her blade at her hip and gently lifted Gyda in her arms. She turned towards the distant city, her armor grating against the torn metal of her friend's shattered breastplate. The sound of a grieving heart. "She needs to be taken care of, and I need to tell Thor I have this under control."

Gyda wasn't the first or even the dearest of loved ones she'd lost during her life, but it wasn't her death so much as all this… this awful mystery surrounding it that cut so deep. Sif was no fool and death was not an abstract concept to one of her profession. She had faced her own countless times and she'd always been afraid and yet she'd known, with a bone-deep, unshakable certainty, that as long as she fought well and died well – and to die well did not mean to die unafraid – then she would reach Valhalla and fight and feast with countless others as they awaited the Last Battle.

To have that certainty stolen was as if the ground beneath her feet, always so stable, had suddenly shifted. It threw everything she knew, everything she was, out of balance.

There was silence behind her, and when she finally glanced back over her shoulder, both the Valkyrie and her mount were gone. Sif scanned the battlefield, noting the scattered, broken arms and armor of Asgardians and giants both, the rusty stains where blood had seeped into the rich earth or speckled the grass bright crimson. It was fading now, like the afternoon, the vibrancy of its life slipping away.

"This is better," she muttered to herself and Gyda, despite the voice in her head saying otherwise. "I don't need anybody to find that Trickster and end his life. I've never needed anybody."

Four
Inge

"Inge? Inge my love, I need your help with someone."

Inge was sitting cross-legged on the grass outside their house, the light from the open door gilding the tops of her cheekbones and nestling golden as a crown among the loose curls of her honey-colored hair. She was singing as she polished her greaves, but now she stopped, looked up, and arched one eyebrow. "The great Brunnhilde, loyal companion and friend to Thor, trusted by the All-Father himself with the souls of the dead, requires this humble shield-maiden's help?" she asked, and a dimple flashed in her cheek.

"There is very little about you that's humble, my heart," Brunnhilde said and took the armor and polishing cloth from Inge's hands, set them aside and then dragged her up and into an embrace, catching her mouth in a kiss to swallow her laughter. Inge pressed against her, though Brunnhilde couldn't feel it through her armor, and she breathed in her lover's scent – oil and wood smoke and sunlight. She held her tighter, fingers lost in the wild tangles of her golden mane, mouth opening beneath Inge's sweet assault. The urge to stay in her arms was strong. Instead, with a deep sigh of regret, she broke the kiss and pulled back.

Inge's sea-green eyes were dark and intent, but then she blinked and grinned. "So, who have you offended this time, O wise and impulsive goddess?" she teased, keeping her arms around Brunnhilde's neck.

"The Lady Sif."

Inge's eyes widened comically, and she stepped out of the Valkyrie's arms. "And you expect me to jump in between the two of you and smooth things over? I have very little desire to get stabbed, thank you very much. It's unpleasant and it hurts."

"Very funny. You know I wouldn't let her hurt you."

"And what if it was you doing the stabbing? You're assuming you're in the right in this mysterious altercation. More importantly, why would you assume I need protecting?" Inge added and put her hands on her hips.

Brunnhilde pinched the bridge of her nose. Today was going from bad to worse. "Inge. My love. My heart. I didn't mean it like that," she began, and then Inge was giggling at her expression and her apology, that damn dimple flashing. Brunnhilde scowled. "This is not the time for teasing, you monster. Inge, really, this is serious. I don't have a lot of time."

"First I'm your entire heart and now I'm a monster," Inge muttered, and then gestured imperiously at Aragorn, cropping the grass. "Take me to her, then, and tell me what you've done on the way. Wait, does this have anything to do with the battle earlier? I know the victory was ours, Odin be praised, but did something else happen?" The humor had fallen from her features.

Brunnhilde nodded. "There has been… an incident. Lady Sif is upset."

Inge gaped again and then scrabbled in the grass. "Let me put my armor on," she said quickly.

"The battle's over, love," Brunnhilde said.

"You said Lady Sif is upset. This is in case of any stabbing." And she grinned again, defusing the building tension.

The Valkyrie gritted her teeth and swung back up into Aragorn's saddle. "Shield-maidens," she muttered.

By the time they reached the city, Inge was no longer amused. Instead, she was as worried as Brunnhilde and just as determined to convince Sif to let the Valkyrie help her recover the lost souls. They found her in the Hall of the Dead, sitting with Gyda's corpse, and Brunnhilde quietly sent someone to fetch Thor. She had a feeling that Sif's stubbornness would need tempering by the God of Thunder's presence.

"Lady Sif," Inge said quietly, bowing to the body and then the black-haired warrior. "I am so sorry for your loss. Brunnhilde has told me what happened, and–"

Sif's head snapped up at that, her gray eyes flashing as they cut into the Valkyrie's, sharp as steel. "What? I said it was a bad idea to tell anyone, I told you not to. I told you that *Thor* told us not to."

Brunnhilde felt herself flush under that angry glare. *She's right. Thor did tell her to keep this quiet.*

She began to apologize, but Sif looked away. "I'm going to

handle this, Inge, I promise. Please don't worry. You and the other warriors need not fear."

"Thank you, it means a lot to know you are taking this so seriously," Inge said.

Brunnhilde blinked, confused and suddenly wary. Wasn't Inge supposed to on her side? But then she noticed Sif subside a little.

"And how will you get the souls to Valhalla when you have retrieved them, may I ask?" Inge continued.

Sif gave her a blank look. "What?"

Inge rounded the marble slab holding Gyda's body and drew Sif to face her, gripping her elbows. "How will you transport the einherjar? How will you collect them, steal them back if necessary? How are you going to save them? Save *us*?" Sif didn't have an answer for her, because of course she could do no such thing; she wasn't a Valkyrie. Brunnhilde kept her expression carefully neutral.

"I know you want vengeance, for Gyda and the others, and for yourself if this does turn out to be Loki," Inge continued, nodding as if Sif's stubbornness was perfectly reasonable.

"It is Loki," the warrior insisted, and then flushed and cut herself off as Thor appeared. "It seems like one of his tricks. And it's the perfect opportunity. He's attacked us before in the All-Father's absence."

Inge let go of Sif and bowed low to the God of Thunder. She licked her lips and glanced at Brunnhilde, who indicated she should defer to Thor.

"My lord," Brunnhilde said.

"Bright-Battle," Thor responded. He folded arms thick

with muscle across his chest and nodded for Inge to continue, his expression closed and unreadable.

"Thank you, my lord," Inge said with more composure than the Valkyrie was expecting. She took a step back so she could see both Thor and Sif. "You're right, Lady Sif, it does seem like one of Loki's tricks," she said soothingly, "and to have taken Gyda no doubt feels like another personal attack against you. If I had ever been so persecuted, it would certainly feel that way to me. I can see how angry and grief-stricken you are, my lady, but because of that, you may not be as clear-minded as you could be. You cannot transport the souls back to Asgard, let alone Valhalla. Brunnhilde can. It would be wise for you to travel together, to face this task together. Not because you need assistance against Loki, but because each of you have skills unique to you."

She gave Sif the honest and trusting smile that had melted Brunnhilde's heart so long before. Sif seemed as powerless to resist it as the Valkyrie was. She even managed a crooked smile of her own in return. Brunnhilde didn't miss Thor's appraising gaze as it rested on the young warrior.

"You can fight the Trickster while Brunnhilde frees the einherjar," Inge continued. "Your abilities perfectly complement each other. Together, you can do this. Alone, perhaps not. And forgive me, my lady, but you risk more than just your life if the threat is bigger than anticipated. You risk Gyda's place in Valhalla and her aid in the Last Battle. From all I knew of your friend, she will be invaluable when Ragnarok comes."

How Brunnhilde loved Inge. Not only a fierce and devoted warrior, but a born diplomat and a ferocious defender of the wronged and the innocent. But to have tamed the Lady Sif upon their first meeting was a feat that perhaps none had ever managed before. Even Thor made no attempt to hide his admiration, and he gave the shield-maiden a nod when Sif sagged and then, low-voiced and ragged, finally agreed to accept Brunnhilde's assistance.

"In fact," the God of Thunder said, considering, "I would like it if all three of you went. As you pointed out, Sif, this affects all warriors. It makes sense to take a third with you, and Inge is both capable and highly skilled. I am impressed, maiden," he added, and Inge's façade finally cracked; she blushed high along her cheekbones, green eyes dancing with pleasure undimmed by the gravity of the situation.

"You do me great honor, my lord," she stammered, bowing again.

"Nonsense. You are young but well trained; you will be subordinate to the Lady Sif, but do not hesitate to speak up if you have an idea. And Sif, my friend," he added, turning from Inge's overwhelmed face to Sif's stony one, "I will make sure Gyda has an honor guard until you return. We will not burn her without you."

Sif inhaled a sharp, surprised breath. "That would… thank you, my lord."

Thor inclined his head as Brunnhilde met Inge's rapturous gaze. The corner of her mouth twitched up and she winked at her girlfriend's clear awe, then focused back on the conversation. "As you wish, lady. All of you, pack your supplies, clean your armor, and get ready to set out in an hour. I presume one of you has a notion where to begin looking?"

"Jotunheim," Sif said, and Inge and the Valkyrie both nodded. "If the mountain giants are our only clue so far – aside from the fact that Loki is half Jotunn himself, of course, and our prime suspect – then it makes sense to go there."

"There's a portal a few days' walk north from here that I can move us from," Brunnhilde said. "It will be easier on you both to Realm-jump from there."

"Good," Thor said, and the shield-maidens both bowed to him. "Sif, I have something for you." He held out a small orb and she approached, curious. Brunnhilde and Inge shifted closer too. It was plain gold – no, not plain, but carved with jagged lines on one side and flowing lines on the other. It rested within a filigree of silver and was strung on a sturdy leather thong at odds with the delicacy of the rest of the construction.

"A Quellstone, one of my mother's inventions. It's… imperfect at the moment, but up against a threat so new and strange, I wish to give you every advantage I can. It has twin powers to break and bind – destroy and heal. They don't hold as much power as Frigga would like, so be judicious. Be *cautious.* It will fade with each use and, ah, apparently they have a tendency to shatter when the last of the power leaves them, so be aware of that."

Sif took it reverently. "Thank you, my lord," she said, and put the cord around her neck, tucking the orb inside her shirt against her skin. There was a bright flash of golden light and she flinched. "Um. Ow?"

Thor chuckled. "It's linked to your body now, so you can direct the breaking or binding as needed. It won't do that again."

Sif thanked him again, and Thor waved it away and turned to Brunnhilde. "Bright-Battle, before you depart, tell me what happened in Valhalla. You saw the Record-Keeper?"

Brunnhilde nodded to Sif and brought Inge's hand up to graze her lips across her knuckles. The Valkyrie followed Thor from the Hall of the Dead to give him the rest of her report and arrange for another Valkyrie to collect the list of names from the troll in two days. Her sister would send the information to her through their mental link, and Brunnhilde would know exactly how many souls they were searching for. A little of the weight slid from her shoulders: they had the beginnings of a plan.

FIVE
THE BRAVEST

Sif didn't know Inge very well; the shield-maiden had come from a smaller town to train as a warrior and had only been in Asgardia for a few years. Their paths hadn't crossed much since she'd qualified from the training school and taken her place in the fifth shieldwall, which hadn't been on duty around Asgardia today. She hadn't seen the battle, and, though her curiosity was almost palpable, she respected Sif's grief and held her peace.

Sif studied Inge from the corner of her eye as the three warriors walked. Inge was relaxed but alert, and even as she chattered quietly with the Valkyrie, her head was always on the move, checking ahead and to their flanks, glancing back the way they'd come every now and then. Perhaps unconsciously, she'd timed her movements to complement Sif's own, so that they traded off which direction to look in and kept their perimeter under constant surveillance.

She was pleased to see Inge's kit was well maintained, and her spear, sword and armor functional, polished and ready.

Inge's shield was slung comfortably across her back, and she didn't use her spear as a walking aid, holding it parallel to the ground instead, with her dominant hand ready to slide along its length into a position to stab or parry.

Even better, the warrior didn't walk at Brunnhilde's side as if their relationship conveyed some status on her, for which Sif was doubly grateful. *You did, those first heady days you were with Thor.* Sif shoved away the thought, her cheeks warm with embarrassment. That had been a long, long time ago now, and she could admit to the folly of youth. Privately, at least.

Inge strode with a long, loose-limbed gait as they took the road north, following back along the path the mountain giants had traveled to reach Asgardia. As the miles melted away beneath their boots, they passed the odd scrap of armor or cloth the giants had dropped on their way to the city.

Sif ignored the quiet chatter between Inge and Brunnhilde and stepped off the road into long grass, a glint of light on a reflective surface catching her eye. It was the metal boss at the center of a giant's huge shield, painted with an eye, a snake and a mountain. She turned it over and saw both the handle and the strap had broken, rendering it useless.

"Find something?" Inge asked and then hummed in appreciation as Sif flipped the item back over. "Their artistry leaves a lot to be desired. And who'd bring faulty kit on an invasion? Giants aren't normally this stupid, are they?"

Sif's memory presented her with an image of the battlefield once all the corpses had been cleared. There'd been a few fallen weapons and helmets belonging to Asgardians, but the rest had been giant gear, and there'd been a lot of it.

She rapped her knuckles on the shield. "Faulty or damaged kit carried all the way to Asgardia itself. Heimdall suspected they Realm-jumped in and then marched to the city, perhaps as a distraction. A mere hundred giants, poorly equipped, marching across Asgard to take on the greatest city and greatest warriors in the Nine Realms?"

"Sounds like a suicide mission," Inge said, running her hand over the broken leather strap of the shield. "But why? A diversion?"

"My brother is watching, and Thor can reach and rally the warriors in any part of Asgard in an instant. Multiple incursions would be the only way such small numbers, armed with poor-quality weapons, could hope to inflict a serious toll on us."

"And yet there'd been no word of another attack before we left. So they *were* sent on a suicide mission," Inge said.

"Perhaps not. They might be a focal point," Brunnhilde said thoughtfully. "If it's a giant or descendant of Jotunheim – someone familiar with the life essences there, anyway – who is seizing einherjar as they die, then the concentrated life force of the attacking giants, the shape of their energy and auras, would act as a beacon to draw the soul-snatching magic to the battlefield. It could be similar to the way I sense the deathglow."

Sif stared fixedly at Brunnhilde.

Descendant of Jotunheim.

Loki.

Her blood heated. It had to be. The Valkyrie had practically admitted that she, too, believed it was the Trickster God committing these terrible crimes. They were finally in agreement, and Sif couldn't help the little shiver of relief that made its way down her back. It would be easier now.

"So there's no reason to send your best fighters or your best armor if the only point is to harvest warrior souls," Inge said. She kicked the shield. "Explaining this. I wonder if the giants knew they were nothing more than bait, sacrificed for some unknown purpose. You killed a hundred of them, and they snatched a single soul. Those are pretty poor odds."

Sif stared at the shield a little while longer, and then climbed back onto the road and began to walk again, faster now. The others fell in on either side. "But," she began reluctantly, because as much as she didn't want to ruin the theory, honesty compelled her to speak. Lady Sif, companion of Thor and the Warriors Three, did not trade in half-truths or obfuscation. Still, it was easier to say while striding along the road with a promised battle at its end. "But this is the first giant attack, and you said the Record-Keeper believed this had happened several times before. There haven't been any reports of other giant incursions in recent months. So, it might not be related to Jotunheim after all."

Brunnhilde arched an eyebrow and then gave her a slow, approving nod. "You're right, but until we have the list of the soul-snatched and how they died, we can't draw any further conclusions. The manner of these deaths may yet connect back to Jotunheim. More than giants live in that frozen, blasted Realm." She held up her palm. "Or they may not. Either way, heading north can only benefit us. I can get us to most places from the Realm-jump point there. I didn't think you'd want to let me jump you without a portal to guide our way," she added with a smile at Sif.

Sif grunted. "Not unless there's no other choice," she agreed, and couldn't quite suppress a shudder. "I can still remember how awful it was, even all these years later."

Inge stared between the pair of them and then gusted a sigh. "You're going to leave it at that? You can't hint at that sort of a tale and then not give me the rest of the details," she pleaded. Her eyes opened wide. "Did you once get into mischief, Lady Sif?"

Sif felt a blush warm her cheeks even as Brunnhilde laughed. "Once?" the Valkyrie teased. "It's been many more times than once."

The warrior gave her an unimpressed stare and then blew out a breath of her own. "Heimdall and I got it into our heads to steal two of the Valkyrior winged horses while on an important mission once," she admitted. "How else do you think my brother got Golden Mane?"

Inge gasped. "You didn't?"

Sif chuckled ruefully. "It was long ago, and we did. My own mount, Bloodspiller, wished to return to the Valkyrior for a time. That's not the point, though. The point is don't ever travel between Realms without the protection of a portal or someone who actually knows how to navigate the between-space," she advised. "The portals are fixed doorways, but even they are painful to navigate for people without the particular magic of the Valkyrie. Or that of a higher god, of course."

Brunnhilde laughed. "They were very young, and traversing that space made them hilariously sick. But that sickness is one of the reasons I'm not Realm-jumping us straight to the portal and then to Jotunheim. The transition to the Giant's Realm is going to be hard enough for you two as it is. No need to make it worse."

They walked in silence for a few minutes, and Sif was mildly surprised that Inge didn't have a dozen more questions for her, but the woman was quiet and seemed distracted.

"Then we are going to Meadowfall?" she asked, after the silence had grown awkward. Her voice was tense.

"Yes. If the giants used Meadowfall's portal, then they'll have passed close enough to the town that the folk there would surely have seen something. And you can check in on your family. As I said earlier, I sensed no deathglow."

"I was born and raised in Meadowfall," Inge said in response to Sif's unspoken question. "It's a large town and well fortified, with a shieldwall of its own. It guards a portal, keeping it safe for those with the ability to use it, and as a result it has often been attacked by enemies jumping in. The chances of the mountain giants – or whoever is controlling them – being unaware of the town's proximity is almost nil. And even if they somehow were, it's a big place with a high wall surrounded by well-tended fields and pasture. Smoke on the wind, regular mounted patrols, and thousands of Åsgardians. There is no way in Hel the giants wouldn't see or smell the town."

"You've been worried about your home and family since we set out and haven't said anything?" Sif asked, shocked.

Inge managed a wan smile. "You are grieving, and a soul is missing. We have enough to think about."

Brunnhilde pulled Inge close in to her side and tucked an arm around her. "Your family are strong warriors, love," she murmured. "Let's not worry until we need to, yes?"

"Yes," the other woman replied, tired and distant. "Because there was no deathglow."

There was little else to say, and they marched steadily northwards for the rest of the day through well-tended fields and wild rolling hills dotted with sheep and sturdy hill ponies. The sky was bright and the sun warm, just enough to offset the chill of an early spring breeze. They camped that night under the stars, eating trail rations around a small fire and taking it in turns to keep watch.

Sif stretched out her legs and put her back to the fire so as not to ruin her night vision, deep in thought. What might come for them next while Odin was away fighting a desperate war of words to weave together the fraying edges of the peace with Vanaheim? Would it be Loki, emerging from wherever he was lurking and meddling, his actions plain for once as he made another bid for the throne? Or would he ever play the puppet-master, fostering dissent and ambition in those who should not have it? Perhaps there would be more mountain giants marching on Asgard's sacred earth and snatching the souls of the bravest warriors.

Sif sat up abruptly and turned to face the others. "The bravest," she said. "Inge, earlier today you said a hundred giants died for one soul, that it was bad odds. But doesn't it depend on the soul? Gyda was stalwart and talented, fierce and brave and true, and that's not just me speaking as her friend. I've fought beside her in a dozen battles. She has – had – a deep and innate understanding of tactics, logistics, the best way to utilize archers and spears and the landscape itself. A born warrior. A born leader. If you could take – and manipulate – a person like that, and you were willing to sacrifice your weakest warriors to do so, wouldn't you? Think what a dozen or a hundred like Gyda could do if you were able to, I don't know, harvest their memories or abilities or whatever it is Loki's attempting with the soul-snatch."

"It would be like fighting the best of ourselves," Inge said slowly and rose to her feet, "the way we practice in training, only for real. If we lost our best and then had to face them again, altered somehow, returned from the dead…" She blinked and then shivered. "I don't like this."

"Nor I," Sif agreed. "Nor I."

"They can't have sent the weakest, though," Brunnhilde said after the silence filled the tiny sphere of golden firelight with foreboding. "The giants, I mean. If they were the worst of their race, they wouldn't have fought as resolutely as they did. They wouldn't have killed enough of our best warriors to harvest souls with the specific skills they were looking for."

The Valkyrie looked deeply uncomfortable as she said it, and Sif didn't blame her – it felt like they were disrespecting those who hadn't been soul-snatched, saying they were unworthy. It must be doubly difficult for the leader of Odin's Choosers to say such things – her entire life was dedicated to honoring the glorious dead, after all. Inge crouched and squeezed Brunnhilde's leg in silent comfort, her thumb sliding over the muscle of her calf.

"So why would our enemies be willing to sacrifice themselves in such a way? Being sent here with faulty kit, marching all the way to Asgardia to face us in a battle they not only can't hope to win, but which they know they're not supposed to?"

"Perhaps they're fanatics," Inge said slowly, even as

she settled again in the grass and pressed herself against Brunnhilde's side, her arm looped around the Valkyrie's waist. "Their cause, whatever it is, is compelling enough that they'll die for it?"

Sif shook her head. She was restless, the muscles in her legs twitching and her heart beating just a little too fast. She wanted to move, to fight. To understand. "Giants are loyal, and they can be zealous in protection of their homes and rulers, in defense of Jotunheim itself, but when they launch an attack, it's usually motivated by reward. What reward can they hope to get if they're killed here?"

"Perhaps whoever is in charge of this has their families held hostage?" Brunnhilde tried. "That might be enough to make them give their lives."

"And Loki is easily ruthless enough for that," Sif growled. "He'll steal anything, do anything, to get what he wants." Inge's gaze flickered to Sif and then away, and she realized she was twisting one of her long, black braids around her fist, pulling it taut, and then letting go. She forced herself to put her hands in her lap. There wasn't a person, warrior or otherwise, on Asgard who didn't know the story of how Loki had cut off her hair in a fit of jealousy when they were young. When Thor had forced him to restore it with magical hair of pure gold made by the dwarves, the Trickster God had stolen it before it could be enchanted, and when he placed it on her head, it turned black. Since then, Sif, whose hair had once been sunlight itself, had hair the color of soot, of ash, of death.

Sif knew it shouldn't matter. She knew that of all Loki's many crimes, it was one of the least. Yet it was so personal, as much a violation of who she was as if he'd carved his name into her flesh for all to see. She was forever tainted by his touch. Forever marked by his whim and temper, like a horse that bore the scars of a cruel rider in its flanks and its wide, shuddering eyes.

In the silence, she squeezed her hands tight together and drew in one long, measured breath. Soon. He would pay soon. For everything.

"Could the soul-snatching magic extend to the giants?" Inge asked into the quiet, her voice bringing Sif back to their predicament and the mystery at the heart of it all. "Brunnhilde, you said that the concentrated life force of the giants could act as a draw for the magic to steal Asgardian souls. Could it, possibly, also summon back the dead giants themselves? Their souls? Perhaps the Jotunn were promised some form of resurrection if they did fall in the fight. Is there any such magic?"

"I know a trickster god who could make the dead live again," Sif said grimly, before Brunnhilde could reply. "It's a viable theory; we shouldn't dismiss it."

"The magic would need to be similar to how we sense the deathglow, but also capable of summoning the soul over vast distances – across Realms, even," Brunnhilde said. "Not even the Valkyrior can do that, which is why we attend on the battlefields and shepherd the dead ourselves. It would take immense power to attempt a magic so vast and complex."

"Again," Sif muttered, but this time too quietly for the others to hear, "I know a god who could do that. And who is arrogant enough to think he should."

She sighed and rubbed her palms over her face. She was

tired, suddenly, of her own everlasting resentment, justified as it was. She was tired of thinking of Loki. Tired of assuming, always, eternally, that he was behind every plot, every tragedy, every mistake. Tired of the hold he still maintained over her.

In fact, Sif realized, she was just tired. Though her strength was greater by far than Inge's or any normal Asgardian's, she had spent the day in combat and then in grief. She glanced across the fire and met Brunnhilde's gaze.

"Sleep," the Valkyrie said softly. "I have the first watch."

Grateful, Sif nodded and shifted to lie back in her blanket again, relishing its thickness now that night had fallen and stolen the last of the sun's warmth. The fire was a comforting presence against her back, and in the distance she could see the twinkle of torchlight from a cluster of farms half a mile down a narrow track. Fields of early sprouting wheat stretched to either side.

It was peaceful, and Sif both craved and mistrusted peace. Every shadow, every tree and solitary standing stone could hide an enemy. Could hide Loki. Grunting, she burrowed deeper into her blanket and refused to dwell on the Trickster God any further.

Staring out at the night, she tried to still the whirl of her thoughts and the knowledge, diamond-sharp, that they still knew so little – not even the sort of trap they were walking into. Resolutely, she closed her eyes and slowed her breathing. Made herself relax. Eventually, she slept.

SIX
Poisons and Glamours

As the youngest and most inexperienced of them, Inge had the dog-watch, and when Brunnhilde woke with the dawn's first kiss of light, a small part of her worried her lover might have given in to the temptation of sleep. But there she was, straight-backed and alert, if drawn around the eyes and mouth.

"Hi," she whispered, pleased and proud and a little shamefaced at her lack of faith, but Inge's face softened as she glanced over.

"Hi," she whispered back and then muffled an enormous yawn. "Does this mean–"

Brunnhilde grinned and stretched. "Come on, get your head down for an hour, if you can. We'll wake you for breakfast." She pulled Inge into her nest of blankets and kissed her. "How are you?"

Inge's bravado cracked around the edges, and her eyes darkened with anxiety. "I'll feel better once we're there."

Brunnhilde winced and, heedless of the early hour, sent

a message to Eira, one of her sisters. The Chooser promised that she would jump to Meadowfall and check the town was safe. The Valkyrie spent another few minutes luxuriating in Inge's warmth and scent before reluctantly getting up. The warrior let out a muffled protest, and then pulled the blanket up over her head until she was nothing but a rumpled tangle of wool and the ends of her hair.

Brunnhilde stretched some more and then built up the fire and set water and dried rations in a pan at the edge. She was thrumming with tension, unable to get the Record-Keeper's words and everything they'd discussed the day before out of her head. She couldn't sit still, so she unsheathed Dragonfang and walked thirty paces out across the meadow to practice sword forms without waking the others.

She felt lighter than normal without her armor, almost light enough to fly as she leaped and spun, parried and attacked – high, then low, then high again – ducking and slashing as her feet carried her across the grass.

She spun again, arcing her blade down in a diagonal cut from face to hip, and a blade intercepted her own, the clang of steel kissing shattering the dawn and startling birds from the trees. Brunnhilde grinned and parried Sif's follow-up thrust, and then pressed into the attack again, forcing the black-haired shield-maiden back four steps, then five, before she flowed like water around her, stepping in a wide arc and coming in on the Valkyrie's blind side.

Brunnhilde laughed as she side-stepped, slapping Sif's sword away with the flat of her hand as she went. Anyone else would risk losing a finger at the move, but she was confident both in her abilities and her opponent's. As expected, the shield-maiden was lightning fast as she recovered and bounded after her. Neither of them wore armor, and both of their swords were razor-sharp, but they fought with a fury and intensity that broke the peace of the morning, trading blows and insults, laughs and whistles of appreciation for a particularly showy or effective technique as they battled.

Brunnhilde was breathing hard, sweat sticking her hair to the nape of her neck, her shirt to her back. Slowly, their laughter faded as they concentrated on saving their breath and maintaining their footwork. It could descend into something far more serious if they let it, and the Valkyrie felt the dimmest flicker of their old rivalry stir in her chest. In their youth they'd been friends and then adversaries and then, eventually, friends again. Even today, they were both competitive by nature and, although Brunnhilde had deep affection for Sif, the urge to press for victory was strong. She pushed it away and tried to find a way to disengage without handing the bout to the warrior or, worse, making the other woman think she was condescending to her.

And then Inge – beautiful, clever, darling Inge – jumped up and down in the corner of her eye. "Breakfast," she yelled. "Eat it before I do."

Brunnhilde looked at Sif, both of them in guard, sweaty and disheveled and intense. She blinked, broke eye contact, and the other woman let out a short huff. They lowered their swords in tandem. The Valkyrie grinned. "Thank you, my lady. I haven't been pushed like that in many a year."

Sif smiled back. "Nor I," she conceded as they sheathed their weapons and made their way back to the camp. "It's a fine way to work out the kinks from sleeping on the ground."

Eira reported in a moment later that all was quiet at Meadowfall. One piece of good news at least. Brunnhilde sat far back from the heat of the fire, already warm enough from her exertions as she relayed the news. Inge relaxed as she handed out the plates, but Brunnhilde sensed the worry she still harbored for her family, now pushed firmly down inside where it wouldn't distract her, despite confirmation that the town was peaceful. Inge dropped a kiss on Brunnhilde's damp forehead and then licked her own lips, no doubt tasting the Valkyrie's sweat.

"Lady Sif, it has been a while since I had the privilege to watch you spar. If you have time, after all this… nastiness is dealt with, there was a move you used back there that I'd love you to teach me, if you have a free afternoon?" Inge's hands fluttered as she described the technique, and Brunnhilde grunted in agreement. It was innovative and had nearly caught her unawares.

Sif smiled at the compliment and Inge's enthusiasm and described the footwork and body position between bites of breakfast. Inge was attentive, but somehow managed to pile more food on all three plates seemingly without looking or Sif even noticing.

When they'd finished eating, Brunnhilde gathered up the plates and the pan to take them down to the stream to wash. Sif stared at her in surprise and there was the slightest flicker of her eyes towards Inge. The Valkyrie arched one eyebrow. "Gods above, you have actually met my girlfriend, haven't you?" she laughed, pointing her chin at Inge. "I'd like to live a little longer yet, thank you. She cooked; I'll wash."

Inge sprawled back on Brunnhilde's blanket and stretched.

"Compromise is the secret to a happy relationship," she agreed with a smirk. "Anyway, I want to know about your duel with Hakurei the Dragon, back when you were traveling with the God of Thunder and Lord Balder. Do the legends tell it true?"

Sif snorted a laugh. "That would depend on whose legends you listen to. Thor and Balder, ah, remember it a little differently to me, it seems."

"Really?" Inge said as Brunnhilde walked away, slowly enough to catch Sif's reply.

"More heroism, less screaming," the shield-maiden confirmed and Brunnhilde laughed to herself. She remembered hearing those tales when they'd first returned from the quest the All-Father had sent them on. She remembered how the details differed depending on the teller and had decided early on that Sif's was probably closest to the truth. Sif had her pride, of course, and had no doubt added some embellishments of her own. Still, she was honest and while she hated being wrong as much as the next person, she would at least own up to her mistakes.

Thor's version, of course, had been one of effortless leadership and restraint, and even now, washing dishes in the cold water of a stream so many years later, Brunnhilde chuckled at the memory of Sif's perfectly arched eyebrow as he spoke.

Sif wouldn't be disrespectful in her telling of the tale, though. Her devotion to the God of Thunder was well known, even though they were now nothing more than good friends. Brunnhilde shook water off the plates and her hands and then stripped off her shirt to wash the sweat from her skin.

She was scrubbing herself dry when Valkyrie Eira contacted her again. "Bright-Battle? You asked my sisters and me to ensure that all those who died outside Asgardia were safely shepherded to either Hel or Valhalla."

Brunnhilde felt her stomach knot. Even through their telepathic link, Eira's hesitance was clear. "Yes. Report."

"There are… three missing. I, we don't know where – Bright-Battle, I don't understand what's happening. How can three einherjar have vanished? How have we failed?"

"Give me their names and histories, their standing within Asgardia's shieldwall," Brunnhilde said instead of answering her.

She scooped up the plates and pan and jogged back to the others as Eira named Gyda and two others, who together made up the three most experienced warriors to have died on the field. She cut the connection with a brusque order to keep the information to herself and dragged a clean shirt from her pack and shrugged into it as she explained what she'd learned to Sif and Inge.

"Thor blast that Record-Keeper," she added. "They told me exactly what I asked and nothing more, didn't mention that Gyda's death wasn't the only one that had felt wrong. Told me that there had been others, yes, but not that there'd been three in yesterday's battle."

"So three, plus whatever is in the troll's list when we get it," Sif said. "Which means that Loki hasn't just played his hand now, with the All-Father's absence. He has been stealthily stealing souls for months. Maybe longer."

"But there hasn't been a war fought on Asgard for years, against giants or otherwise," Inge said as she rolled the blankets and strapped them to the packs. "Not even a skirmish in the last six months. So how, who, can these dead be?"

Brunnhilde stamped out the fire, settled her pack over her shoulders and gestured, and the three women set out at a fast walk. It was something that had bothered her too, ever since the Record-Keeper had brought it up. "My sisters and I haven't been called to more than isolated incidents in the last year," she confirmed reluctantly and then sent the Valkyrior a quick query. Their responses came quickly and were couched in worry. By now they all knew that something was wrong.

"Beast attacks mostly. Giant eagles, or packs of wolves targeting individual warriors. Something unidentified in a lake. Arguments that descended into duels and then death." She shook her head. "Now that I think about it, that makes no sense: warriors of Asgard's shieldwalls would never engage in death-fights with each other."

"And these are only the deaths you know about, where the souls were successfully retrieved," Sif said, wincing at the accusation in the words. She brushed her knuckles against the back of Brunnhilde's hand in apology. "So, others must have died and been soul-snatched without the Choosers being aware. If it was a single deathglow, quickly vanished, perhaps it wouldn't be so easy to sense?"

Brunnhilde stared ahead. The bright sun of earlier had vanished behind a thin layer of cloud, softening the edges so that the vibrant green took on the gentle hue of polished jade. The forest to the west was dark with shadow and bright with blossom. Skylarks called high above their heads, an unceasing song that she struggled to follow, its notes coming so fast they were only heard in the aftermath. It was too beautiful and perfect to be considering such horrors. And yet she had to.

"That's not how the deathglow works. Whether it's one soul or a thousand, they burn as brightly. Impossible to ignore. Impossible not to react to – it's built into us. A Valkyrie would be as likely to miss a deathglow as she would be to lift Mjolnir."

"Then perhaps," Inge began, and her tone was heavy with such dread that Brunnhilde stopped and faced her. The skylark's song continued unabated, incongruous against the sudden tension. Inge grabbed her upper arms, squeezing hard. "Perhaps there is something wrong with the Valkyrior. Something blocking your abilities to sense the deathglow. A poison or magic?"

Brunnhilde's stomach dropped into her boots at the implication and at the naked worry in her lover's face. "I'm fine, my heart," she reassured automatically, and then stopped. Thought about it. Two pairs of eyes fixed worriedly on her as the Valkyrie sought inside herself for her magic, and for any wrongness bound up in it. She could still feel the connection to her sisters, and to Odin himself. Physically, she was strong and relaxed, pain-free and alert. She could sense Aragorn cropping grass back at home, and the thin skeins of magic connecting her to Dragonfang and Geirr, her enchanted spear.

"I am. I'm fine," she confirmed, and Inge's shoulders climbed back down from around her ears. She spared a quick moment to pull her in close and drop a kiss on the crown of her head. "But that doesn't mean the other Valkyrior are unaffected." She ran through what they'd told her again and grimaced.

"No souls collected at death have then vanished from Valhalla, but Gyda's soul was never sensed in the first place. So whatever magic is being used against us may be interrupting our perception, not trapping it within ourselves, but instead… blinding us to the dying. The pattern so far is that once we sense them, they make the journey and then stay there. So, the issue may be with our perception in the first place. But not from an internal ailment," she added before Inge could start to worry again.

"And the All-Father is not here to examine the magic that grants you your abilities," Sif said, kicking at the hard-packed dirt of the road. "This just gets better and better. Or worse and worse, depending on whether you're us or that damned Trickster." There was an edge of fury in her voice, but a glimmer too, along that edge, of reluctant approval. Brunnhilde understood: it was hard not to appreciate such a complex plan, even if they could only see a part of it so far. There was no shame in respecting a worthy foe.

"Would Thor be able to sense anything?" Inge asked, breaking into Brunnhilde's thoughts. "He could examine the Choosers and see if any of them are having their abilities blocked."

The Valkyrie was already shaking her head. "Affecting Valkyrior would be both dangerous and difficult."

"Could it be the warriors themselves?" Sif tried as they began to walk again. The morning had lost its charm, and unease was leaping between the three of them, winding them tighter with each theory until they thrummed like Thor's lightning. "Could Loki have cast a glamour over them that screens their souls? Using the focus of the giants' presence, their life essence, to mask the deathglow in some way, or to direct the glamour to certain individuals."

She snapped her fingers, suddenly animated. "Gyda had traveled out of the city not long before she died. Perhaps she was poisoned on her journey, something done to her that not only masked her deathglow but made her weaker. Made it more likely that the magic – and the giants' lives – wouldn't be wasted when it came to battle."

"I can ask Thor to examine some of my sisters and, with your permission, Gyda too, to see if he can feel anything. It may be worth asking Lord Heimdall to examine them as well. His sight may pierce any veil or glamour cast upon them." Despite her words, Brunnhilde didn't think it would be this simple, or that they would be so lucky. She wasn't usually one for despondency, but she didn't think this was going to give them the answer they were seeking.

"Absolutely," Sif said, unaware of the Valkyrie's inner turmoil. "We should enquire whether any warriors have gone missing, too. The souls aren't being snatched from Valhalla itself, so the missing that the Record-Keeper mentioned must have come from somewhere. Lone warriors being killed on the road between towns, or even small parties guarding trade goods, perhaps. Their absence might not be noted for months."

The Valkyrie gusted a sigh. "Those souls may not have ended up in Valhalla anyway," she pointed out reluctantly. "We have a working theory that it is the bravest and brightest being stolen, and this doesn't fit that theory. On the other hand, it would account for why we didn't notice them disappearing."

"Every hour we end up with more questions and fewer answers, it seems," Inge said as she scuffed her boots through the grass at the side of the road. "It could be the Valkyrior; it could be the warriors; it could be neither; it could be both. It could be Loki, or it could be someone else." She held up both palms as Sif bristled. "I'm sorry, Lady Sif, but it's true. The signs certainly indicate him, but we'd be remiss to make assumptions without evidence. If the Record-Keeper keeps his promise, though, we should have the list tomorrow. Hopefully that will help us identify the being behind these foul attacks."

"For now," Brunnhilde added in quiet support of her girlfriend, "we have to treat this as any other incursion from an unknown source. If we assume, we could end up wrong-footed."

Sif looked from one to the other and quirked a smile. "I see you're ganging up on me now. It's just hard for me to think it might be anyone else. After everything."

"I know," the Valkyrie replied. "And I appreciate your willingness to listen to alternate theories. Especially after everything."

Inge was silent for a few steps, and then she pointed to a tree a mile distant. "Race you," she yelled, and broke into a sprint. The other two paused for an instant, surprised, and then grinned at each other and set out in pursuit.

Born diplomat, this one. Gods, but I love her.

SEVEN
Dread Revelations

Aside from the confirmation that Meadowfall was safe, they received no further intelligence by way of Brunnhilde's telepathic link with her sisters that day or the next. By the time evening rolled around, Sif could feel frustration beginning to gnaw at her.

The Record-Keeper had said they needed more time to produce the list, ordering the Valkyrie Brunnhilde had sent to return later. Brunnhilde herself had been tempted to Realm-jump all three of them straight to the Hall of Records, jump-sickness be damned, to threaten the vile creature until they complied, but Inge had talked her out of it. Once she calmed down, Sif realized that Thor had been right to send Inge with them. The shield-maiden was clever and quick-witted and refreshingly didn't hold the raven-haired warrior in awe, for which Sif was grateful. She was also meticulous, her inexperience making her cautious, which balanced out Sif's hastiness and Brunnhilde's growing concern for the missing souls.

But Inge, too, had worries of her own. Despite Brunnhilde's repeated assurances that Meadowfall was still safe, she grew quieter and more withdrawn as the hours passed.

They camped in an old farm that had been abandoned decades before, the wheat and oats growing wild and unharvested and slowly seeded through with wildflowers, shrubs, and small trees. It sat in a dip in the land, with low hills rising all around until it felt as if they were in a giant bowl with the sky spreading pink and peach and golden above them.

Sif lay on her back a short distance from the camp to give the others some privacy. The grass was long and lush and dampening with evening dew, but she didn't mind. She chewed a stalk of ryegrass and let the sky wash through her soul, its grandeur and majesty reminding her of her small place in the Nine Realms, no matter her history or reputation. It cleansed her of anger and grief, scouring her out until she was empty and merely sad. Clear-headed.

Inge called not long after the sun vanished that supper was ready, and Sif made her way back to the cheery circle of firelight and her companions. "How much further to the portal?" she asked when they'd eaten, cleaned up and laid out their blankets.

"Three more days. We can make a short detour into Greenside tomorrow to pick up the latest news and some more supplies," Brunnhilde said.

"Don't you mind the slowness of the journey?" Sif asked curiously.

The Valkyrie was silent for a while. "Sometimes," she said eventually and then smiled at Inge, "but this one has taught me to enjoy moving at a slower pace. It isn't just the considerations of the jump-sickness for both of you; this way we have the chance to think things through and perhaps gather further intelligence from the towns we stop at."

Sif cocked her head to one side and jerked her thumb at her own chest. "And a slower journey prevents me being reckless, eh, old friend?"

Brunnhilde laughed and held up her hands. "There is that," she acknowledged. "It was, perhaps, suggested to me by Thor that time for your anger to cool would be time well spent."

"Even after all these years," she said, but without heat. "So little faith."

"His exact words were, 'she's at her deadliest when she's calm, and that's what you'll need to fight whoever's doing this,'" the Valkyrie said.

Sif blushed, cleared her throat, and stood hurriedly. "Get some sleep," she said, her voice rough. "I've got the first watch." She stalked out on her first lap of the perimeter, her ears burning, and pretended she couldn't hear the soft laughter behind her.

As ever, Brunnhilde felt tension trickle through her spine when she openly entered a city, town or village. Although Dragonfang was invisible when sheathed, her armor clearly identified her as one of the Choosers of the Slain. A Valkyrie wandering into town had a certain effect on the populace, particularly the warrior class, who had a tendency to lay hands on weapons immediately to ensure an honorable death if she came for them. It always made things tense, and with everything they already had going on, Brunnhilde didn't want tense. But at the same time, she wouldn't glamour herself as they entered Greenside. They needed information, and if the warriors stationed here knew it was a Valkyrie asking, they would be more likely to answer quickly.

The combination of Brunnhilde's armor and Sif's distinctive midnight hair drew all eyes and caused a storm of whispers to follow them as they made their way through the busy, brightly colored marketplace into the center of town. Inge walked between them, shorter, slighter, appearing almost as an afterthought. She seemed more overawed than annoyed that they garnered so much attention, however.

Sif's face was carefully blank as the crowd parted before them. Shoppers squeezed between the stalls, and even the children were pulled without protest out of their path. A shieldwall commander pushed through the crowd towards them, waving. He was tall, with long mustaches plaited and beaded, and the rest of his face shaven. The hair at his temples was braided too, a rich strawberry-blond shot through with silver, though he moved with the grace of a young man.

He blanched when he saw Brunnhilde, almost stumbling over his feet before recovering. He hauled a smile onto his face and saluted. "Lady Sif, honored Valkyrie, and fair shield-maiden, I confess I did not expect such an eclectic group of warriors, but I thank Frigga you've come, nonetheless, and so quickly. I am Commander Olafson of the Great Northern Wall."

The three warriors exchanged a glance, and Brunnhilde gestured for Sif to handle the conversation.

"What brings you to Greenside, commander?" Sif asked, as he ushered them towards a building and into a wide, low-beamed room of desks. An intricate mural had been painted on the far wall. A few desks were occupied by scribes transcribing the Legends of Asgard into beautifully worked scrolls for apprentice storytellers, but Olafson snapped his fingers, and they collected up their papers and fled.

"What brings me to Greenside?" he repeated when they were all seated. "The deathless, of course. Isn't..." he trailed off, his face falling. "Isn't that why you're here? We sent messengers two days ago. I thought..."

Brunnhilde's stomach flipped over. "Speak," she snapped, and Olafson looked at her and hesitated, confusion tinging to suspicion.

"This is the leader of Odin's Choosers, and Inge of Asgardia's fifth shieldwall. You know me, I presume. Please, tell us what is happening at the Great Northern Wall." Sif's voice was calm and polite, but it crackled with authority, and any doubts Olafson had vanished at this confirmation of their statuses.

"Forgive me, Lady Bright-Battle," he said to Brunnhilde, his fingers touching the engraved hammer he wore around his neck. The Valkyrie ignored the gesture. She was long used to people warding off impending death when they recognized her. Instead, she tilted her head slightly towards Sif, reminding him of her question.

"What are the deathless, commander?" Sif continued, and the man jerked his attention back to her.

"If only we knew," Olafson said miserably. "There've been isolated attacks all along the Great Northern Wall over the last weeks, warriors being picked off or small scouting parties set upon and slaughtered." He gestured at Brunnhilde. "Of course, you know this," he said, and the Valkyrie had to clench her jaw at the visceral horror that swept through her. *I know nothing of this.*

"I don't," Inge said smoothly, and Brunnhilde breathed a silent prayer of thanks at her intervention. She hadn't wanted to have to lie or, worse, admit she didn't know what the commander was talking about. "I'm a simple woman in the company of these fine warriors. How many losses, do you know? And for how long exactly? What is Asgardia doing about it?"

"A few dozen so far, but those few who manage to survive all tell the same story…"

Brunnhilde's ears began to roar, Olafson's voice fading out. *A few dozen. So far. A few dozen so far.* She sent a frantic call to her sisters, asking how many of the souls they'd escorted to Valhalla recently had been from the region around the Great Northern Wall. The responses were quick, but incomprehensible. None. No one had been called that far north by a deathglow in the last half-year.

Impossible. No, no, no. Impossible!

Bile rose in the Valkyrie's throat. Not one single soul sensed, not one single Valkyrie in attendance upon the glorious dead. Soul-snatched, every one of them.

Brunnhilde swallowed hard. Her fingers had knotted together in her lap, but nothing she did could force them to unclench.

"…what do you mean, exactly?" Sif was demanding.

Olafson was wretched, wringing his hands in a rare

show of helplessness for a warrior of his evident standing. "Exactly that, my lady. They are deathless. They don't die. Or perhaps they're already dead, we don't know. It's a very recent development, though. Before, the deaths were from ordinary incursions, albeit in unprecedented numbers – a band of ragged dwarves, a wandering giant. But these are… the deathless have only come for us in the last week. They're horrific, great beings that appear half-elf or half-troll or half-wolf, sometimes. The other half is always giant. And their eyes. All their eyes are the same." His voice had dropped to a whisper with the last words.

"What about their eyes?" Sif asked. Brunnhilde, even amid her turmoil, was impressed that the black-haired warrior hadn't yet accused Loki of being the architect behind these slaughters. Perhaps she was as off balance as the rest of them.

A few dozen so far.

She sent a command to one of her Valkyrior to go to the Record-Keeper again and not leave until she had the list of the souls who'd *died wrong,* as the troll had put it. If her sister needed to threaten, she was welcome to. If she needed the authority of the God of Thunder standing behind her with Mjolnir, she could go to him and request that too. *Tell him I sent you, but get me that list.*

She blinked back to the room just as Olafson licked his lips and wrung his hands some more. "Familiar," he whispered in the end. "Their eyes are familiar. Known. Torvald, one of my steadiest warriors, swears that the deathless he fought last week was his brother, killed the month before that–" his eyes flicked to Brunnhilde, and she managed a tiny inclination of her head and even that was a lie, an awful lie. She had no idea who Torvald's dead brother was "–but it couldn't be, could it?"

"It certainly doesn't make any sense," Sif said, drawing Olafson's attention away from the Valkyrie. "This is a new and frightening enemy from the sounds of it, and these strange fancies are most likely just the stress of combat, especially as you've said these creatures are immortal. And that, really, is what we need to focus on. How have any of your warriors managed to survive if their enemies won't die? What strategies have you adopted to counter them? We will need to spread this knowledge far and wide if these incursions increase and the Great Northern Wall is further tested. With the All-Father absent, we must pool all our knowledge and expertise."

It was a nice deflection, and Olafson seemed to accept it, because he began talking about strategies and how dismembering these creatures seemed to be the only way to end their threat. Severing the limbs and head appeared to destroy them; anything less and they simply kept going.

"I can imagine that is not only extremely dangerous but also very distressing for your warriors, particularly if they themselves are grieving their glorious dead, as Torvald is," Sif said, with more diplomacy than Brunnhilde had heard from her in a long time.

The Valkyrie sent a mental command for twenty of her sisters to move immediately to the Great Northern Wall's patrol area. It was a permanent shieldwall, much like those warriors stationed in Asgardia, Meadowfall, and the larger towns and cities. It had been set up because the northern regions were so wild and sparsely populated that enemies had discovered they could infiltrate and move large numbers into position without being detected. Now, the warriors who patrolled that vast expanse of hill and forest were always on the move, traveling unpredictable routes to prevent themselves being easily bypassed. They were effective, and they were some of the toughest warriors on Asgard. They had to be, because they spent weeks out in the wilds without guaranteed backup.

And they are afraid.

The responses came in, and the Valkyrie stopped her wild speculations to pay attention to them. She commanded her Valkyrior not to reveal their true nature unless and until they felt a deathglow, and instead where possible should travel with the larger scouting parties or shadow them out of sight. At all times, they must be ready to perform their duty and report in to Brunnhilde with their observations if battle was joined with these deathless warriors.

"Perhaps we should speak to this Torvald," Inge whispered as she leant close to Brunnhilde. "I can ask him for his brother's name, and you can ask the Choosers if they've escorted him."

The Valkyrie's shoulders tensed. "I already have," she breathed. "None of them have been called north."

Inge's fingers dug in to Brunnhilde's wrist with shocking force. "None?" she hissed. "But he said–"

"Enough," she warned, and her lover bit off the rest of her words. Inge was pale, her pulse jumping visibly in her throat. Whatever number the Record-Keeper was going to give them was going to be far higher than they'd anticipated. If Sif had never seen what happened to Gyda, who knew how much longer this sacrilege might have continued. How many they might have lost. The troll would never have volunteered the information, either. That creature was bound to Odin's will, but they were sly enough to do their duty exactly, and no more.

Brunnhilde stared at the mural on the wall of the Norns deciding the fate of every living Asgardian. She wondered how many threads of life they had cut already, and how many more rested within the blades of their shears. A chill prickled from her scalp to the soles of her feet.

It couldn't be a coincidence that these deathless creatures had arrived not long before the mountain giants who'd marched to Asgardia. Surely they were all being controlled by the same person. Brunnhilde was finding it harder with each new revelation to convince herself that the mastermind behind this could be anyone other than Loki.

She understood suddenly why Sif's anger against the Trickster God never seemed to wane, how it could continue, curled patiently in her stomach, an ever-present warmth. Whoever was responsible for the soul-snatching – *Loki, Loki, Loki* – had just earnt the Valkyrie's eternal, undying enmity. They had stolen the honor from her life's purpose; they had made her complicit in their atrocity. It didn't matter that she hadn't known – *she should have.* She had failed the dead, and every day that passed without bringing an end to this horror, she continued to fail them. Brunnhilde's fingers itched to draw Dragonfang and Realm-jump directly to wherever Loki was cowering and bring him to justice – or to death. Silently, she took a deep breath and concentrated back on the conversation.

"We'll need to see the corpses of these deathless creatures," Sif said. "Unless you've already burned them."

Olafson sucked one of his mustaches into his mouth and chewed it thoughtfully, the beads braided at the ends clicking against his teeth. "We have to burn them as soon as we can, because otherwise their… bodies put themselves back together," he said.

Brunnhilde blinked, convinced she had misheard. A glance at Sif's and Inge's faces told her otherwise.

"But if you come back with me, I can send you out with a patrol and you'll run into them sooner or later. That's a guarantee." Olafson's tone was bitter.

"That might take days," Sif said. "I'm sorry, I don't think we have time for that. We are on urgent business for the God of Thunder."

The commander spat out his mustache. "More urgent than this?" he asked, disbelief etched across his face. Sif folded her arms across her chest and leant back to glare at him. "Ah, of course, of course, my lady," he muttered and then his shoulders slumped. "Someone will come soon from Asgardia, I hope. Someone who can tell us what these things are and if there is a better way to destroy them. My warriors are some of the best, but they are… growing afraid."

Inge looked between her and Sif, the question clear in her eyes. Should they go to the Great Northern Wall?

The Valkyrie's own instincts were torn, but the soul-snatched had to take priority. "Help will come soon," she said. "How many of these deathless creatures have you destroyed so far?"

Olafson slumped a little more. "Nine. They appear,

annihilate a patrol or scouting party, and then vanish again. They don't steal, they don't make demands. Their only desire appears to be slaughter. One of the survivors said that her patrol was twenty strong and wiped out, with the exception only of herself, by just three of these things. Arrows bounce off them, sword cuts seal themselves back up. Severing limbs with a single blow is the only method we've found to slow them, as I said. And to stop them completely, we have to take off all the limbs and the head. Otherwise…" He held his hands out shoulder-width apart and then meshed them together. A shudder rippled through him. "Some of them keep talking even after they're in pieces. Hence the fire."

They were all quiet for a while. "No wonder your warriors are afraid," Inge said. "And yet also so courageous, to go out on patrol again and again. You must be very proud. We would like to pray for the fallen, with your permission. And the living, that their hearts and arms remain strong and true."

"Even the Valkyrie?" Olafson asked, skeptical.

Brunnhilde bristled until she realized his words came from a place of fear and exhaustion. "Especially the Valkyrie," she said quietly. "If you would allow it."

The commander seemed to hear his own words echo in his head, because he blinked hard and then agreed. "Forgive me, my lady," he said hurriedly, and she noted he touched the amulet at his neck again. "I've no doubt the glorious dead would be most honored. And the living."

Guilt and nausea twisted in her again, but she forced them away and even managed a small smile. She'd be praying for forgiveness and that their souls might make themselves known to her so that she could find them and bring them to Valhalla as they deserved.

There was little to say after that. They left Olafson writing another letter to the palace in Asgardia begging for aid, a courier standing patiently at his side.

"You could jump us to the Great Northern Wall," Inge said as soon as they were outside. "We could take a day to search. I won't let the jump-sickness affect me."

"Another dozen warriors might have their souls snatched while we're there," Brunnhilde hissed. "Another dozen I'll have failed."

Inge gasped and reached for her, but the Valkyrie strode away through the market stalls.

"This is typical of Loki," she heard Sif say to Inge as they hurried to catch up. "Throwing random, seemingly unrelated challenges at his enemies to prevent us putting together a plan. Our task is to find…" she trailed off as they worked their way through a thick knot of townsfolk. Brunnhilde slackened her pace a little and held out her hand behind her. A second later, Inge curled their fingers together.

"I'm sorry," the Valkyrie murmured.

"No, no," Inge said quickly. "I wasn't thinking. Lady Sif is right. We have our mission and we can't let ourselves be distracted from it. Like the commander said, it might take us days to find these creatures and we don't have that time to waste."

"Whereas we're guaranteed to run into them wherever Loki is," Sif said from behind them. "Brunnhilde, of the dead Olafson spoke of, how many–"

"All of them."

Sif swore under her breath and Inge tightened her hold on her hand. They fell silent as they bought extra supplies and two horses. Brunnhilde summoned Aragorn, and the winged horse spiraled down out of the sky to land just outside the town limits. They mounted up and headed north again, though more fields of tall crops, swaying green and golden and serene. The Realm was too peaceful for the atrocities occurring beneath its skin.

Brunnhilde pushed Aragorn into a canter. And then a gallop.

EIGHT
MEADOWFALL

They rode until night fell and they could no longer see the path beneath their horses' hooves. They made a cold camp and Sif insisted on taking the full night's watch. She was restless, her mind still processing everything they'd learned or suspected so far, picking away at the mystery of the deathless and worrying at the numbers Olafson confirmed had been killed so far. A night of standing watch would allow her to analyze it and give Brunnhilde some much-needed time with Inge: they all had burdens on their souls now, of people lost or lamented. The last thing the others needed was four hours of standing watch alone and working themselves up into a frenzy of guilt and grief. If they could find some rest in each other's arms, then it would be to the benefit of all three of them.

Sif walked a wide, silent perimeter around the little camp as the stars came out and the temperature cooled. An owl hooted as it flitted on soundless wings above them, and Sif looked up, but it was invisible in the blackness. There was a squeak as a bat's life ended in its crushing grasp.

Is that how Gyda felt? she wondered, and then shoved away the thought like it was an over-friendly drunk on the street.

It was a long, still night, and when dawn came, the shield-maiden had made no further sense of the many confusing things they'd learned, despite her hours of wakefulness. She had worked out what had been gnawing at her, though – and almost wished she hadn't.

Sif doled out cold rations, and they ate as they rode, the silence heavy and pensive until the black-haired warrior abruptly broke it. "Commander Olafson said the deathless have been attacking his patrols for a week. Heimdall saw the mountain giants coming, but he never mentioned these monsters, at least not in my hearing. I think if he'd seen them, Thor would have told us before sending us on this mission."

There was nothing but the sound of hooves on stone for long moments. "How is that possible?" Inge asked, a plaintive note in her voice.

"My brother sees all living creatures moving within the Realm." Sif shrugged tiredly. "And yet he has not seen these enemies. Whatever they are and whoever has sent them, they must somehow be glamoured against Heimdall's sight."

The others had no theories or suggestions that might explain how the Far-Seeing had not spotted the creatures attacking the Great Northern Wall, and the mood darkened still further.

"Talk to me about Meadowfall," Sif said abruptly. Brunnhilde gave her a warning scowl. "How many warriors, how high is the wall, what are your defenses like?" she persisted.

Inge was silent for a few seconds and then began to speak, her voice a monotone. Soon, though, she warmed to the topic, detailing the weapons caches and archer platforms within the town and the sentry towers on the road between Meadowfall and the portal. She spoke of the cleared approaches to the town that prevented ambushers from scurrying close under tree cover and how the walls were sunk twenty yards below ground level to defeat sappers.

Sif listened as some of the animation returned to Inge's voice, absorbing the layout and typical deployment of defenders that the warrior sketched with her words even as she swept the terrain around them for dangers. She nodded approvingly as she listened, and even Brunnhilde paid close attention; the Valkyrie's skills were better given to individual combat, whether against one or more opponents, rather than taking a place in a shieldwall. Neither sieges nor full-scale battles were her area of expertise, but she drank in every one of Inge's words.

"It sounds excellently fortified and defended," Sif said, when Inge finally fell silent. They had dismounted to allow the horses to rest, and now all three walked abreast with the animals meandering behind them. "I can think of no changes I would make to the deployment of your warriors or placement of supplies and weapons caches. The killing zones sound perfectly set up, and each archer station has overlapping fields of fire. Meadowfall can clearly withstand a determined and sustained assault. It doesn't surprise me that you passed your training in Asgardia with ease when you come from such a community."

Inge blushed a little and ducked her head, but she managed a smile that had a hint of realness to it as she glanced over. "You honor me, Lady Sif."

Sif snorted. "Please, you don't need to use my title all the time. Just Sif is fine."

Brunnhilde winked. "See? I said she likes you," she teased, and Inge went even pinker.

"No, I don't," Sif said, pretending a scowl, "it's just easier to yell 'Sif' in battle, so she'd better start practicing now."

Inge's face fell, and Sif waited a second, and then laughed and bumped their shoulders together. The other shield-maiden went spectacularly red but managed a rueful chuckle of her own.

Brunnhilde narrowed her eyes and dragged Inge to her. "Monster," she breathed at Sif. "It is impossible that anyone could dislike my perfect little cherry blossom, my sweet little–"

"Odin's eye, get off me," Inge said, struggling. "You're so embarrassing. Lady Sif, I mean Sif, don't listen to her, please." She wriggled out of Brunnhilde's embrace and stalked a few paces ahead. "Gods, you're both awful, you know that?" she demanded over her shoulder, but her lips were curving in a smile. She gave a theatrical shake of her head. "I'm embarrassed for you both. Is that what passes for humor in goddess school?"

Sif arched a black eyebrow at Brunnhilde. "And you call me reckless," she said as if insulted. "I should teach her a lesson she won't forget. Such disrespect."

The Valkyrie snorted. "This one's a real berserker," she said fondly. "But I'll have to ask you to refrain from drawing steel on my girlfriend. It wouldn't really set the right tone if we're going to be working together."

"And there was me thinking you were defending my honor

purely out of love," Inge said with a theatrical pout, but she slowed enough for them to catch up.

"Love or self-preservation, it's hard to tell the difference sometimes," Brunnhilde said with a shrug. Inge gasped in outrage and the Valkyrie clapped her on the back so hard she stumbled forwards a step.

"Hela, sweetheart," Inge complained, "we're not all as strong as you."

"Very true," Brunnhilde said blithely, earning a snort from Sif.

"That's it, I'm going to talk to my horse. You're both, and I cannot stress this enough, terrible role models and even worse examples of Asgardian seniority." Inge made a show of pausing until her mount came alongside her, and then she slung her arm over his neck to murmur in his twitching ear.

"What?" Sif began, concerned that her mood was real until she caught Brunnhilde's eye. The Valkyrie winked.

"I did warn you she was a handful, yes?" she whispered. "But thank you. You've helped her remember how well defended her home is, and the banter has eased her heart a little. She's a lot more worried than she will admit, even to me."

Sif smirked and then dipped her chin at the Valkyrie, not wanting to explain that she hadn't just done it to comfort Inge. It was rare that Sif's motives were altruistic when they lived in a world that contained evils like Loki. If it did come to a siege of the town or a confrontation outside it, she had to know as much of the layout as possible before they got there. The last thing she'd need in the middle of a battle was to take a turn down a blind alley or fall into one of the concealed pit-traps outside the walls and end up at the mercy of creatures who had none.

The warrior was aware that she could be cold and distant, that her dedication and duty were sometimes seen as insurmountable obstacles between herself and the Realm, but she'd long ago made peace with that aspect of herself. Her barriers were in place for a reason. They kept Sif – and others – safe, much as her newfound knowledge about Meadowfall would keep her and its inhabitants safe if she needed to take action.

It had felt good, though, to tease and be teased in turn. Perhaps Inge's wasn't the only heart to be soothed.

Everything changed just after noon when Brunnhilde lurched to a stop, her eyes going wide and distant. She vaulted into Aragorn's saddle, and the winged horse skittered sideways to give himself room to unfurl his vast wings. They leapt into the sky.

"Deathglow," she said to Inge as a golden haze rose from her skin, hair and armor. The woman vanished and the goddess sat in her place, both a warrior and a comfort to warriors. "Run," she ordered, and vanished, Realm-jumping to Meadowfall, now only five miles away.

"No, no, no," Inge was whispering, her face gray with shock. "Please don't be this, please."

Sif grabbed her upper arm hard enough to bruise. "Run," she snarled, echoing Brunnhilde's order. "They need us."

They scrambled into their saddles and kicked their horses into a gallop. They'd never be able to cover the full distance flat out, but one look at Inge's pinched face told Sif she wasn't capable of rational thought.

The horses began to blow after two miles, and Sif shouted to Inge that they had to rein it back. "If your mount has a heart attack, you'll be on foot the rest of the way," she added as the warrior shook her head.

She thought, for a few brutal moments, that Inge would indeed ride her horse to death, but instead she let out a frustrated shriek and reined back to a canter. Even that pace would be too much soon, but the black-haired warrior would deal with that when it happened.

For now, she replayed the town's layout and defenses in her mind and extrapolated theories on what they'd find when they arrived. If it was giants again, they'd have little difficulty surmounting the walls, even with warriors lining the top and hacking at them with blades and spears. Once they were in the town, panicking civilians were going to hinder any sort of defenses the shieldwall could put in place. It would be fragmentary, most likely, too many warriors to each giant as they tried to prevent it reaching past them to screaming children and the like. Plus, the logistical issue of moving troops through streets that were quite literally filled with beings four times the size of the defenders.

Or it might be these deathless monsters Olafson spoke of.

Sif clenched her jaw. Next to her, Inge's hands on spear and reins were white-knuckled. "Easy, warrior," Sif snapped in her commander's voice. "I need you cold. If you can't be, you should wait here."

Inge's face was furious as she glanced across.

"You're a warrior of Asgardia's own shieldwall. Don't you

dare disappoint your instructors or your family by charging in wild. *Do you understand me?*" she added when the other woman didn't seem to register anything Sif was saying.

Inge's mouth worked and then she nodded, her nostrils flaring as she slowed her breathing and then, for a miracle, her horse too.

"Good," Sif said and saw the praise bolster her flagging composure a little more. But: "We go where we're needed, warrior, not where you want to be. Do you understand that?"

A muscle jumped in Inge's cheek, but she nodded again.

"I know," Sif said, perhaps too quietly for the other woman to hear over rushing wind and pounding hooves, "but this is what we do. When war comes, we are warriors first."

The horses were barely above trotting speed when the town came into view, at first visible just as a twisting column of black smoke connecting earth to sky. Next the wall, strong and sturdy and… broken in at least two places. There were indeed giants milling around, some outside, others already within the town, a few stretched in death on the earth. Around them were scores of figures, running and fighting. The air above Meadowfall was full of winged horses as dozens of Valkyrior descended on the town.

Sif flushed with cold at the sight, dread coiling within her, before she realized what Brunnhilde was doing. So many Valkyrior on the battlefield and within the town would minimize – hopefully – the number of souls that could be snatched. Relief chased the dread: at least if she fell here today, she stood a chance of reaching Valhalla.

Brunnhilde appeared in the air above them, the wind from

Aragorn's great wings battering at them as they hovered. "The defenders at the westernmost breach are beginning to crumble. Go there!"

Sif met her eyes in acknowledgment, and the Valkyrie and her steed vanished again. Inge angled off the road and across the field towards the pile of rubble that had once been a smooth stretch of wall. Sif followed, her mind sinking into that cold, precise place from which she could analyze, evade and kill without thought, a being of pure reaction and pure focus.

Fear flickered around her edges, and she embraced it and used it, a whetstone for the blade of her righteous fury.

Everything Olafson had told them about killing the deathless – if these were such – came back to her, and she alternated between staring at the creatures besieging the town and soothing her exhausted horse as she followed Inge across the pasture.

Other creatures fought alongside the giants, a ragtag mix of dark elves from Svartalfheim, trolls and dwarves and giant wolves, and even… Sif's breath caught in her throat. Her hands squeezed the reins hard, pulling her horse to a halt, before she recovered and urged him on again. And even something that looked very much like a demon from Muspelheim. No wonder the defenders were close to breaking.

"With me," she called ahead to Inge and then kicked free of the stirrups and dismounted, unsheathing her sword. "*Asgard!*" she screamed and raced across the turf and threw herself upwards onto the demon's back. It was shorter than the giants flanking it, but not by much, and its back was corded with muscle that controlled the vast, leathery black pinions half-unfurled to either side. It was probably a commander, and it was by far the most dangerous enemy on the field.

Sif landed on its shoulders and anchored herself by wrapping her free hand in its lank hair. She leaned out and back, and her sword ripped into a wing, shredding the delicate flesh stretched between the widespread digits.

The demon roared and belched smoke and flame, twisting to try and reach back between its wings to grab her. Sif ducked, the skin of its back already burning through her trousers it was so hot, but she clung on and slashed again, deep into meat and bone this time. If she could ground it, it would be far easier to kill. She could worry about how in Hela's name Loki had seduced a demon to his cause later. If there was a later.

Sif managed a third strike and felt a bone in the wing break. The demon roared again and flung itself into the sky. Its wing dragged uselessly and it fell back to earth, twisting belly-up in the air as it did. Sif tried to jump clear, but the ground was coming up fast and she was only half out from under it before they both hit the ground, the demon's scalding hide and immense weight slamming her into the dirt.

Her sword skittered from her grip as the demon writhed on top of her, trying to turn over and get its hands on her without letting her escape. Sif was face down. She spat out grass and dirt and braced. Straining every muscle, she pushed up, lifting herself and the squirming demon until she could plant a knee and then throw herself forwards, slithering like an eel from beneath it.

The warrior rolled once and lurched to her feet, scanning the ground for her sword.

"Blade!" screamed a voice, and she looked up as Inge threw the sword at her and then leaped past to ram the tip of her spear into the demon's wing, pinning it down.

"Don't," Sif began, but the demon flexed, ripping the pinion free and knocking Inge into her. They went down in a tangle of limbs. By the time they'd scrambled to their feet again, the demon was up – and it was angry.

Only a sustained blast of fire from the demon's throat would harm Sif, but Inge didn't have the same innate defense. Sif threw up her shield and dragged Inge behind it just as the jet of white-hot flame blasted down, driving them both backwards, the shield heating in seconds until it glowed red.

She hauled Inge even closer, angling her own body between the blast and the other warrior. Her sword arm pulled Inge's head in against her side as strands of blonde hair vaporized in the heat. The shield's handle was becoming unbearably hot, and panic was evident in the tight fists Inge clenched in the material of Sif's sleeve before the demon finally ran out of fire.

As soon as the flames went out, Sif swore and hurled the shield directly at the demon's face, as much to distract it as to get the shield out of her hand. It took strips of blistered skin from her palm as it went, and she hissed in pain. "All right?" she barked at Inge and received a shaky nod in return. The warrior's face was scarlet from the heat, sweat streaming down her face, but she didn't hesitate to follow when Sif raced back into the fray.

There was a change in the battle at this part of the town

wall: with the demon distracted, Meadowfall's shieldwall worked to seal up the gap in the tumbled masonry with a three-deep line of armored warriors. Unfortunately, it meant sealing Sif and Inge on the outside too. Trapped with nowhere to retreat to and surrounded by some very large, very angry foes.

"Guard my back," Sif said to Inge as they ran. "Keep an eye out." She pointed with her sword and got another nod from Inge, steadier this time. "If I yell 'fire', you run," she finished, and didn't wait for a reply.

The demon thumped the earth with its fists and then opened claw-tipped hands that could each encircle her waist with ease, beckoning and mocking both. The warrior let her lips peel back from her teeth and threw herself underneath the first sweeping blow, a claw snipping several inches from the bottom of one of her braids it passed so close. The remainder of the plait came loose as she straightened, sword in one hand and knife in the other, to dive between its legs, blades flashing.

The sword curved around to rip into the back of the demon's left leg, while the dagger sliced through the side of its right knee, and then she was on her feet behind it, ducking its spiked tail and cutting again. Hamstringing it. Sif leaped back as blood hot as lava poured out, hissing and smoking as it touched the ground. The grass blackened into char, and small fires began to burn.

The demon lurched onto its knees, bellowing. The edge of one wing, tipped with a black claw as long as her arm, arced down out of sky towards her. Sif watched it come, then stepped sideways, grabbed the edge of the wing in her knife-hand and climbed up the side of it. She reached the nape of its neck and wrapped her legs around its throat. Locking her ankles together, the warrior squeezed with all the power of her thighs. Sif brought the sword around the front of its throat and locked the cross-guard of her knife against its other end and pulled.

The edge, honed sharp enough to split light, dug in under the demon's chin, and she rocked it across its throat, burrowing the blade ever deeper. There was a scalding rush of demon blood over her legs, and Sif snarled in its ear as the pain began to bite. One of its hands came up, clawing at her leg, its talons screeching down her greaves with a sound like tearing metal, and then Inge was there, lunging with her spear for the demon's belly.

The sword in Sif's hands was getting hotter, the burning blood on her legs inching closer to agony, to having to let go, when the blade finally severed its windpipe, and blood and flame gouted from the wound.

"Fire!" she screamed at Inge, and the shield-maiden didn't hesitate, flinging herself away from the demon. Sif unwrapped her legs, ripped her sword across its throat one last time and then backflipped off its body as it began to fall, crumpling forward into its own burning. Its wings shivered, flapped once, and then it was still.

Sif lurched in a circle, checking for danger, and then dropped into the long, lush grass and rolled, smearing the blood off her legs. She'd still had her pack on her back this whole time – no time to drop it – and now she shrugged out of it, found her water bottle and upended half of its contents onto her legs, washing away the last of the blood and soothing the flesh. Her trousers were burned through in several places, the flesh beneath raw and stinging.

She drank the rest of the water and then, after checking her surroundings again for imminent danger, she dug the Quellstone out of her shirt and examined it. Just a trickle of healing magic to soothe the worst of the burns?

No. The orb's energy reservoir was limited. She'd heal in a few hours; she could bear the pain until then. Resolutely, Sif stood and scanned the battlefield, forcing herself to concentrate on something other than her injuries. She caught a flash of sunlight on steel, abruptly cut off by a looming shadow out in the meadow, and began to run again, away from the wall this time.

Inge.

The shield-maiden was ducking away from the slow but unstoppable fall of a massive ridge of earth conjured by the mountain giant she was facing.

The blonde warrior slid out of range, and Sif bellowed a wordless warning – an elf of Svartalfheim was coming up on her blind side, their sword raised. Sif threw her own, spinning end over end in a silver blur. It took the dark elf between the shoulders, impacting hilt-first, not blade. It was enough to send them sprawling forwards in the grass with a shout, and Inge jumped sideways, twisting like a cat in the air, before punching the tip of her spear through the elf's ribs. Even from here, Sif heard it scream – not just from the wound, but also that it was dealt with iron, unbearable to elves.

Sif slowed and beckoned, and Inge snatched up the sword she'd thrown and charged back towards her. The giant had either lured or forced her back from the wall, but she was far too exposed out here. They were almost out of arrow range if anyone up on Meadowfall's wall had shafts to spare in their direction.

"Are you hurt?" Sif asked.

Inge was dirt-stained and sweaty but calm enough that Sif's respect for her increased. "I'm all right. Let's get inside."

"You let the giant distract you," Sif said as they headed back towards the city, checking all around for danger.

"Seemed like the bigger threat," Inge replied.

Sif snorted. "The biggest threat is the one that kills you, no matter its size. Keep your awareness focused out wide, not just on what's in front of you."

Inge just nodded, but Sif knew the lesson had been learned.

The burning demon had forced the attackers away from that section of wall. "With me," Sif said and sprinted straight at it. Beyond the corpse was the breach, and warriors were taking advantage of the smoke and flame to hastily stack broken blocks of masonry in the gap.

"Two from Asgard," Sif shouted as archers trained their weapons on them from above. The bows didn't waver, tracking their advance, until someone shouted Inge's name. All of a sudden, they were being beckoned forward, told to hurry. Sif chanced a look behind and found six, no, eight, elves on their tail. "Sorry," she muttered to Inge, grabbed the woman by shoulder and thigh and hurled her bodily forward with all of her strength. The shield-maiden let out a surprised shriek and then she was tumbling down the far side of the scree of broken wall.

Sif flung herself after her, springing high and landing upright on the treacherous stone. It shifted warningly under her weight, and she jumped again, landing on the clear ground of the killing zone inside the wall.

They were in Meadowfall. And Meadowfall was in chaos.

NINE
DEATHLESS

Smoke and flame and collapsing buildings. Smoke blinding her, screams deafening her. People dying. Everywhere, people dying, even civilians not destined for Valhalla, whose departing souls she had to walk past with her eyes averted.

It was rare that a battlefield would also be full of non-combatants, and Brunnhilde was reminded how little she liked it. Guilt twisted in her, but she had her duty, and she was determined to do it. Ahead of her, a girl not yet a woman was wielding a kitchen knife in the doorway of her home, slashing desperately to hold back a lithe, tall elf armed with a wickedly curved blade and a wickedly curved smile. Behind the girl were two others, far younger, clutching each other in the dimness of the house.

The elf lunged past the girl's slow and untrained defense. She gasped in pain, slashing with her knife even as she sank to the floor and scoring a cut to the elf's forearm. The elf leaped back with a startled oath. The girl didn't see Brunnhilde step up behind the creature and ram Dragonfang through its back because she had collapsed, her fingers loosening on the knife handle. The Valkyrie knelt quickly and tightened them again, placing hand and knife on the girl's chest until her soul and her last breath left her. This one was a warrior, if not in name then in spirit, and Brunnhilde gathered her soul close and pressed her face against her shoulder so she wouldn't see her dead form, the dead elf, or the other shrieking girls in the house.

Quicker than thought, she transported the soul to Valhalla and deposited her into the care of one of her sisters with a kiss to the brow and a warm, proud smile. It was all she could do. She blinked back to Meadowfall; the corpses were still there, but the children were gone.

Other Valkyrior stalked through the flames and smoke, invisible to all but Brunnhilde and the dying. They, too, were seizing souls at the instant of death and whipping them away to Valhalla before some of them had even registered they were dead. Brunnhilde had stationed a score of her sisters at Odin's Hall to take charge of the souls as they were delivered, to calm them and explain events to them. It was the most she could do for the glorious dead, because she needed as many Choosers of the Slain on this battlefield as she could summon.

She *would not* lose any more souls today. The urge to unsheathe Dragonfang and fight alongside the people of Meadowfall was almost overwhelming in its intensity, but already she had done more than she should. To stand by and let those whose lives were destined to end do so was the hardest part of her duty, especially knowing that if she and all the Valkyrior fought, they might turn back the tide of this uncanny collection of warriors. She hesitated to even call it an army, for there were beings that were normally mortal enemies fighting side-by-side. Elves with blue skin and pointed ears fought in step with shaggy, badly armored giants and heavily robed trolls.

Still, it was not her place to fight. It was not her purpose, given to her by the All-Father himself. She wanted to do it anyway.

Inge's soul was a bright spark in the corner of her heart, and Brunnhilde knew both where she was and that she lived. If she wasn't careful, she'd lose focus and drift through the chaos towards her lover without conscious volition, to watch over her and keep her safe. The knowledge that she had a duty that was more important felt like a betrayal.

She's with Sif. And although she is my heart, she is only one warrior. I cannot – I will not – lose others because my attention faltered. And she's with Sif.

And she's a fine shield-maiden, fast and strong and deadly. Trained with Thor himself.

To love a warrior was to understand mortality in a way Brunnhilde normally didn't. It would be easy – and completely inappropriate – to swoop in and save Inge if the Valkyrie ever thought she needed it, but that would only convince the shield-maiden that she didn't trust her to save herself. That she doubted her ability, her skill and passion and dedication. That she wasn't a true warrior. And if that happened, Inge might begin to doubt herself, too. And doubt on a battlefield was as deadly as a blade beneath the ribs.

Only the thought of Inge fighting was a blade beneath *Brunnhilde's* ribs. Every single time. She remembered her girlfriend's rapt attention when Sif had spoken of fighting the dragon Hakurei and Balder's insistence on coming to her aid as if she was incapable of defending herself. She put herself in Balder's place and Inge in Sif's and winced. No. Not an option.

It couldn't stop her worrying, though.

Brunnhilde halted to allow a knot of warriors to charge past her down the street towards a raging mountain giant with at least a dozen spears protruding from his torn leather armor. Again, she fought the itch in her fingertips to draw her sword. Valkyrior did not join the battle unless expressly ordered to by the All-Father or the God of Thunder. She couldn't intervene again.

Unless I went to Thor. Unless I asked for permission.

One of her sisters appeared on the other side of the street, but not to collect a soul. "Bright-Battle," she said, "the Choosers in Valhalla are reporting a deathglow rising further south. Greenside and its surrounds."

Brunnhilde stopped and stared at her, her heart pounding with sudden wildness. Commander Olafson's face floated before her, telling them of the deathless, of the lives being lost along the Great Northern Wall. She cast out with her own senses and yes, there it was now that her focus wasn't so intently on the town around them. Unmistakable.

"Twenty Valkyrior are already stationed at the Wall," she snapped. "Out with the patrols. Are they responding?"

"Of course, Bright-Battle. But at least one soul has already… been snatched."

Brunnhilde swore. "How do you know?"

"Eira saw it happen."

She swore again and then closed her eyes, sending a message to all her sisters and commanding a dozen from Meadowfall to make for Greenside and the Great Northern Wall, with the rest to redouble their efforts. As soon as they confirmed, she contacted Valkyrie Eira and demanded to be shown what had happened. Brunnhilde's senses were swamped with another vision, another setting. Someone else's emotions. Their panic.

Eira, watching a patrol from a distance, glamoured and invisible as she trailed the warriors through lush hills and forested glades, until they rode into an ambush that even she hadn't spotted. Blue-eyed, blue-skinned elves rose from concealment on two sides and let loose arrows to bring down riders and horses, racing into the chaos with curved blades rising and falling.

The warriors, fighting back and realizing with growing horror that these elves, far taller and bulkier than normal, were deathless – that wounds healed and broken bones knitted and only dismemberment would stop them. Realizing that such a tactic would take too long, too many warriors working in concert to destroy one deathless, that they were outmatched even though they weren't outnumbered.

Eira, moving in close on her winged steed, dismounting in time to catch a soul in her arms as it left its body. Lifting it to her mount and glancing back at the pull of another deathglow. This warrior, a man, his eyes widening in despair even as his body slackened in death.

Eira reaching instinctively towards him, only for a shimmer to rise all around his form, the faintest iridescence like a rainbow reflected in dark water. Watching his chest rise with a ragged inhalation – and then nothing. The iridescence winking out. The warrior's body no longer alive, but also not dead. His soul and his last breath were gone.

Eira, torn between duty to the soul she'd Chosen and the body of the fallen warrior, consumed with panic and fear, retreating back to her mount and hastening to Valhalla, her mind a riot of emotion.

Brunnhilde blinked and was back in Meadowfall. She had one hand against the wall for balance and her chest heaved with ragged breaths and borrowed panic. *Thank you, Eira. Continue your duty.*

It wasn't enough, but it was all she could muster. Sif had spoken of a shimmer rising from Gyda's body, and the lack of an exhalation, too, fitted with her testimony and Brunnhilde's examination of the warrior's corpse. By sharing Eira's experience, she had as close to firsthand knowledge as she could get. Only it told her nothing new.

She blinked again. *What did you feel?* she asked the other Valkyrie. *Anything strange?*

She was reminded of the pause in the Record-Keeper's reply when she had asked them if there had been anything about Gyda's death that stood out. A scent that was also a color and a sound, the troll had said. And Brunnhilde's own observation, that the memory of Gyda, the shape of the echo of her soul, had been wrong. These were what she was searching for in Meadowfall. If Eira had sensed the same, then it would be proof that what was happening in the north and what had happened outside Asgardia, at least, were linked. If she sensed that same here, if she could find the thread of power that allowed the soul-snatching to occur, she might be able to follow it back to its source – to Loki. She reminded herself they didn't know if it was him for sure, and that the identity didn't matter anyway. Whoever was doing this would face justice.

Eira hesitated for so long, Brunnhilde thought she'd lost the connection somehow. And then: *a… sort of tugging. As if the soul was being ripped free but the power that was doing it wasn't quite precise enough to target him alone, and so the edges of it reached me too.*

Another pause, and then an outpouring of grief.

It hurt.

Brunnhilde swayed, the wall taking more of her weight. *As soon as you are done there, go directly to Asgardia and find the God of Thunder, Frigga and Heimdall too, if you can. Tell them everything; spare no detail.*

She felt Eira's assent and then snapped her focus back to Meadowfall, casting her ability to sense the deathglow wide and following it, running now, dodging the fighters who couldn't see her, leaping over them when she couldn't get past the whirl and clash of combat. The urge to pause at every skirmish in case a warrior was mortally wounded was strong, but she had to follow the deathglows she could sense. Had to make sure that those, at least, were properly taken care of and not abandoned to wait next to their own corpses for a Valkyrie – or something far more sinister – to scoop them up and take them away.

She Chose seven more souls before she heard back from Eira: Thor was heading to the Great Northern Wall to fight alongside the warriors there. He linked to Brunnhilde herself moments later for an update and, when the Valkyrie asked to be allowed to fight, he agreed. But the other Choosers at Meadowfall had to continue in their duty.

Thank you, my lord. I understand, she said.

Do not lose the city.

We will not.

Brunnhilde called Aragorn to her, unsheathing Dragonfang as the winged steed landed in the town square where she stood. She jumped into the saddle and let the glamour of invisibility fall from them both, then sent the horse galloping straight at a knot of dark elves. She urged the animal on, and he leaped into the air at the last instant, just as her enemies were bunching to face their approach. Aragorn's hooves flicked out as his wings lifted them, striking two elves in the face and killing them instantly. Brunnhilde leaned out of her saddle to swing at a third, cleaving into shoulder and neck in a spray of blood.

Her mount landed delicately on the far side, wings outspread, and then kicked backwards, catching a fourth elf in the side and spinning her away into the wall to collapse, boneless.

Brunnhilde reined him in a circle, a savage grin twisting her mouth. A grin that faded as all four collected themselves and stood. She noted the similarities from the elves she had seen in Eira's vision: too tall, too broad, their usually delicate features writ large on heavy skulls.

Aragorn's hooves and her own sword were smeared with blood, but there were no visible wounds on the elves as they separated to come at them from opposite sides, the blue and green eyes gleaming.

They were deathless. And she was outnumbered.

Ten

Blood-Washed Night

The shieldwall's commanders had bowed to her experience once they realized who Sif was, and they'd spent the day working together to organize the defense: they knew the city, and, based on Commander Olafson's testimony, she knew how best to deploy the scattered forces against the deathless.

Not that all of their enemies were deathless. The demon from Muspelheim certainly hadn't been, for which she'd offered a fervent prayer of thanks to Frigga once it was over and she'd been able to think of something that wasn't *die, demonspawn Hel-beast* and *please, please, let me live through this.*

But the combination of enemies made defending against them more complicated, not less – their forces didn't always know who or what they were facing with each new threat. To assume an enemy was deathless because they were taller than average – the only factor they had so far found the creatures had in common – meant employing slashing and severing strokes, which left warriors open to more refined counterattacks. But merely running a blade through a deathless did nothing but give it an opportunity to kill you. And most of the time, the deathless were each supported by a trio of mortal fighters. Each quartet formed a lethally effective fighting force and as the day wore on, neither Sif nor the shieldwall commanders had found a workable counterattack.

The defenders were hemmed in to their own city, struggling not to be pushed back so they didn't bring the fight to the civilians hiding in the center of the town. Battle was becoming siege, protracted and desperate. The enemy's numbers were impossible to accurately calculate in the night along with the running battles through the streets. Their own losses were likewise uncounted. But too high. Sif didn't need to know the numbers to know they were too high.

Stinking bonfires were littered throughout the town, their flames kept hot so that the dismembered deathless could be burned before they could resurrect. Brunnhilde had burned three of the elves she had killed, but she brought the fourth back for Sif and Inge to examine during one of the lulls in the fighting. They'd been sickened by how the body strove to put itself back together again whenever its disparate parts were in close proximity.

In a horrible experiment, Brunnhilde had collected the head of a different deathless killed at the wall and placed it next to the pieces of the dismembered elf. Nothing happened, and they'd all slumped in relief – if the deathless could reanimate using body parts that weren't their own, there would have been little hope for the survival of the city.

Sif had discovered no traces of technology or magic, nothing that might explain how they were the way they were, and the Valkyrie had confirmed that no deathglow rose from them as they died.

Unable to learn anything more without risking the half-elf, half-giant deathless returning to life again in the middle of their defensive position, Sif burned it and rejoined the fray. Brunnhilde circled overhead on Aragorn, winking in to deal a decapitating blow to disrupt the enemy's formation before jumping back out again. Spreading herself thin, covering as much ground as she could.

Night had fallen with stunning swiftness, or so it seemed. One moment, they'd been clawing their way into the city past the burning corpse of a defeated demon, and the next they were squinting through a flame-lit blackness that hid more than it revealed. And still the attackers came. Out of that blackness. Out of nowhere.

Inge had gone wherever Sif and the shieldwall commanders needed her to, though in every lull between attacks, she had asked for news of her family. No one had seen them since well before dusk and she'd been growing steadily more brittle as the hours passed. When Brunnhilde and Aragorn landed, both exhausted, Inge took one look at the Valkyrie and flung herself into her arms.

"I want to find my family," she said in a small, apologetic voice. "I'm sorry, I'm sorry, but I need–"

"Go," Sif said with a weary nod. "I pray that they are safe. You have one hour."

The Valkyrie slid a bloody, armor-plated arm around Inge's waist and walked her away. Sif watched them go with something like envy and a lot like exhaustion. Then she turned back to the wall.

The defenders were shattered, drained, and still standing. At this section of the wall, they'd lost perhaps a third of their number, and nobody knew how many civilians had so far died in the streets as they fled the invaders. No one could bear to know, not right now. That knowledge could well steal the spines from them, and they were all that stood between the city and annihilation.

Because that's what the attackers, deathless and mortal, seemed to want, as they reportedly had along the Great Northern Wall: souls and annihilation. They made no demands, they required no one to bend their knees in acknowledgment of a new god, a new overlord. They came to destroy and to snatch souls, nothing more.

Inge hadn't been the only one to slip away to check on family and friends during the infrequent lulls in the fighting. Sif knew the feeling well – she'd fought alongside loved ones more than once and was familiar with the grinding, ever-present fear that gnawed on the insides like a wolf every time she'd lost sight of them on the field.

And now Gyda is dead.

She swallowed down that voice and the guilt, thick and syrupy, that tangled in her throat and threatened to choke her. One thousand right choices in a battle would never outweigh one wrong one, if it led to a death. But Gyda's death hadn't been as a result of anything Sif had or hadn't done. It wasn't her fault, and the rational part of her knew that. It was just a shame that the rational part of her was currently occupied with scanning the darkness beyond the wall, intermittently lit by pale silver moonlight, for the enemy coming to tear them apart. It left the irrational part of her far too much time to snarl her in a web of lies and negative emotion. Almost, she fancied Gyda's missing soul and breath were hovering just behind the nape of her neck, stroking cold fingers across her skin, judging her. Condemning her.

Sif hadn't slept in thirty hours and she'd been fighting for nearly twelve of those; self-doubt was spreading like slow, insidious poison through her system. With determined focus, she scanned the expanse of ghostly pasture just visible to her night-adjusted eyes and forced herself to think of the defenses and weak spots in the city wall and how one might counter the other in such a way that they would live until dawn and then beyond.

Sif knew there were Valkyrior in Meadowfall, lurking on roofs and behind knots of fighters, ready to steal away the dead before they could be snatched by Loki's unknown magic. She knew it was the right thing for them to do, but how she wished those scores of fighters could drop their glamours and help turn the tide, their abilities as demi-goddesses and prowess with blade, spear and bow shoring up the fraying determination of the shieldwall's surviving warriors. Or, if not fight, then at least form an impenetrable ring of steel around the huddled, fearful non-combatants who had gathered in the city's center to wait for life or death to claim them.

"Here they come!" someone shouted, and Sif hurried forward, the promise of violence wiping every doubt and puzzle from her mind. In comparison with ordinary Asgardians, her abilities were as far out of their reach as that of the Valkyrior, but even she could feel the slowest rusting of her speed and strength prior to both failing. Not yet, but perhaps not too many hours in the future.

Civilian builders had been piling the shattered remnants of the breached wall back into the gap during the lull, wedging blocks together to form a stable base and slapping mortar on it. They ran now, vanishing into the roads leading to safety. The mortar hadn't even begun to dry yet, but the pile of rubble was a few yards higher than before, meaning the city was that little bit more secure. Sif would take what she could get.

"More torches," she shouted. "Fire arrows to the second marker."

Scores of flaming arrows arced into the night like determined, angry fireflies, to crest and dip and drive down to the earth a hundred yards out. Their tiny pinpricks of light were hidden and revealed, hidden and revealed, by the advancing, racing enemy as they passed the tiny torches. Two or three lucky shots hit bodies, but none of them dropped, instead ripping out the burning shaft and coming on. Deathless? Or berserker?

"First marker," Sif bellowed, and another arc of fire split the night sky with streaks of yellow, orange, red. "Twenty seconds," she shouted, and the warriors hustled forwards, out past the broken wall onto the field, shields and spears in front, the second row angling their shields overhead. A third and fourth row waited behind, ready to brace against any charge that threatened to push them back.

Sif herself anchored the line on the right – the most dangerous place in the shieldwall, as she didn't have anyone to her own right whose shield could protect her. The commanders had the center so they could pass orders in both directions, and the left-hand anchor was the jagged spill of rock that had collapsed outwards from Meadowfall's wall.

She'd had a succession of warriors to her left as the afternoon had faded into evening and they'd formed line again and again, including Inge, but this one was another stranger. A young and clearly frightened stranger. Sif tapped her shield against his. "Sif," she said with a grin, "and we're going to look out for each other, yes?"

"T-Trig," he stammered, and his returning smile was ghastly and devoid of humor. "I hope to be worthy to fight at your side."

"I hope so too," Sif said cheerfully, though everything about him made her stomach sink into her boots. "How about you lift that shield because they're only a few seconds away now, yes? That's it, warrior. Spear ready, feet rooted, strong stance. Good. We've people behind us, don't forget. We're not alone."

She didn't have time for more. The torchlight gleaming around and above her limned the faces and teeth and armor of the fighters charging them. She spared a single glance along the line of advancing troops and huffed out breath. Looked like the giants were going to be causing trouble to her left, which made a nice change. Sif locked her shield against Trig's and put her shoulder into it, sank her hips, and dug her toes into the ground. *Four, three, two, one…*

The impact rocked her onto her back foot. She sank a little lower to counter it, snarling and jabbing with her spear, slicing open a face whose race she couldn't identify in the half-light even as she felt the warriors behind brace and then shove her forwards again. It had been something like a troll, but too tall, its eyes burning blue.

Oh, Thor's hairy ass, she thought as the creature's face sealed itself up.

They'd discovered it throughout the day, and it might explain why Commander Olafson's warriors at the Great Northern Wall had been convinced they knew the deathless they faced. While most Asgardians had eyes in a hundred different shades of blue, or grey, or green, all the deathless they faced shared the same intense blue stare. This one was no different.

"Lock shields," Sif roared at Trig as he stumbled sideways, flailing and opening a gap between them. The boy gasped and slammed his shield back across, barely deflecting a wicked, jagged-edged spear that would have opened one or both of them, armor or no.

The maybe-troll let out a high-pitched, choking laugh and attacked again. Sif rammed her spear into its throat and tried to rip it sideways, to begin the decapitation that would stop it. It grabbed the shaft in long-taloned fingers and leaped backwards, wrenching the weapon away. Sif had to let go or be pulled into the darkness. She swore and unsheathed her sword, its shorter length putting her at even more of a disadvantage out here on the lonely, unprotected end of the line.

"Spear?" she snapped to the warriors behind her, but no weapon was passed forward.

Again, the pressure of Trig's shield left hers and she stepped to her left, trying to re-establish contact. Was the entire line shifting, or just contracting as warriors fell and left gaps? Why wasn't the second line stepping into those breaches? Even the third or fourth? Why were they crabbing sideways?

Whatever was causing it, the further left they moved, the more exposed became the breach in the wall they were defending. It wouldn't be long before the enemy could slip around her and over the rubble and into the city. If she lost contact with Trig or the warriors behind, alone among the enemy… Sif shoved the thought away, knowing that insistent little voice would kill her as surely as a blade through the heart.

The troll-thing came back in, spear gone from its throat and no evidence that she'd ever ripped it open but a dark dent. It, too, had a sword, this one jagged, the false edge designed to catch hers and disarm her if it could twist its wrist just right. On another warrior, it might have worked. She exchanged a quick flurry of blows, mostly defensive as she maintained contact with Trig, who stepped left again. Sif didn't have time or breath to shout down the line to correct their slow drift, because the deathless troll was on her again, close in this time, its blade insinuating its way past hers as she let the shieldwall's movement distract her.

Sif whipped her shield laterally across her body, deflecting the jagged blade and parrying it further with her sword as she slapped the shield back against Trig's before anyone could take advantage of the gap.

Or so she thought. The boy coughed and then stumbled, the weight of his shield on hers slipping.

"Trig! Stay with me, warrior! Stay with me," she tried,

but the troll-thing was on her again and she couldn't spare even a blink in Trig's direction. A thin whine came out of his throat, and his shield slipped some more. Sif dodged left and jammed herself tight against him, hampering his spear arm, but he wasn't doing anything other than standing there with the tip pointed at the dirt, so it didn't much matter. A flicker of feathers in the corner of her eye told her the story of his coming death: he had an arrow in the right side of his chest. The side her shield was supposed to cover.

"*Second line*," she screamed as she parried again, then ducked a diagonal cut that would have split her skull. "*Step up!*"

Nothing. No one. Trig stumbled when her weight shifted away from his. His face was gray, eyes already unseeing.

"Valkyrie! We need a Valkyrie!" she bellowed, and with a swift plea for forgiveness, she thrust at the deathless with her sword to push them back, sheathed the blade and stole the spear from the boy.

Trig staggered again, and this time he fell like a tree, making no attempt to save himself. *Please, All-Father, a Valkyrie for him. Please.*

Sif jumped over him, slamming her shield into that of the next warrior along, shortening the line again, but it was that or be cut off, surrounded, and then cut down. This warrior was steady and fast, which in turn steadied her, and between them they took off both the troll's arms and half-severed its neck. A thick fountain of blood spouted into the night to fall as a hot, sticky rain, but still the deathless came, shambling now. From the corner of her eye, she saw its arms writhing weakly on the ground, trying to return to their owner. She stamped on one, then hooked her boot beneath it and kicked it away. The warrior next to her ran his spear through the troll's chest, impaling it and then angling the weapon down, forcing it onto its knees. Sif cut through the rest of its neck, caught its head by its stringy hair, and flung it directly into the path of a charging elf. It tripped and fell, and the woman it was facing impaled it through the back with her spear, pinning it to the ground and then taking its head off with her axe. The other limbs followed.

There was no one in front of Sif. She sucked in air, three deep draughts, and then took one step forwards and twisted. "Line right, five paces. Say again, line right, five paces," she screamed, hands around her mouth. Distantly, she heard it repeated. "On three. Three! Two! One! *Line right!*"

To Sif's immense relief, the line came with her, and they crabbed sideways as they fought, switching to defense only until they were in place. Three steps, four… five. She breathed a sigh of relief that turned into a grunt as something impacted her shield and knocked her balance backwards over her heels. She stepped her left foot back and braced, ducking into protection and unable to see what was on her. The blow came again, off-center this time and spinning her shield out of alignment, exposing her left arm and hampering the spear in her right. Sif started to shift, turning half-on to get back behind her shield, when the bite of a blade gouged at her left arm, just above her elbow. Blood sheeted down her arm as the weapon – jagged-edged – tore out of her flesh. No clean cut, that, but one designed to cause as much damage as possible.

Sif's shield drooped despite her best efforts, severed

muscles trying valiantly to perform their task, and she came face-to-muzzle with something that appeared to be part wolf. Thick fur sprouted from beneath its clothes and armor, and its face bore a long muzzle with sharp, yellowed fangs and a red, slavering tongue. Big triangular ears stood up from its skull, and its humanoid hands held two serrated blades.

"Hela, what are you?" Sif grunted, shocked and disgusted, battering her shield into its sensitive snout and smacking its leg with the haft of her spear. It was too close for the long weapon, its dark fur and leather armor having concealed its approach. She bashed at it again, pushing against it as she prepared to drop the spear and snatch her sword. Agony was sliding up her left arm now, washing into her chest and neck and head with every pulse of her heart. Blood flowed freely to drip off her elbow.

Groaning, she forced her arm up again, then dropped her spear, kicked the demi-wolf in the gut as it came in with those twin blades again, and ripped her sword free to meet them edge-on above her head. She parried the left blade, took the impact of the right on her shield – gasping with pain as the torn muscles juddered – and cut back, her sword tip slicing down and into the creature's lead thigh, opening fur, flesh and muscle.

It staggered back, a half-human howl breaking from it. Sif took a step after it and ran it through, her blade punching out of its back. She twisted her wrist, opening the wound, and dragged it back out, waiting for its next attack. Surely it was deathless. To her surprise – and not a little relief – it collapsed, wheezing and whimpering through its muzzle, and then died.

It was the last death along Sif's part of the line. In the flickering, intermittent torchlight, the shield-maiden watched the enemy retreat. How many more attacks could they resist before the shieldwall collapsed? What was happening in and around the rest of Meadowfall?

Sif turned to go and find out, and instead found herself on one knee, sword dug into the ground to break her fall, and her shield slipping from her other hand. She heaved in great lungfuls of air as the world spun lazily around her. She closed her eyes against a surge of nausea, and then forced herself to stand. Sif sheathed her sword and clamped her hand around the collar of Trig's chainmail, hissing pain between her teeth. She staggered for the breach, the corpse bumping along behind her. She staggered for the safety – however fragile – of the city.

Eleven
To Hold the Portal

"There she is."

They hurried towards the black-haired warrior sitting on a pile of rubble and staring blindly at the chaos around her. "Sif? Sif, it's Brunnhilde and Inge. Are you alright?"

Sif looked up slowly, her eyes dull and far away. After a long moment where it seemed she didn't recognize them, her gaze sharpened. "Brunnhilde? Did you get him? The boy Trig, in the front line not long ago? Out there, he was next to me, took an arrow to the chest." Sif stood and seized her arm in a hot, wet grip. "I moved my shield. I shouldn't have, the arrow wouldn't have gone in otherwise. I brought his body but… did you get him? Is he safe?"

"Sif, you're bleeding," Brunnhilde said, prying the bloody hand off her elbow. She leaned closer. "We need to get that looked at. You're going to need stitches."

The warrior glanced down at her arm with utter indifference. "It'll heal. Tell me you got Trig. Tell me he hasn't been soul-snatched."

A few of the warriors around them looked over at that, their brows furrowing at the unfamiliar term, and Brunnhilde felt her stomach tie in knots. "Shut up," she breathed, low but intense. "We don't talk about that here."

"Then answer me," Sif hissed, clamping her hand back around her wound as Inge made a small noise of distress and began to fuss.

"I didn't. Let me check in with the others," the Valkyrie said after a long pause. She had to remind herself Sif was wounded and felt guilty that a boy was dead and so her temper was shorter than usual. They were all tired. Still, she closed her eyes and sent the request to the Valkyrior in Meadowfall and, while she waited, debated what she'd tell the warrior if the answer was that he had, indeed, been stolen.

"There's a medical station set up half a mile away," Inge was saying. "They'll be able to clean and treat that. Can you walk?"

Sif arched an outraged eyebrow. "Yes, but I'm not going. There could be another attack any minute. I'm needed here."

"Lady Sif," Inge tried, but Sif cut her off with a wave of a bloody hand. "Then I'll stitch it, if you'll sit still for five minutes for me?" Inge asked.

Sif blew out a long breath but then sat again with her left arm presented to the meager light. "Did you find your family?" she asked belatedly and let go of the wound to put her hand tentatively on Inge's vambrace.

"Thank you, we did. They're safe. Well, my parents are fighting, and my brother too, but the others are safe."

"I'm glad," Sif said, and seemed to mean it. Inge ripped open the warrior's sleeve and poured water over the wound.

She wiped it gently, though it began oozing blood again immediately. It was deep and nasty, and though Sif healed far faster than normal Asgardians, it would limit her movement for a few days. Brunnhilde tapped Dragonfang's hilt as she watched and waited for her sisters to give her an answer. Inge gave the water bottle to Sif and gently bullied her into drinking the rest. She knelt before her, fumbling in the pouch on her belt for needle and catgut, squinting to get it threaded.

"Sorry if this hurts," Inge murmured and then pinched the edges of the wound together and jabbed the needle through. Sif winced but held still, and soon enough her eyes glazed over again as she drifted on the waves of fatigue.

The Choosers of the Slain in Meadowfall reported in, and Brunnhilde breathed a sigh of relief. The boy Trig had been collected and escorted to Odin's Hall. His soul and last breath were safe. She turned to Sif to tell her, but Inge stood up and shook her head. Sif was slumped, chin on chest and spine curved inwards, upright and fast asleep. The wound on her arm had been bandaged.

"Well done. Did you drug the water?" Brunnhilde breathed into Inge's ear before kissing it.

Inge swatted at her arm. "Of course not. She's just tired. Have to say, though, I've never actually seen someone fall asleep while being stitched up. I'm impressed."

"That one doesn't do anything by halves," the Valkyrie agreed. "And Trig's soul is safe," she added. "So at least we can reassure her about that when she wakes."

"Oh, that is a relief. I was next to her in the line when she was anchoring it earlier today. I'm not sure what was more frightening, her or the enemy. She's like Thor's lightning come to earth. But cold."

Brunnhilde guided her a few steps away from the sleeping warrior. "Don't let her hear you say that; she'll be impossible to live with," she grumbled, but without heat. Inge managed a tired smile. It was easier to tease than to think of her lover being near the end of a shieldwall, in the greatest danger. "How are you feeling now?"

Inge smiled and pushed her hair behind her ear. "Better now I've seen my family and know they're safe. Tired, though. Sore."

"You should try to rest as well, love," Brunnhilde said.

Inge snorted. "We all should. That includes you. How's Aragorn?"

"I sent him back home so he can rest in safety. He can jump back here in the morning if I need him. Now, you sit with Sif. I'm going to check how the warriors on the other side of the city are doing."

"But you need to rest," Inge protested.

Brunnhilde steered Inge back towards Sif and pressed her down until she was sitting. "I was riding Aragorn all day. I've got a lot more energy than you. Sleep now. Sleep while you can." She dropped a kiss on her sweat-lank hair. "And when the enemy comes again, stick with Sif. Protect each other."

Inge tried to protest again but yawned instead. Brunnhilde seized the opportunity to duck away into the shambling crowds of warriors and those civilians – builders, doctors and cooks – who were alternating between bustling around them and casting fearful glances out through the shattered wall and into the night.

In truth, Brunnhilde was nearly spent, the effort of Realm-jumping herself and Aragorn for hours on end – even if it was only over short distances – draining her powers. She sent out a tendril of connection to her steed and encountered only the calm warmth of his full belly and sleeping mind. It soothed her to know he was well and lightened her steps a little. At least one of them was safe.

Much of Meadowfall was silent and dark as she strode through it, the residents locked within their houses, no fires or lanterns lit to advertise their presence. Others had fled those properties built in the shadow of the wall to retreat deeper into the town, away from the incursions that had spread to three sides of the city. Even here, though, nearing the parks and markets in the center, everything was still, dark, and eerie. She could sense life – not the deathglow, just the presence of living people – all around her, but saw no one. Even stronger, she could sense fear hanging over the city, like the smoke from a million chimneys had formed a choking blanket over everything.

Brunnhilde passed through knots of warriors slumped against walls and each other, too tired to search out shelter or even a blanket. Most slept, but a few watched her pass with dull, indifferent eyes. It was strange to be visible to the living on a battlefield, and even stranger not to be watched with apprehension in her distinctive armor. She strode among them exuding as much confidence as she could muster, her head held high and proud, as if the monsters besieging the city were barely worth her notice.

She smiled and nodded at every warrior who made eye contact and paused at a small fire four had set up in a courtyard to exchange quiet words and slap some shoulders. It wasn't strictly her place to do so, but in her experience, all warriors reacted the same to a show of strength from their own side. At the very least, it couldn't hurt.

The warriors around the fire also gave her the latest intelligence from this side of Meadowfall. Their commander was dead, but her second-in-command had taken over and was doing a fine job. There had been no further giant sightings, and despite the elves' athleticism and climbing ability, no further incursions beyond the wall.

Deathless and mortal, trolls and giants and, most worryingly of all, perhaps, light elves fighting alongside dark elves. *Light elves fighting at all,* she reminded herself. While the inhabitants of Svartalfheim were openly martial in nature and had attempted to conquer other Realms more than once, those who lived in Alfheim were secretive. What little was known of them indicated they were playful and peaceful, and their use of and proficiency with weapons was limited.

For light elves to have been seduced into this army – whether as deathless or mortal – was even harder to believe than the fire demon's appearance that had nearly roasted Inge and Sif alive when they first arrived. A demon's presence among hybrid monsters and deathless warriors dedicated to slaughter was understandable – light elves associating with any of those things was not.

How had they been bribed or coerced into joining this cause? Were their families held hostage, as Inge had believed to be the case with the mountain giants outside Asgardia? Was Alfheim itself under threat? From what little Brunnhilde knew of them, light elves wouldn't go to war for something as paltry as mere wealth. Surely they were here against their will?

The Valkyrie heard the clash of arms and screams of pain from the road leading off hers and she drew Dragonfang and broke into a sprint. She didn't have answers to the mysteries, but she had a blade and the will to use it.

A dozen warriors were strung across the width of the street, fighting a desperate holding action against at least eight elves. Behind the small line, four others lay in crumpled, bloody heaps of armor and clothing, motionless. As the Valkyrie closed the distance, she felt the deathglow rising, and swore when a shimmer began to rise from the furthest from her. *Soul-snatch!*

Brunnhilde Realm-jumped directly to the body. The Valkyrie stretched out hands and power and grasped at the soul. Its eyes opened wide, mouth too, as if to ask the Valkyrie a question – and then it was gone.

Brunnhilde felt something – an awful tugging, as Eira had described, a lance of agony through her chest and flashing into every limb. It was as if there was a vortex at her center, straining to pull her through into somewhere else. For a wild moment, she thought about letting it – it would at least take her to where the missing einherjar were – but she suspected that if she did, it would only be her soul going. She would have no corporeal form wherever she ended up. She would be helpless.

So, she fought back, dragging her disparate components back together, settling her mind, breath and soul firmly within her flesh. When she had control of that flesh, she threw herself backwards, away from the corpse.

Brunnhilde hit stone hard, hip and shoulder and then the side of her head as she failed to break her fall. Dragonfang was flung from her grasp to skitter across the flags towards the opposite wall. She felt weak, disconnected from everything, as if she was floating a few inches above her body. Instinctively, she cloaked herself from the view of the still-battling Asgardians. If they looked back to see a Valkyrie sprawled insensate among corpses, the panic that was already bubbling in them would overflow.

The deathglow from the other three figures crumpled on the stone was still there, but no Choosers of the Slain came to them; they sensed Brunnhilde's own presence and thought the souls to be safe. She rolled onto her knees, the night spinning and flipping as she did, and then forced herself to stand. With effort, she composed herself into the merciful, compassionate Valkyrie and then accepted the souls as they exited the bodies on their last breath, murmuring praise and comfort and reassurance that they were going to Valhalla, that they'd fought gloriously and that they and their names would live forever.

She jumped them direct to Odin's Hall and handed them off to one of her sisters with a reverent bow for each of them, and, she hoped, no sign of haste. Then, she gathered herself and jumped back to the fight, fury licking dark, poisonous flames in her gut. Snatched from beneath her very palms!

Brunnhilde retrieved Dragonfang and then dropped her glamour in the very middle of her enemies. They had control of the entire street now, but her appearance left them blinking, gaping, and in that instant the defenders regrouped and charged. The elves – all of them from Alfheim – howled and converged on her. With the icy control for which Lady Sif, not she, was famous, the Valkyrie spun into a lethal dance of whirling blade and crushing leaps and stunning blows.

Within seconds, the defenders had surrounded the elves, who surrounded Brunnhilde, and between them they cut their enemies to pieces. These hadn't been deathless, and they died easily once Dragonfang and Asgardian spears and swords found their flesh. Not as easily as peaceful inhabitants of Alfheim should – these elves had been trained, and their howling rage and twisted features were unnerving. Brunnhilde was sure, now, that they were being controlled somehow.

For a brief moment, she regretted killing them all; perhaps they should have kept one alive for questioning. She made a mental note to see whether any other defenders had mortal captives and if they'd learned anything from them.

She checked in with the warriors who'd fought alongside her and then made her way to the wall on the east side of the city, confirming to the commanders there that the western side was still holding despite multiple breaches in the wall. They'd fared no better here, and some of the foe had managed to set more fires as night fell. A dozen civilians had died of smoke inhalation in a large meeting house; more had been injured by fire or collapsing masonry.

Annihilation, she reminded herself. This enemy wanted nothing except to destroy – and to snatch souls where possible. Brunnhilde wasn't sure how much longer they could hold out.

Heimdall, if you're watching this, send word to Thor. We need him.

It was a futile plea. Of course Heimdall was watching. But Thor had been called to the Great Northern Wall hours before. He wasn't coming; they were on their own.

Wearily, Brunnhilde set out to walk the perimeter of the city, lending aid wherever skirmishes were being fought or warriors pushed back. Everywhere she went, the defenders were grim-faced and determined, but fear was curling in around their edges. The attacks came randomly out of the darkness, their numbers never seeming to shrink despite how many they killed. As if there were always more waiting their turn to fight.

She heard variations on the same story wherever she went. They faced overwhelming numbers, but whoever was in charge was sending them in slowly, forcing the battle into a drawn-out siege, a slow attrition that sucked at the defenders' energy and spirits. A creeping fear that grew and grew. What would happen when they were too tired to fight? What would be done to them?

The best and brightest won't give in to that fear. The leaders – the ones Loki wants – will keep rallying and fighting. They'll stand out as targets for soul-snatching even more as the siege wears on.

The cold calculation of it was sickening, but Brunnhilde pushed it away. If Loki were sending a constant stream of fighters to wear them down, then she knew where these enemies must be coming from.

The Valkyrie turned down a dark, abandoned alley and glamoured herself, then took a few seconds to rub at her face and re-tie her hair. Then she unsheathed Dragonfang and transported herself to the Realm-jump point, appearing a few dozen feet from the tall, carved menhirs that marked it. Half a dozen dark shapes were clustered together on the road from the portal to the city. The pillars themselves were glowing, the magic visible to the goddess' eyes. Readying to bring more enemies into Asgard. A score, a hundred, a thousand, she didn't know.

She had to close it. Now.

The Valkyrie sprinted between the ornately decorated pillars and reached out with her senses. The portals were linked through the between-space to places across all Nine Realms, and while she couldn't tell where this one was opening to, she felt the familiar brush of its magic as it prepared to disgorge more enemies. Brunnhilde herself could Realm-jump from and to anywhere, but the portals were a way for those without her ability to move across Realms – like the elves who had startled at her sudden appearance and were now watching her with wary confusion, perhaps expecting her to use the portal to jump to safety.

She didn't. Stretching her arms to their limits, Brunnhilde braced her palms against each pillar and began to channel its power into herself, forcing shut this door between Asgard and the other Realms. She was only just in time – she caught the shiver of life and magic on the other side and forced them back and away, tossing those who'd been about to emerge back into the between-space.

It began as a faint buzzing in her palms and fingertips. Then, it became a pleasant tingle that moved slowly up her wrists into her forearms and then on, biceps into shoulders into her neck and jaw and skull, down through each individual rib, shivering through her lungs and heart, lower into her waist and hips and thighs and calves and feet.

Brunnhilde gritted her teeth so they wouldn't vibrate and eventually shatter. Her vision began to blur until she had to close her eyes. The portal's power seeped faster through her palms into every fiber, breath, and beat of her heart until she thought she might just shake apart and fly away into the night.

A long, stuttering exhale, edged with the faintest groan of protest, eased from her clenched jaw. Through the fluttering of her eardrums, she heard the elves shouting in consternation. Tensing the muscles of her face, she opened her eyes and tried to focus: they were running towards her across the turf, their swords glimmering in the faint starlight.

All-Father, looks like this armor you gave me is going to be put to the test.

Brunnhilde dropped her chin so they couldn't easily slit her throat and tensed every muscle in her body. She flashed a warning to her Valkyrior, showing them what she was doing, urging them to continue their duties when she fell. Inge's face filled her mind's eye and, despite the tension in her jaw, she grinned and then roared at the oncoming elves, urging them to do their worst.

One elf pulled ahead of the others, his lips lifted into a snarl of vengeful triumph. Brunnhilde shouted a wordless challenge at him. He leaped into the air, bringing his curved blade up above his head in both hands. He'd split her skull as he landed.

The Valkyrie watched him come. When his leap was irreversible, his trajectory set, she slammed the sole of her right boot into the pillar, let go with her right hand and caught the blade as it arced towards her face. Bright, fierce pain seared through her hand and into her arm, all the way to her shoulder. A yell burst from her mouth, but the sword was suspended above her and the elf, his movement arrested by the sudden stop, dangled in the air for one surprised instant. He let go of his blade and landed, catlike, at her feet.

Brunnhilde's arm was already moving, and as he rose fluidly from his crouch, she ripped his own sword across his face. The elf screamed and stumbled back. Brunnhilde tossed the weapon in the air to catch it hilt-first and decapitated him with a single, clumsy blow. More luck than intention, for the muscles in her hand had been severed and her fingers were loose around the hilt. Still. One down, five to go.

In the seconds before the others reached her, the Valkyrie threw the sword, end over end, to take the next elf in the chest and pin him back to the ground. She swapped sides – pressing her bleeding hand to the right pillar and her left foot to the other to continue channeling the portal's power. She drew Dragonfang with her off-hand.

The portal's magic was still increasing in strength within her, blurring her vision and dampening her hearing, but she didn't hesitate. Four elves. One sword. One Valkyrie.

Brunnhilde grinned. The others had slowed their approach at the sight of two of their own already down, and now they spread out so they could come at her from two sides. From behind.

The two elves in front of her stopped, just out of range of her sword, when a blade opened up the hamstring of her supporting leg from behind. Brunnhilde kicked off the ground and spun herself upside down, supported only by her right hand and left foot against the pillars. The elf who'd cut her was gaping, and her hesitation was just enough for the Valkyrie to stab her through the throat and then lop off the arm that came up in instinctive defense.

The second lunged for her. She drove him backwards, but then those on the other side closed in, hacking at her limbs, and she had to come down out of the pivot to counter. One tried to sever her arm, but her vambrace was made of Asgardian alloy, and the dark elves, of course, couldn't bear the presence of iron. Their weapons were hard oak and glass – wickedly sharp cutting edges, but brittle. Brunnhilde tensed her forearm within its armor and the blade shattered, though her hand skidded in its own blood down the carvings on the pillar until she tightened it again.

A blow against her back had her lurching forward, boot and hand scrabbling to maintain contact. This time she didn't spin upside down, just braced and kicked backwards. She missed, but she heard the elf hiss and skitter away. The portal's power had built to unbearable levels, and Brunnhilde was almost blind and deaf with it, relying on instinct and a warrior's senses beyond those of the normal five to keep her alive a few seconds more.

Alive, but not victorious. Another cut, to the back of her upper arm just beneath the pauldron, and more Valkyrie blood flowed. She tried to lash backwards with her blade; again she missed. Next, cuts at the back of both legs, weakening them until she had no choice but to drop her sword and slap her hand against the pillar to support her weight again.

Inge, forgive me. I love you.

Slowly, gently, she slid to her knees, the portal's power close to overwhelming. Every muscle shuddered, every bone resonated to a different pitch. Brunnhilde's head tipped forward onto her chest. Every second she channeled this power was a second Meadowfall lived. A second more that Inge lived. She would give them as many of those seconds as she could.

The elves in front of her crouched, grinning in savage, merciless amusement. Brunnhilde peeled back her own lips in a ghastly parody of a smile and then, driven by something beyond her, she sucked in a deep breath and screamed at them.

More than just breath and voice blasted her foes. Some of the energy from the portal blazed out of her in a great coruscation of green-edged light. It struck one elf in the chest and the second half-on. The first simply vanished, there one blink and gone the next. The other… well, the part of him that had been struck with the energy vanished, just like the first. The rest of him… did not. One arm, most of a leg attached to a jagged slice of pelvis and hip, and one ear quivered for a sliver of time and then collapsed to the grass.

Brunnhilde stared, some of the agony in her bones and muscles having faded with the expulsion of power, and then she began to laugh, great ragged whoops of amusement, edging close to hysteria.

The surviving elf behind her sliced across the back of her neck. The Valkyrie jerked and felt hot blood pour down behind her back-plate, soaking into her hair and her shirt. She made a sound, and her vision faded in and out. Another blow, and then the sound of a bowstring and another impact that had her jerking on her knees.

Brunnhilde's hands slid from the pillars. The portal's energy stopped pouring into her in a scorching, agonizing rush. Its sudden absence was almost as painful, an awful emptiness unable to distract her from the deep wounds the elves had made in her flesh. The portal was open again. Unprotected. Unguarded.

The Valkyrie tried a final time, one trembling hand rising to the pillar flickering in and out of her blurring sight, but then the last of her energy – and the last of the portal's energy – rushed out of her. The last thing she knew was her cheek slapping cool, bloody grass.

Twelve
The Promise

The sun was high when Brunnhilde woke, her consciousness swimming up into increasing layers of pain and bewilderment. Was the battle still raging or had they won? Could they have lost?

Where was Inge?

It was that last thought that propelled her into consciousness. She groaned. Instantly, there was movement nearby and she tensed, gasped at another flare of pain. Her eyes were still so heavy, but adrenaline coursed through her system.

"Brunnhilde? Lover? Can you hear me? How do you feel?"

The Valkyrie managed to unstick one eyelid. Inge hovered over her, her face so close she could feel its heat and the tickle of an escaped strand of honey-blonde hair against her temple. "Mmph," Brunnhilde managed.

The force of Inge's kiss nearly pushed her over the edge into death, but she managed to cling on through it and even smile when the warrior released her mouth with a happy, relieved little laugh. The smile earned her a dozen more featherlight kisses, to her brow, cheeks and the tip of her nose. Eventually, Brunnhilde fought one hand from beneath the blanket to push her away. The gesture woke every muscle from slumber into screaming agony, each its own unique pitch, until she was thrumming with a symphony of hurts. But she was indoors, in a bed with bright sunshine sliding in through wide windows. No one was trying to kill her. It was nice.

"Alive, then," she croaked, and even speaking was painful. She wondered, for one embarrassed moment, whether she'd been screaming as she'd held the portal shut.

"Scare me like that again and you'll wish you weren't," Inge scolded, but her eyes were shiny with emotion. "Idiot."

"Rude," Brunnhilde breathed, but put her scabby knuckles against the warrior's cheek. "Love you."

"Love you too," Inge murmured and finally sat up straight with a hiss she tried to hide. Brunnhilde saw why immediately, but Sif was on the other side of the bed and shoved the Valkyrie back down as she tried to rise, her horrified gaze fixed on the sling and the wrapped arm nestling within it.

"It's just a broken wrist! Don't worry, it's already been set. The doctor says it will heal well and without complications. Besides," Inge added with a warning growl, "you don't get to say a word. Not after all this," and she made a broad gesture with her good arm that encompassed the bed, the blankets, and Brunnhilde herself.

"Rest a bit longer," Sif added. "We need you."

The Valkyrie managed to tear her attention away from Inge at that. "What's the latest?"

Sif leaned back against the wall with her arms folded, still dressed in her armor, which was filthy with grime, smoke, and blood in varying shades from various races. "They've pulled back. It was dawn when we drove them off from the city, back towards the Realm-jump point. It looks like they'd been reinforcing throughout the battle. When you shut the portal and their numbers began to fall, they panicked."

Brunnhilde nodded, glad to have her own theory confirmed.

"You were… unconscious by then, but nothing was coming through to Asgard – or if it was, you dumped all the energy you'd held as you let go. There's a circle of blasted earth fifty feet wide around the portal. It's likely that if anyone was in the between-space at the time, they were shoved off-course or killed. Who knows where they'll end up, if they ever find a way out?"

"Killed… Asgardians?" Brunnhilde tried, and made to sit up again. Sif shoved her back against the pillows, though the Valkyrie made her work for it this time, pain be damned. "Sif?"

The shield-maiden shook her head. "A few of the first arrivals alerted by the Valkyrior were injured, but none killed. Any surviving enemies around you took the full force of the blast."

Brunnhilde grunted. "I remember," she said sourly. "They fought without honor."

Sif gave her a wolfish grin. "Asgard's enemies always do. The attackers retreated, waited until we'd brought you here, and then circled around to the portal and fled. With the All-Father's grace, they've been beaten soundly enough they won't come back for a second attempt."

"A few Valkyrior offered to follow them, thought they might be able to pick up traces within the between-space, but the God of Thunder told them not to," Inge said. "Lady Sif would have gone with them."

Brunnhilde nodded. "Of course you would have, but Thor was correct in this. You and my sisters would have jumped straight into a staging area for a battle. I can bring us out a little way off from that, somewhere hidden." She shifted and forced herself up to sitting despite Inge's protest, biting back a groan and plastering a smile in its place. From the unimpressed look on her girlfriend's face, she was fooling no one. "So, how long was I out?"

Sif squinted at the light spearing in from outside. "About twelve hours."

"Then aside from some lingering stiffness and some new lines on my skin, I should be pretty much healed," the Valkyrie said. She held her breath against the pain and shoved back the blankets. She was only in her underwear and many, many layers of bandages, but she twisted her arm until she could see the back of it and pulled away the gauze covering the slice there. An angry red line greeted her, but nothing more. Good enough. Her right hand worried her the most, damaged when she'd caught the elf's glass blade edge-first. She flexed the fingers, and they responded, the nerves and muscles protesting but intact. She made a fist, slower than normal, but her fingers closed all the way. She'd be able to hold and wield a sword, and that was all she needed to know.

Sif nodded and pulled at the tear in her own sleeve, showing a not dissimilar freshly healed scar. "Ready when you are."

"She's bloody not," Inge swore. "Just take a bit more time, will you? Eat? Bathe, at least. Both of you." She wrinkled her nose, and Brunnhilde found she couldn't argue with that one.

"It's two hours before noon," Sif said. "We can spare a few more hours, but not much longer."

"I saw a soul-snatch last night," Brunnhilde said quietly, and the air in the room grew thick with tension. Sif's fingers dug into her own biceps, their tips paling at the force of her grip. "I felt it as well, some of it. So yes, Sif, a few hours to eat, wash and clean armor, but no more, because we have to end this. *We have to*. I don't know how many others might have been taken during the battle, but… Thor was fighting at the Great Northern Wall, and not even he will have been able to save everyone."

Brunnhilde paused and then continued. "I think it's prudent to assume that we're going to be looking for scores or more of stolen einherjar by this point. While a Valkyrie shouldn't escort more than one soul at a time, as much for the soul's honor as anything else, we can if we must. But each one will weigh me down a little more, so once we find them, they're going to take a toll on me. And the longer we wait, the more there might be to free."

Inge sat next to her on the bed and slid her arm around her shoulders. "Not your fault," she murmured. "We all did what we could. We'll find them. But are you sure you can manage so many?"

"I'm absolutely sure," the Valkyrie said. "But you…"

Sif came around the bed to face them, her lips tight but her face soft and regretful. "Not with that broken wrist, warrior," she said calmly. "Stay here with your family and help the shieldwall and civilians secure the city."

Inge slumped. "I knew you'd say that," she muttered, though she turned a beseeching expression on Brunnhilde, large, soulful eyes that the Valkyrie always, *always* struggled to deny. Which was precisely the point. She clenched her right hand and focused on the spike of pain.

"No," the Valkyrie said gently, and softened it with a brush of lips against her temple. "You can't hold a shield like that, and you know it. Sif's right: Meadowfall needs you. Your family, too. Look after them, yes?"

"But I wanted to come with you," she began. "Fight for you and Asgard." Her eyes flickered to the leather thong visible around Sif's neck.

"I know, my love. But no. We can't," she winced, "waste the Quellstone's power and you don't heal like us. I'm sorry."

"Always with the goddess stuff," Inge grumbled. "I could still help."

Sif clapped her on the shoulder. "You look after the city. I'll look after the Valkyrie."

Inge's smile was wan. "You better."

Sif ducked her head as if taking the warrior's threat seriously. "You fought bravely and well. If we knew for sure the amount of power in the Quellstone, I'd absolutely use it to heal you so you could come with us." She backed away before Inge could say anything else. "Four hours, Brunnhilde. No longer. I'm going to find the armory, some food, and a bath, in that order. See you at the west gate."

She opened the door, and the groans and cries of the wounded drifted into the little room as she slipped out like a wraith. Brunnhilde shifted decisively. "There are people more hurt than me that need this bed and the doctors' attention," she said. "Take me to your family's home if you insist on me resting any longer," she continued, forestalling the inevitable protest. "I'll eat all their food, use all their water for my bath, and sit still for at least two hours while I clean and repair my armor. You can't ask for more than that."

Inge muttered something that sounded like "I can" under her breath. Brunnhilde swallowed her smile at the petulance in her lover's face. She dressed carefully over her bandages – no point unwrapping them if they didn't hinder her movement; she could well have need of them in Jotunheim – and together they walked slowly out of the room.

The Valkyrie tested the strength and mobility of her legs. The wounds she'd taken to her hamstrings had healed inside and out, but the muscles remembered the pain of being severed and protested even this gentle pace. It would fade soon enough, and she could ignore it even if it didn't.

Inge insisted on carrying Brunnhilde's armor. The divot taken out of the top rim of the backplate reminded her she'd been shot in the back. Even on her knees and bleeding, the last elf had been too afraid to approach within striking distance. She grinned, savage and triumphant.

She wondered what might lie before her and Sif in Jotunheim, with its windswept, icy peaks and frozen, empty terrain. Where they might be by the time dusk fell on another landscape out of another sky. It was where they had to go, if they were to find Loki.

But here in Meadowfall, with Inge at her side, birds were calling high above, and there was the distant, unexpected laughter of a child, as if unaware of the devastation that surrounded them. Life and light and people moving stone towards the wall, taken from collapsed buildings or those that had burned. Resilience. Recovery. Determination. Everywhere they walked, people nodded at her and Inge as if they'd done something bigger or more impressive than any of the warriors who made up the city's shieldwall. The urge to cast the Valkyrior glamour over herself was strong; she suspected her expressions were as raw as her body felt. She resisted the temptation.

Inge was recognized several times on the walk to her family's home, greeted with relief and smiles and words of defiance. Brunnhilde's heart swelled with pride and gently, when Inge was at her most distracted, she stole back the sack containing her armor so her girlfriend could respond to the gestures with her good hand, the other hanging in a snowy sling that caught the Valkyrie's eye every third step.

Warrior. Skilled and fierce and deadly. She's fine. She'll be fine.

It had been a long time since Brunnhilde had loved this intensely, and the force of her worry was a constant stone on her chest, thorns pricking at her throat. She strove for some of Sif's cool detachment, how easily she seemed able to put duty before all else. She was sure, in the quiet, private places of her heart, that Sif felt and feared and loved as deeply as she herself did, but she kept those emotions firmly locked behind the shield of duty and devotion to Asgard and its rulers.

As a Valkyrie, deep feelings were essential – to properly honor the glorious dead required a complete immersion in the triumph and devastation of their deaths, the ability to experience those feelings just as intensely as the newly gathered soul – but she sometimes wished for her friend's facility to push her emotions to the back of her mind until she was in a safe place to experience them.

Instead, she stared at the shattered city as they passed through it, at the sections charred and broken and bloodstained standing mere feet from others that didn't even have a scratch on the stonework. There were corpses in some of those buildings, she knew. She could both sense and smell them, but most already had people picking desultorily through the wreckage, their faces blank with shock and a surfeit of fear. She made herself feel both the victory and its cost, in equal measure.

Brunnhilde was glad to reach Inge's family home, not only because it was intact and most of her kin had assembled there, but because she didn't have to look at any more devastation. It was selfish, but she was tired, and had nothing in her future but more death, more horror, more crossing of steel and will and sinew. She knew it as intimately as she knew the movement of breath in her lungs or the quiet whisper of blood in her veins.

Death stalked her, and so did the deathless. And for the first time in her long, interesting life, she couldn't be sure she would escape unscathed.

Sif stripped off the last of her bandages and flexed her arms, stretched her back and shoulders, and then redressed. She added her armor and dropped into a low squat before jumping up and down. Nothing grated, stuck, or fell off. It was second nature by now, but she made herself focus.

She'd seen more than one warrior die because of an armor malfunction in the middle of a battle.

Everything was secure, and the pack on her back was light and slimline, containing rations and water, a torch, fire-striker and rope. Although they were heading into the frozen wastes of Jotunheim, she had nothing more than a fur-lined cloak rolled into a bundle and secured to the bottom of her pack. With luck and the gods' grace, they wouldn't be there long enough to die of cold.

Probably because we'll die of giant.

Sif pushed away the thought with a half-smile, half-grimace as she headed to the west gate. The thought had contained the humor and cadence of her brother Heimdall's voice. She wished, with sudden intensity, for the chance to see him again before they jumped to the Realm of Giants.

Ridiculous. He's probably watching me right now.

Sif let the smile claim her face this time and pinched together her thumb and forefinger in the secret sign they'd had since they were children: I see you. She couldn't, of course, but she trusted he could see her and would reciprocate.

The shield-maiden was torn from her thoughts by Brunnhilde and Inge's arrival, as well as at least a hundred warriors of Meadowfall's shieldwall.

"They'll guard the portal after we're gone," Brunnhilde explained, forgoing greetings. "It would drain too much of my energy to disable it now. So, anyone comes through that isn't us gets stabbed first and questioned second."

Sif pursed her lips. "Sounds good. We ready?"

Inge exhaled hard and then stepped forward to grip Sif

with her good hand. "Take care," she said, and if she had to visibly swallow more words, Sif didn't blame her.

"You too. Guard this city well. My friend."

Inge acted as if she hadn't heard the tiny pause and pulled Sif into a hug she wasn't expecting and wasn't sure she deserved.

Sif huffed into honeyed curls and hugged her back, touched. "Don't worry until there's a reason to. I'll make sure she does the same. I promise."

"Thank you, Lady Sif," Inge said and bowed her head, then shook it when she tried to protest. "No. In this, you deserve your title and everything that goes with it. I know you'll be safe. I know you'll keep her safe and..." she glanced at the warriors watching and lowered her voice, "you'll complete the task the God of Thunder set you. Come back to us."

Sif cleared her throat. "I will. *We* will." She turned to the waiting warriors who would guard the portal, giving Brunnhilde and Inge the illusion of privacy. "If it looks like you're going to lose control of the portal, evacuate the city," she told them. "Fight a holding action here for as long as you can." The warriors fell silent and listened, wide-eyed.

"Don't worry about us – Brunnhilde can jump us in somewhere else if necessary. But you'll hold this as long as you can," she repeated, and the huddle nodded as one. Sif nodded back, standing straight and proud, projecting confidence, and saw them respond to it. "We'll do what we can to prevent anything else coming through, but we don't know what exactly we're jumping into."

"You have our back, Lady Sif," said a grizzled warrior with more gray than blond in his beard. "And we have yours, that I swear."

"I thank you for it," Sif said, and then Inge was moving past her, away from Brunnhilde.

She was clear-eyed and straight-backed, and she spun smoothly to face them and then led everyone gathered in a salute. "Frigga guide your steps, and the All-Father lend strength to your arms," she said.

Sif felt another flicker of surprise, but she returned the gesture, as did Brunnhilde. Their gazes caught and held as they turned together to the Realm-jump. The corner of her mouth ticked up in silent question; Brunnhilde blinked in readiness. They stepped forward as one, between the pillars, the Valkyrie reaching out to take her hand, and Asgard vanished.

Thirteen
Jotunheim

The between-space was every and no color, directionless, void and matter and chaos, both an eternity and an instant. And then, suddenly, they were out. Sif might have doubted it as her sight was assaulted by a whirling maelstrom of white, gray, and black, not unlike the viciousness of the between-space itself, but it was accompanied by the scream of wind against her back and a cold bitter enough to send pain into any exposed skin.

She sucked in a breath and instinctively tightened her grip on Brunnhilde's hand as the world spun and flipped around her. Nausea tightened its grip on her stomach as her body adjusted to the movement between Realms; she could barely see Brunnhilde, even as close as she was.

"Rope," Sif screamed, jerking the Valkyrie right next to her so they touched at shoulder and hip. "Rope up, or we'll lose each other. In my pack."

Brunnhilde squinted at her, watching her lips move, and then nodded. Sif turned to give the Valkyrie access to the bag on her back – the world lurched sickeningly again and she breathed deeply – and thanked the gods for her foresight. She'd expected to need it for tying prisoners or abseiling down rockfaces, but this was even more important. They couldn't risk getting separated. Swiftly, Brunnhilde dragged the coil from her bag and tied one end around her waist and the other around Sif, making sure it didn't snag on their weapons. They checked the tightness of the knots and then Sif dragged on her cloak for good measure. Brunnhilde had one too, its collar lined with fur.

"Which way?" Sif bellowed over the howl of the wind. The Valkyrie held up one hand and then closed her eyes. Sif felt the tingle of power stretching out around them and held herself still and quiet. The light was diffused – up above the storm, it was still daylight here, for which she was grateful – and in the snowlight she watched frost form on the metal of her armor.

Brunnhilde gripped her arm and then pointed. The shield-maiden had no clue which direction it was, but she nodded anyway. When the storm ended, they'd have a better idea of where they were, but for now, she trusted the Valkyrie's ability to sense Asgardian souls and set off in her footprints, letting the taller woman break trail. The wind was from their left, lashing their faces with ice and snow and wind sharper than a blade. They were both in heavy trousers and tunics beneath their armor, both cloaked, and, within an hour, both shuddering with cold.

Sif had been to Jotunheim several times, in all seasons – cold midsummer and vicious winter – but this felt extreme. A thread of anxiety began to unspool in her gut: they might freeze to death before they ever reached their destination. It was ridiculous, of course. They'd withstood far worse and for far longer during their long lives, but the worry of it simply wouldn't go away. Sif concentrated on Brunnhilde's back and the loop of rope joining them together. She had to keep shaking it to crack the ice building along its length.

After another hour, Sif insisted on taking the lead. Breaking trail was hard work, and it was best they share that burden so that neither one was unduly fatigued if – when – it came to a fight. "You don't know which way to go," the Valkyrie shouted.

Sif leant in close. "Then steer me if I go off course. Teamwork, remember?" She blinked snow from her eyelashes. "We need to be sensible about this."

Brunnhilde gestured into the whiteout. "None of this feels sensible!"

The shield-maiden managed a laugh, the sound torn from her mouth by the gale. "Loki's lair is bound to be warm and out of the wind," she shouted back, as cheerfully as she could. "May as well get there as soon as we can, to thaw out if nothing else."

Brunnhilde grinned and then spat out a mouthful of hair as the capricious wind shifted direction. She gestured Sif ahead of her. "I'll tap your upper arms to steer you," she yelled, and they set off again. The warrior's supple leather boots came up to her mid-calves. The snow came up to her knees and slid inside her greaves and then her boots, melting against her shins and sliding down to soak into her thick socks. It didn't take long for her toes to go numb, but she ignored it the way she ignored the fading ache in her muscles that was all that was left of the strains and cuts she'd suffered during the battle for Meadowfall. The burns she had endured fighting the demon were still the most tender of her ills, and she found herself wishing, a little masochistically, for the remembered heat of its burning blood.

The exertion did much to keep her core warm, but her extremities were slowly freezing despite her abilities. Regulating body temperature wasn't an ability gifted to Asgardian gods. Fortunately, stoically ignoring the elements very much was, and despite the storm and steadily deepening snow, neither woman complained as they pushed on.

An early dusk had fallen, and the wind was, if anything, even stronger when Brunnhilde took the lead again. The ground began steadily to rise. Despite their superior night vision, the violence of the storm was such that they continued forward almost blind. The storm winds deafened them. It felt as if everything was conspiring to slow them, stop them, and leave them unprepared for danger.

Sif let Brunnhilde concentrate on direction and any threat that might be coming from ahead. She put her head on a constant swivel, checking their flanks, squinting into the snow and the darkness for a telltale gleam of eyes or torchlight, the hint of a voice on the wind or the crunch of a foot on snow.

"Deathglow's getting stronger," Brunnhilde paused to yell, waving an arm forward. Sif nodded and felt her heart beat a little faster. She stepped in the Valkyrie's footprints, checked left and right – and paused. Movement. The cold had frozen her sword in its sheath, and she wasted a precious second wrenching it free and then she spun all the way around, facing back the way they'd come. She stared into the storm.

Nothing.

The warrior closed her eyes and stretched out with her senses, searching for a hint of body heat, a sound on the edge of hearing. There. The whine of steel cutting through the air, the tiny *tink tink* of ice crystals bouncing off metal. Her blade came up in a parry even before she opened her eyes. Her hands and wrists, arms and shoulders registered the shock of impact and, an instant later, the jerk of the rope as Brunnhilde kept moving away from her. She rocked under the sudden blow, boots slipping beneath her, and her enemy – a giant – struck again as Sif was scrabbling to set her feet, hampered by the deepening snow.

She managed to bat away the blade, but not far enough, and then the rope around her middle tightened and in a single, unexpected yank, pulled her off her feet. Sif flew backwards, and her enemy's sword thunked deep into the snow where she'd been standing. She landed on her back and immediately sank, and then floundered up out of the snow to find Brunnhilde at her side. Dragonfang flashed in the murk.

The darkness was alive and it was angry. Huge figures and long reaching blades arced out of the night and the storm. She and Brunnhilde spun back to back. If the rope joining them was cut and they got separated, they'd lose each other in the whiteout. And if that happened, the only thing waiting for them would be a lonely grave beneath a skin of snow.

Sif ducked a whistling blade, skidded and turned her lack of balance to her advantage, planting her left hand in the snow and kicking the giant swinging for her in the knee, dropping it so hard it toppled over. She flipped back upright and brought her sword down two-handed, cleaving its heavy skull. Blood was a black spray in the gloom. It didn't get back up again. Not deathless. Or that one wasn't, at least. She couldn't risk assuming they'd all be the same.

In fact, it was more likely the rest of them were deathless, and she'd just got lucky with this first one. Her heart kicked against her chest, adrenaline and fear mingling crystal-bright in her veins. She sucked in air so cold it was like a knife to her throat and then blinked desperately.

Loki has sent his deathless for me.

The certainty of it settled into her bones, the knowledge that she couldn't defeat these foes, that this was it. This was where she died, in the snow and the cold of Jotunheim, roped to a raging Valkyrie who would cut her loose as soon as she became dead weight. Panic tightened Sif's throat and began to narrow her vision. Her breath whistled and her hands inside her gloves were locked rigid and inflexible around her sword hilt.

No.

No, I will not die like this. I refuse.

I am Lady Sif, friend and companion of Thor himself and of the Warriors Three. Loki will never choose the manner of my death. Loki will not win. Not today. Not ever.

Sif parried on instinct, fast and easy, as loose as if she was on the training field with a bunch of new recruits. At her core sat a bright, sharp-edged diamond of terror, threatening to crack and flood through her. The warrior ignored it, parrying again, spinning and ducking as her feet kicked up clouds of snow to be whipped away by the wind and replaced with more. Finally, she could see that the giant's skin was pale blue, and his armor was thick ridges of ice plated across his chest, lower legs and forearms. His weapon was a spear made of ice. When her blade shattered it, he simply conjured another from the elements. This was his land, and his magic.

Sif needed space to move and roped to Brunnhilde she wasn't going to have that. But if she lost Brunnhilde in the storm…

The giant threw his spear. Sif dodged, but the rope pulled her up short and she felt the kiss of ice, so cold and sharp it was only the heat of blood running in the next second that convinced her it had laid open her scalp just above her ear.

The diamond of her fear cracked, but she ignored it, slashing back behind her. The rope parted under her blade, because it was separate or die. Sif ran at the giant. She let the momentum of the downhill slope lend her speed and then she leaped, flinging herself through the storm with her cloak billowing behind her. She landed sword-first on the giant's chest, the blade shattering ice-armor and plunging into flesh colder than that of a corpse. She dangled from the hilt as ice fell around her, all three feet of the blade buried in him, then braced her feet on his stomach and tore it back out.

The giant roared and made a grab for her, and she kicked off and somersaulted, red-clotted steel flicking out for his leg as she landed in a spray of snow. The giant stumbled backwards, and she missed. His hands came together, and a spike of ice erupted between her feet. Sif threw herself at him again, the spike just clipping her heel as she dodged, but she managed to recover before sprawling facedown. The next spike reared up in front of her as the giant kept backing away, and Sif got another half-dozen paces before realizing he was trying to draw her further from Brunnhilde and out into the lonely, lethal dark.

She used the next spike of ice as a launch pad, running up the side of it, twisting in midair and landing, catlike, facing back the way she'd come. She set off again, sprinting back towards the hard-to-see figure of the Valkyrie ducking and slashing between two more frost giants. Panic flared in her gut as Brunnhilde went to one knee, then dropped flat and rolled, scrambling back up just before the ground beneath her exploded into a hundred flying spears of ice.

Sif ran faster, a wordless shout bursting from her as the Valkyrie vanished behind a cage of ice. Brunnhilde burst out moments later, but she was thrown immediately into a frenzied defense as both giants attacked again, pressing her hard and herding her off the path they'd been taking. Further from Sif.

Sif was going to be abandoned, trapped here in the cold and the dark with no way to save the stolen einherjar and no way home. Brunnhilde slipped and fell, then vanished as a storm of icy projectiles peppered the ground where she'd lain.

Sif shouted again, higher-pitched with shock – *she's Realm-jumped; she's left me* – and the fear that had been steadily building since their arrival surged. Instinctively, her mind reached for the magic held in the Quellstone. She channeled it, speeding it down her arm into her sword. Then, she jumped to strike the closest giant through the back and into its heart. If she could clear the field of enemies, Brunnhilde would come back for her. *Please, Brunnhilde, please come back.*

Ice-armor shattered, grating and screaming under her sword's impact, and the Quellstone flared bright gold, the magic blasting through her blade and into the giant, super-bright and super-heated, filling its veins with lava.

The giant stiffened, traceries of bright yellow light swarming through it. It tried to move, tried to scream, but instead exploded into steam and bone and blood, flying apart with a wet boom. Sif was thrown clear, landing hard on a section of frozen, iron-hard ground that had been stamped clear of fresh snow. The breath was knocked from her lungs, but she rolled, absorbing the impact and coming back to her feet with only a wince.

The second giant turned on Sif with a roar of fury. Brunnhilde flickered back into view as Sif began scrambling backwards, stunned by the how the Quellstone's power had coursed through her and staring at the manner of her death coming for her.

The Valkyrie appeared next to the giant and hacked half through his huge thigh before he even noticed her. He fell with another roar. Sif could do little but watch as the Valkyrie hacked at him again, vanishing as he made a grab for her and reappearing on his other side to make another cut, this time deep into his ribs. Each time the giant reached for her, Brunnhilde Realm-jumped somewhere else, until eventually he gave a last, pathetic wail and slumped.

Sif, dizzy with exhaustion, turned into the darkness where the third giant had lured her. She could see him, on the edge of her sight. She lifted her blade and pointed it at him. It shook, but he still ran.

And then they were alone.

Brunnhilde was bruised, but she wasn't broken. She stood

with Sif, both of them leaning on their swords and panting out huge clouds of mist among the wreckage of corpses and pools of red- and black-stained slush.

"We're getting close," she gasped into a rare lull in the wind. "They wouldn't have hit us so hard otherwise."

"Didn't send their deathless, though," Sif pointed out. "What if we're in the wrong place?"

"We're not. I can feel the… not the deathglow as such, but the echo of it. I can feel the souls." She bit her lip on any further words. Sif didn't need to know that the souls were horribly, agonizingly aware of where they were. That they were hurting, and desperate and afraid. That *something* awful was being done to them. And, even worse, that in the hours they'd been in Jotunheim so far, one of them had… gone blank. Not vanished, not ceased to exist, just become unresponsive. Uncaring. The Valkyrie didn't know if it was a defense mechanism or something worse. Some external force being exerted on it and changing it.

The thought filled her with a horror far deeper than she'd felt when the giants had loomed out of the darkness to attack. Shame and fury warred with worry, with a slow-burgeoning fear that they'd be too late, too weak, too incapable. She swallowed it all down.

"We should hurry," she rasped instead of giving voice to her fears. Sif nodded and knotted the cut ends of the rope, securing them together again. "How are you feeling after using the orb?" she asked over her shoulder as they began again to climb the slope.

"Battered from the inside," Sif called back as the wind picked up again. "I can still use it, but I'd prefer to have a couple of hours to recover first. And the more I use it to break, the less power it'll have to bind – to heal. If we need it."

"I didn't think you'd use it in battle at all, let alone… this early on."

Sif said something that sounded like "I thought you'd left me," before clearing her throat. "You were facing two of them and you were slowing. I didn't have a choice."

Brunnhilde resisted the urge to lick her lips: in this weather, the saliva would freeze and crack her mouth. "Do you want to find somewhere to hunker down and rest until you've recovered? Might be safer."

Sif was silent for a dozen steps and then she pulled Brunnhilde to a halt with a gloved hand on her sleeve. She pointed. "There's an outcrop there. Let's get out of the wind. We need to talk."

Brunnhilde frowned but let the shield-maiden tug her over into the paltry shelter. The wind dropped as they squatted, and just the lack of it made her feel instantly warmer.

Sif dragged her cloak tighter around her and then stared down at her hands for a few seconds. "Safer," she said eventually, meeting the Valkyrie's eyes. She took a deep breath and nodded once, decisively. "I think we're being manipulated somehow. Don't ask how, because I can't sense anything, but I've been constantly anxious since we arrived. A little thread of it, growing stronger every hour that passes. I was convinced back there that I was going to die, that I'd never win against them. Convinced that Loki knows I'm here and had sent warriors specifically to kill me. Then I saw you disappear and panicked again. Thought you'd abandoned me and that's why I reached for the Quellstone. Because you're right, I did use it early and we don't know how many charges it contains. I've put us at a disadvantage, and we've only just got here." She huffed, annoyed, and then managed a self-deprecating smile.

"These are not normal emotions for me, and that was a poor tactical decision on my part. I can say without arrogance that I am an exceptional warrior, and also admit that you're better than me. And yet, these decisions, these worries…" Sif spread her hands and trailed off.

Brunnhilde chewed the inside of her cheek. "Yes," she said shortly. "The worry I felt for the soul-snatched on Asgard was – how can I put this – normal. Deep and abiding, but a mix of concern for them and anger at myself and the other Choosers. Guilt, of course, but a rational guilt. But as soon as we arrived, that guilt became all-consuming. I've been telling myself I don't deserve the All-Father's trust, and that I am the last person who should have come here, that I'm not strong enough to do this. I'm afraid to do this. And that fear–"

"Has spread?" Sif interrupted.

The Valkyrie nodded.

"For me too. I'm scared, Brunnhilde. I very rarely get scared. Not like this. Nothing we've faced here in Jotunheim has been unexpected or something I haven't dealt with before. None of it should inspire the fear that I'm feeling, but I can't help it. I'm scared."

Brunnhilde blew out a breath and slumped back against the rock protecting them from the wind. "I think you're right. Something – someone – is manipulating our emotions. I'd thought it was just me, until you spoke," she added, deciding honesty was needed here. She fidgeted with the edge of her cloak. "I thought I was feeling what the souls are feeling. They're scared, Sif. Deeply. I thought my connection with them was amplifying my own fear, but you can't sense them. Yet, you feel as I do."

Dismay and grief flickered across Sif's face, and Brunnhilde watched as she deliberately packed them away. "All right," Sif said, determination limning her tone. "So how do we deal with it? Do we just suffer through, or what?"

They could, Brunnhilde supposed, but just the thought of it worried her – and now, of course, she didn't know if that worry was genuinely hers or something more. "No," she said, and Sif grunted and nodded immediately. "We have to keep talking. Any sudden spikes in emotions could be a sign of this manipulation, whatever it is. I've been stretching out my senses ever since we jumped in to make sure we're going in the right direction, and I can't feel any sort of energy reaching out to us. There's nothing unusual."

She paused. "What if… what if there's something wrong with my–" she began and Sif shoved her knee, cutting her off.

"There's the first example of why we need to keep talking," Sif said fiercely. "There's nothing wrong with your senses, Brunnhilde. I can't feel anything either, so whatever is doing this is outside our experience or abilities. Just because we can't feel it doesn't mean it's not there. Yes?"

The Valkyrie rubbed her gloved hand against her face, trying to thaw the frozen flesh. "Yes," she said firmly. "Thank you."

Sif grinned and then stood. Immediately, the wind hit her in the face, and she squinted, her previously neat braid of ebony ripped apart by the gale so that strands flared and streamed around her face. A wound near her ear was sticky with blood, but seemed to be healing.

Brunnhilde stood too, the gale like a hand against her back. "Not far now," she shouted. "An hour at most at our previous pace. And… while I appreciate that blast of golden power you sent at those frosties for me, I know there isn't an infinite supply of it. I'm not going to leave you here, all right? Don't be reckless with the orb."

Sif shuddered once, whether at her words or the cold, and then clapped her on the arm. "I'll take point," she said, gesturing into the night. Gently, Brunnhilde turned her shoulders so she was facing in the right direction. Sif flicked her a rueful smile and set out.

The snowdrifts grew shallower the higher they climbed, until it became clear they were in the mountains. Tundra became rock as they labored upwards, and the rope now was more to prevent one of them tumbling back down the slope than to not lose each other in the storm, which faded as they trudged on. The night cleared and the temperature dropped even further, a million unfamiliar stars glaring down at them as they scrambled onwards, dark shapes against the thin white blanket of snow and ice over rock. It was cold enough to hurt, the air like knives in their lungs and against exposed skin, as if those distant, sharp-edged stars were cutting into them.

FOURTEEN
THE CAVERN

The deathglow was a beacon to Brunnhilde's senses, dragging her forwards like a parent with a recalcitrant child. She couldn't stop even if she wanted to. How many souls were there? What was she going to find, row upon row of the glorious dead somehow imprisoned, hurting and afraid, begging for a release she could not give them? That she was too weak to give them? *No.*

She embraced a rage colder than the bitter air and climbed faster until she was side by side with Sif. She pulled ahead, fingers going to the knot in the rope as it pulled taut between them. Faster. Had to go faster. Sif tugged the rope, a sudden sharp drag Brunnhilde couldn't feel through her breastplate, but which stopped her, nonetheless. She stumbled and turned with a snarl.

"What?" Her voice came out louder than she intended and far harsher. "We don't have time for your hesitance. The einherjar are crying."

Sif flinched but then she patted the air, sinking to her

haunches and gesturing for Brunnhilde to do the same. When the Valkyrie refused, Sif dragged on the rope between them, forcing her into a reluctant squat. "Alright, talk to me. What are you feeling?"

"We don't have time for this," the Valkyrie snarled again. "We have to – or they'll, there are so many – come on!"

"What are you afraid of?" the warrior demanded instead of getting up. Brunnhilde wanted to shake her, wanted to leave her behind. She had to get to them before anything else happened. Her hand dropped to Dragonfang's hilt. Sif rose fluidly, keeping her own hands very visible. "Tell me what you're afraid of," she commanded again, gently this time.

"I'm not afraid," Brunnhilde growled and then paused. Her eyes went to her hand, now wrapped tight around her sword hilt. "Oh."

Sif's mouth twisted in sympathy.

Brunnhilde shook her head hard. "But I didn't even feel anything happen. I just suddenly had to…" she paused and bared her teeth. "I just suddenly had to run in there heedlessly to save them, because otherwise we'd lose them all. I'd lose them all. No time to plan, just run."

"And you still haven't let go of that weapon, my friend. What is it you think I'm going to do?"

The Valkyrie released her sword hilt with a gasp. She felt a blush sting her wind-bitten cheeks.

"Whoever's doing this is clever," her companion said quietly, interrupting Brunnhilde's stuttered apology with a wave of dismissal. "They're targeting you this time because you're a Valkyrie. They can't hide the einherjar from you, so they're using them as a lure, making you worry about them and not about yourself. Or me." She shook her head as Brunnhilde opened her mouth to apologize again, shame twisting in her.

"Don't worry, I'm not blaming you. This manipulation is subtler than I thought, twisting thoughts as well as fears. We need to keep this rope on as long as possible. It keeps us connected, meaning it keeps us communicating. It should stop either one of us from doing something rash."

"Yes," Brunnhilde said, more relieved than she liked to admit. "Yes, let's do that. And… something else. Those were frost giants back there."

Sif nodded, a line of puzzlement between her brows.

"There weren't any frosties outside Asgardia or in Meadowfall, Greenside or at the Great Northern Wall. And these weren't deathless."

"You think we ran into a bunch of unaffiliated frost giants through sheer bad luck?" the warrior asked.

"Perhaps. Perhaps not. Whoever is behind all this – Loki – has managed to ally light and dark elves, trolls and demons. Perhaps it's not a stretch that they've got frost and mountain giants working together. But it didn't feel like that?" She phrased the last sentence as a question.

Sif nodded. "You're right. It didn't. It wasn't as if they were stopping us from taking this path. They weren't between us and our destination. They saw us; they attacked. Though I did lose one in the final moments, so we should be wary of further ambushes." She looked about to offer an apology of her own for that, but Brunnhilde nodded before she could say anything.

"I was already assuming anything we encountered here

would be an enemy, but I can't say I'm thrilled by the idea we could end up stuck between opposing giant clans. The frosties might not have anything to do with the deathless, but I've no doubt whose side they'd choose if it comes to another battle against Asgardians."

Sif's face was grim in the starlight. She pointed ahead. "What are the chances that once we break out of the snowline – and I don't even want to wonder right now why the higher we climb the less snow there is; not even Jotunheim's climate is normally this strange – we'll be out of their territory?"

"It would make sense," Brunnhilde said slowly, staring ahead. "Though, yes, it's the only thing about this that does. But it could also eliminate one potential threat." She paused for a long moment, a bizarre thought tumbling through her head: that whatever was affecting their emotions might also be twisting their perceptions. How could you climb uphill and yet come out of the snowline? What if they weren't heading the way they thought they were? Before she could second-guess herself, the Valkyrie held up a hand to forestall any questions and then closed her eyes, seeking outwards with her senses. The deathglow was there above them; they were definitely moving towards it, whether or not it turned out that "above" was correct. Whatever their eyes and ears told them, Brunnhilde had to believe in this. If they didn't have this as a guide, they would fail and then they would die.

Feeling a renewed sense of determination, she opened her eyes. "Let's go."

They got their answer to the mystery a few hours later. The air grew decidedly warmer as they climbed, until the snow vanished, and the rock underfoot grew slick with melt instead. They exchanged a few concerned looks, a few wild speculations, but little more. Brunnhilde's senses were bent towards the deathglow. She had little focus to spare for anything else, though Sif dragged her from her obsession regularly to check in with her and keep her on mission. The Valkyrie was glad for her concern.

A few leagues higher and Sif removed her cloak and rolled it back up to secure beneath her pack. "I don't like this," she muttered as they paused for a short rest. They were on what was clearly a faint trail winding ever higher, ever steeper, up the mountain's flank. They'd passed the middle of the night, and dawn was only hours away.

"Nor I," Brunnhilde agreed, "but it isn't much farther. At this rate, we should be there just before sunrise." She stared at the sky, the trail ahead and behind, and then the shield-maiden.

"Yes," Sif said immediately. "We can risk a Realm-jump now. We're close enough, and while the night camouflages us against the bare rock, we'll be way too visible come dawn. Can you jump us to the deathglow?"

Brunnhilde closed her eyes and quested towards it, seeking to see around its edges this time, to sense the snatched souls' environment. There was a… blur, a barrier. Something in the way.

"They're underground," she said eventually. "They're inside the mountain. It's not impossible to jump us straight there, but we'll be emerging into an enclosed space without any time to analyze what we're up against, who, or how many. There's a slim chance I would jump us into solid rock, as in we emerge inside the rock itself, killing us instantly. If we walk, we can check the ground and the approaches for ambush points or a force that could end up following us in and trapping us there, especially if there's some sort of jump-dampener. I've seen them before and they're… unpleasant."

She frowned. "Also, the jump-sickness might affect your use of the Quellstone, and I'd rather we had that as a backup for whatever we face in there. I don't want you throwing up and then passing out when you could be protecting my back."

Sif shook out her shoulders and flexed her hands. "Fair point. All right, there are too many risks to chance it. But if we're not jumping, we should run. Shave some time off our approach just in case they are aware of us. If they believe us to be three hours away, I'd prefer to get there in two and surprise them."

"That we can do," Brunnhilde agreed. The urgency to reach the souls was thrumming beneath her skin, an impossible itch she couldn't reach. And yet. "Keep an eye on me," she said, as Sif settled her pack and weapons firmly. "In fact, you should lead. Just in case."

The warrior's face softened, and she gave the Valkyrie a reassuring pat. "No problem. Count your steps or your breaths if you're getting worried. Talk to me if you start feeling anything. I'll do the same. We don't know what's going on here, not just with the soul-snatched but with our own reactions, our own feelings. We need to stay aware."

Brunnhilde nodded. Any initial embarrassment they'd felt after the frost giant attack about their swelling fears had faded. They were facing something that could manipulate their responses, force them to feel things they wouldn't normally. There was no shame in being afraid, whether it was genuine or created in them. What mattered was how they dealt with those fears. What mattered was that they could still function. If they forgot their purpose, or forgot their caution, none of them – whether living or dead – would make it out of here.

The reminder was potent, clearing the last of the fog from Brunnhilde's mind.

They began to run, their boots scuffing stone, and the terrain rocky enough that soon they were dislodging stones to rattle downhill, slipping and scrambling as the slope steepened. The miles vanished beneath them until it seemed as if they climbed the night itself.

And then another soul blanked, vanishing from the conjoined deathglows and their awful clamoring for aid, for answers, for rescue, all a constant bright pain in the Valkyrie's mind. Brunnhilde stumbled, badly, as the absence slid into her awareness like a knife. She gasped and went to one knee, jerking Sif to a surprised halt and pulling a grunt from the warrior's mouth as she skidded in the scree.

"Brunnhilde? Brunnhilde, are you alright? What is it?"

The Valkyrie felt the terror of the other einherjar wind even tighter around her, twining with her own. They too knew that one of their own had vanished, and not to the Halls of the Dead. Not to glory or to honored memory. She was dimly aware of Sif's voice, of her hand gripping the back of her neck, squeezing in wordless comfort. Aware of the bright sting of a cut knee through her trousers, of the strange warmth of the rock beneath her hands and the awful void of a soul taken – for the second time.

Warmth? Brunnhilde tried to focus on that instead, on the external world that could fight and stab and kill them. Sweat was trickling down her back but not, she realized, just from their long uphill run.

"Brunnhilde? What is it?" Sif's voice was clearer this time, striving for calm but with an undercurrent of tension. "Talk to me."

The Valkyrie felt an irrational urge to conceal the truth from her friend, an almost overwhelming need for silence. She pushed against it, testing its edges and its limits, and then pushed past it. She didn't believe that the need was her own and spent too long thinking about it – yet another distraction, she realized, when Sif shook her, hard and unkind. "Valkyrie!"

"Gone," she gasped, the word a shuddery exhale. "Another one's gone. I don't know where. I don't know who. They're there, and afraid, and then… nothing. Blank."

Sif squatted and put both hands on Brunnhilde's shoulders; she couldn't feel them through her armor, but the woman's thumbs pressed gently against her neck as warm reassurance. "Take a deep breath and then tell me. In detail."

"The stone is warm," Brunnhilde said instead. "That explains the lack of snow, anyway. It can't be a volcano, though, can it?"

Sif stared at her as if she was uttering demonspeak, and then blankly put one hand down on the rock. She frowned, dragged off her glove and replaced it. "Hela's teeth," she swore. "How?" She twisted to look up at the mountain looming over them. "No smoke. Not a volcano. Something inside is heating it." She shook her head. "Not important right now. Tell me what happened."

Haltingly, the Valkyrie told her what she'd felt and could still feel as they both stood and began walking uphill again, the need for movement pressing at them.

Sif's lips were bloodless and her fists clenched by the time the Valkyrie had related all she'd sensed.

"I don't know who it was, Sif. I promise. If I did, and if it was Gyda, I would tell you. I wouldn't keep that from you."

The other woman nodded, a jerky up-down as if she was a puppet. "I love my friend," she said quietly, "but it's not just about her now. It wouldn't make a difference even if it was Gyda. Or it shouldn't make a difference," she amended, at Brunnhilde's questioning glance. She blew out a deep breath. "Honesty, of course. Thank you. I am trying. The truth is there are too many who've been snatched now. It would be selfish and cruel for me to prioritize Gyda over all the others. We are here to save everyone. I just hope that with whatever this, this *blanking* is that you're feeling, we can still succeed at that."

Dread and reluctance coiled in Brunnhilde's gut. "That's my aim too, my friend," she said quietly. "And it's one I'll gladly die for. But we have to be honest about what we can accomplish."

Sif turned a gaze, as fierce as an eagle's, on her. "No," she snarled. "Those are not your words. They're not. We are going to save every last einherjar. We are getting them to Valhalla and ourselves home to Asgard. That's what we're doing. Whoever that voice in your head is," she added, fingers digging into Brunnhilde's biceps, "it isn't yours. It belongs to whoever is trying to manipulate us. You need to decide whether you're listening to me or to that stranger whispering lies. Well?"

The fire in Sif's voice brought a reluctant smile to the Valkyrie's face. "On the basis I don't want an early death at the hands of an ally, I'm going to say you," she managed, and the levity balanced them both, granted them a measure of clarity. "Thank you, Sif," she added. "Your candor has never been so necessary. No Valkyrie would ever abandon a soul. My words shame me."

"No," Sif said again. "They are not your words, so they can't shame you. Besides, we don't have time. If you want to bury yourself in self-recrimination, wait until we've completed our mission. Hel, I'll bring a shovel and help you dig. Until then, we guard each other's words, and we watch each other's backs."

Brunnhilde nodded and bit the tip of her tongue. A part of her was screaming that she should be the one saying these things, that she was letting Sif take charge. The rest of her stamped the thought to dust. It didn't even matter if it was true – those words were a blade she wielded against no one but herself, and she couldn't afford to bleed.

Sif shot her an amused glance, one corner of her mouth quirking up. "Can you imagine going through this with someone else?" she asked. "Balder, or Heimdall, even Thor? 'Tell me your fears, O God of Thunder, that I might soothe them.'"

Brunnhilde couldn't swallow her quiet laughter. "That would never work." She clapped Sif on the back. "I'm glad it's you, shield-maiden."

The other woman winked. "Same, Valkyrie. My brother would have died of tight-jawed, embarrassed stoicism by now."

"And Thor would rather smash himself in the face with Mjolnir than admit to anything that might be considered a weakness."

Sif chuckled again. "I'd pay good money to see it, though."

Brunnhilde laughed, but when Sif cast her eyes to the sky in involuntary anticipation of a rumble of thunder, the Valkyrie twitched and did likewise. It didn't come.

"Made you look," Sif teased, and Brunnhilde elbowed her, though not hard. "Run?"

"I don't think we need to," she said and pointed. Up ahead, the grayness of the mountain and the black of shadows was interrupted by a vast, inky expanse. Taller by far than either of them, taller than a giant, it appeared circular. "That's not a natural occurrence," she said in a low voice. "I think it's a cave entrance."

It was still a quarter-mile ahead, cast into sharp relief by the icy glare of the stars. They stopped and then crouched down, staring uphill, both at the entrance and all around it. Sif tapped the back of her hand and then pressed her own palm flat on the stone. Brunnhilde copied her and nodded; it was even warmer than it had been a few miles below.

The Valkyrie quartered the landscape below them. She could see where the snowline started, how the deathglow had led them through the foothills and then up the flank of this monstrous mountain whose summit was lost even to her keen sight. There was no movement on the trail below, or to either side, and she turned back to examine the way ahead again. "Looks clear to me," she breathed.

"Let me scout it," Sif replied, untying the rope from her waist with only an instant's hesitation. "You stay here. I'll be back in half an hour, no more." She must have seen the skepticism on Brunnhilde's face. "And if I'm not, come to my rescue, yes?"

"If I have to do that, I'm never letting you forget it," Brunnhilde threatened.

The warrior rolled her eyes and shrugged, and the Valkyrie watched her lithe form slip into the shadows until she vanished.

FIFTEEN
THE MOUNTAIN'S SECRETS

Sif slipped through the darkness like a blade. She extended her senses for movement, sound, even body heat other than her own, straining into the darkness that was on the cusp of becoming dawn.

She didn't take the direct approach, stepping off the path as soon as she left Brunnhilde behind and looping far to the east. The ground was more broken here, slowing her further, but she willingly sacrificed speed for stealth. There was no movement on the trail or at the cave mouth the closer she got. Sif didn't trust it. The snatched souls were in there, which meant their quarry was in there, and Loki was never one to leave himself unguarded. Even his vast arrogance didn't extend to considering himself safe while being in possession of dozens of einherjar that he knew Asgard would come for one way or the other. He would have taken all the necessary precautions. And yet the cave mouth was unwatched.

It had to be a trap. Sif was of the opinion most things were, which is why she was still alive. Up close, the cave mouth was even bigger than she'd estimated. Easily twice the height of the tallest giant. Sif crouched fifty yards east of it and studied the trail and the entrance for long, slow minutes. No movement. No sound. Not the slightest hint of light in its gaping maw. Whatever had the einherjar in its grip was deep, deep within the mountain itself. The eastern sky was indigo, the stars beginning to lose their sharpness, when Sif made her way back to the Valkyrie's hiding place.

Brunnhilde was tense until they made definite eye contact, Dragonfang loose in her hand. "How are you? What are you feeling?" she whispered as soon as Sif settled in at her side.

The warrior blinked. "What? Fine. Honestly, I feel fine. It's impossible to see anything in there – no flickers of light, no movement of giants or warriors or anyone. No noise. If it wasn't for the deathglow, I'd have said it was abandoned."

"So, we just walk in?" Brunnhilde asked, skeptical.

"Well, I was thinking more of creeping in, but essentially, yes. Dawn is coming, and while that will give us light to see into the cavern entrance, it will also outline us to anyone in there. If that is a mountain giant nest, they'll know every inch of it no matter how dark it is. We are going to be at a disadvantage no matter what we do, so we may as well just get on with it."

The Valkyrie stared past Sif towards the cave. "I can't decide whether that's reckless or not, but it's not as if we have much choice. At least once I'm in there, I should be able to sense whether there are jump-dampeners. If not, then even if we are spotted it doesn't matter – I can just move us somewhere else."

"And if you can't?" Sif asked, fingers clenching and unclenching with the need to move.

Brunnhilde patted her sword hilt. "We do it the loud and bloody way," she said.

"I like it," Sif said with relish. "Come on. The longer we wait, the more likely it is that other souls will blank, as you termed it. Let's get in there. Let's *fight*."

She stood, but to her surprise Brunnhilde dragged her back into a squat. She shook her off, tried to stand again. This time the Valkyrie hooked her fingers into the high collar of Sif's breastplate and yanked her to her knees.

"Get off me! Let's get in there and make them pay, make them give us Gyda and the others and then kill them all – oh." Realization crashed through her like a wave. "Oh," she said again, in a whisper this time. "That's not me talking, is it?"

"Even you're not this reckless, Sif," Brunnhilde said, her voice quiet but kind. "And you're definitely not bloodthirsty."

They sat in silence for a few breaths as Sif examined her feelings, the urgency in her mind, turning it over as if it was an unknown object. "I couldn't tell," she murmured at last. "It… my thoughts, my feelings, they still feel like mine. There's no, no *signature*, nothing about them to indicate they're not coming from me. I couldn't tell."

"Neither could I, earlier. That's why we need to stay together. That's why we need to listen to each other. We need a word, something we both know, but which is going to have no context for anything we discover down there. If one of us says the word, the other one must stop what they're doing – as long as it's safe to do so. It can be a failsafe, a vow we make to each other that cannot be broken. I say the word, you just stop. You say it, I stop. No matter what."

Sif stared at her, suddenly aware the Valkyrie's features were much clearer than they had been. Dawn had broken. "All right," she said slowly. "Sounds good. A bond unbreakable. An oath sworn in the All-Father's sight. But what's the word?"

"We need something neither of us is likely to shout in a combat situation," Brunnhilde mused.

"I love Loki?" Sif suggested, and the Valkyrie snorted a laugh. "But no, I make no oaths that require those words. What about Aragorn? He isn't here, and it's not something either of us is likely to forget. If either of us shouts it, the other one must step back, must stop and think."

Brunnhilde nodded. "Aragorn. Perfect. And we can't use the rope now – we don't want to get into another fight while tied together – so this will serve as a way to keep us close to each other, prevent one or the other from running on ahead. I hope." She held out her hand, and Sif clasped her wrist in the warrior's grip. "Are you ready?"

"Ready," Sif said. "Let's go. Follow me and stay low."

She led the Valkyrie at a crouching run, the same route she'd taken before, east off the path and in a loop that brought them back in to the cave entrance from the side. The sky was lightening fast, but they found shadow among some tumbled boulders from which to check the entrance one last time. Brunnhilde tapped her arm twice as the signal to confirm there was no movement behind them and it was safe to proceed. Ahead was similarly empty, and with no other reasons to hesitate, the shield-maiden slipped between the rocks and into the shadows of the cave.

Warm air. It was the first thing she noticed. The tiniest movement of air against her cheek and brow, easily missed were it not for the temperature difference compared with outside. Her toes and fingers began to tingle in the sudden warmth. She stripped off her gloves and tucked them into the back of her belt. Whoever was in here liked their comforts, and Sif suppressed a derisive snort. Loki had grown both indulgent and complacent. She looked forward to the coming confrontation.

Unconsciously, she sped her steps, but seconds later Brunnhilde was tugging on her sleeve. She glanced back and saw the other woman's frown. Sif's mouth twisted in irritation – at herself, not the Valkyrie – and she slowed again, creeping along the right-hand cave wall, fingertips brushing the stone as the darkness grew ahead of them.

They were barely fifty strides into the mountain and the light was almost entirely gone. Sif closed her eyes, sending out her other senses. If they were going to be blind soon enough, best get used to it now. She slowed further, feeling the way with her boots and hand and hearing, aware of Brunnhilde only a pace behind from the soft shush of her breath stirring against the back of her neck.

The sound and space ahead of her abruptly changed, and Sif opened her eyes again. There were two passageways branching off ahead, to left and right. Both appeared perfectly circular, hand-carved rather than natural. To the left was the faintest glow of light; to the right the tiniest echo of sound, right on the edge of hearing, vanishing as soon as Sif concentrated on it.

Left to light? Right to noise?

Sif turned around and pressed against Brunnhilde, lips at her ear. "Realm-jump ability?" she breathed. The Valkyrie twitched her head against Sif's: a nod. The shield-maiden closed her eyes in a brief, wordless thank you. "Which way?"

"We should probably split up," Brunnhilde whispered against the side of her face, "just to be safe."

Sif shook her head hard enough that their temples knocked together. "That's the opposite of safe, Valkyrie. We are absolutely not doing that, and I will invoke the name of your stupid horse if I need to."

Brunnhilde tensed and then exhaled. "All right, the deathglow is overwhelming, being honest, pulsing at me from all sides, but a little stronger to the right, I think. There's… something, though, to the left. I can't quite make it out but it's… familiar." She jerked and looked in that direction. "*What is that?*" These words were even softer, not meant for Sif. The Valkyrie shifted as if to pass her, and Sif grabbed her arm.

"We go right. And no splitting up, either. Ever," she added as the Valkyrie's gaze slid from hers and across to the leftmost tunnel again. "Souls first, justice second. It doesn't matter what or who we encounter down there, even Loki. Souls first. Justice second. And this is me, Lady Sif the Reckless, who has an undying need for vengeance on that thrice-damned Jotunn, saying that. Think about what that means before you argue."

She felt Brunnhilde shift her weight, fidgeting, and then nod. "Souls first. You're right. Thank you." She clenched a fist and one of her knuckles cracked. "I hate this," she whispered fiercely. "How are they doing it? How can they just make me forget my duty so easily that I need to rely on someone else, someone not even a Valkyrie. It's humiliating."

Anger flared deep in Sif's gut. It took her a few seconds to breathe through it, to not spit out that Brunnhilde should go left then, if she was so desperate to. *Not my thoughts. Not hers, either. She didn't mean that. It's not because it's you that she's humiliated, remember that.*

Despite herself, her heart thudded against the cage of her ribs. *Calm, Sif. Be calm. This is a battleground. Be strategic.*

"Don't think like that. Focus on the mission, on the souls. There will be plenty of time to get angry once we've got them all to Valhalla safely and I've delivered you to Inge without a scratch. I don't fancy facing her wrath if I come back without you."

Brunnhilde's laugh was more breath than sound, but the unnatural stiffness in her shoulders released, and Sif congratulated herself on finding a way to cut through the Valkyrie's spiraling thoughts. "I never fancy facing Inge's wrath," she agreed. "Alright. Right-hand tunnel, double back if we have to. Souls first, justice second. That's the plan."

"That's the plan," Sif agreed, and led them off towards the source of the strange sound. Her palms were slick with clammy sweat, an unpleasant mix of adrenaline for whatever was to come and anxiety that Brunnhilde would vanish as soon as she turned her back. She had to trust the Valkyrie wouldn't. Here, in the dark, in the nest of their enemies, trust was all they had.

They crept around the curve of the cave into the right-hand tunnel, the thin light of dawn vanishing as they rounded the corner. Ahead, the dark was absolute, but the sounds were the slightest bit clearer. She couldn't tell what they were, not yet, too full of their own echoes to make sense, but she got the impression they were… unhappy.

Sif let the fingertips of her left hand stroke her sword hilt and then skate backwards for the long, curved knife in its sheath against her armored spine. The movements were for comfort more than anything, her right hand maintaining contact with the tunnel wall so they weren't completely without an anchor in the darkness. Brunnhilde tapped her back, reassurance she was there, her fingernail making the quietest *tick* against her armor. The sound was so slight it was hard to believe how much weight and meaning it carried, but it fueled Sif to keep going.

Right to noise or left to light, the decision made only by the Valkyrie's assertion the deathglow might be stronger in this direction. They didn't have any better ideas, but the warrior couldn't help but think that she was leading her friend into an ambush.

Gods and demons, but Sif hated being right. And also shockingly, horrifyingly, wrong.

The muffled sounds had resolved into a voice, intermittently pausing as if for questions they couldn't hear, and it was, indeed, unhappy. And familiar. Sif felt a second of bewildered incomprehension, the sense of dissonance so strong that it stopped her in her tracks, and then Brunnhilde let out a wounded sound, punched from her chest on a stuttering exhalation, before charging past her towards the new light emanating from a doorway a few hundred yards ahead. The source of the voice. She ran with no hesitation, no stealth, and no planning.

Sif sprinted after her, because if they were going in blind, then they needed to have each other's backs from the start. She knew, down to her bones, that Brunnhilde was going to need her when she was confronted with whatever was happening in there.

The light grew as they raced forwards with swords drawn, the Valkyrie pulling ahead despite Sif's best efforts. Brunnhilde's fear was so palpable it was a taste in the back of the shield-maiden's throat, a bright, jagged thing that made it hurt to breathe. The voice came again, defiant but twisted high and desperately young with the promise of pain.

"You are going to pay for this," it screamed – and then screamed in truth, and suddenly Brunnhilde was gone. Realm-jumped.

Sif forced herself to move faster as the screaming was overlaid with shouted alarm and then the distinctive grunts and scuffles of violence, lost beneath Brunnhilde's bellowed war cry, and the unmistakable sounds of metal cleaving flesh.

The light was clear and steady, burning from the room off the tunnel's left-hand side, and Sif saw the shadows of figures struggling, though the only shouts were coming from the Valkyrie, not her opponents. Sif sprinted around the corner with her sword drawn. The urge to leap to Brunnhilde's side was overwhelming, but instead she put her back to the wall and tried to make sense of what she was seeing.

Elves, trolls, even some humans from Midgard, at least a dozen from what she could make out, ran at Brunnhilde, acting as a screen for others who continued to work behind them. The room was long and set up like an infirmary with high metal tables dominating the floor, most of them holding a huge, twisted body, at least twice the size of the workers bending over them. The workers appeared oblivious to the fight erupting by the entrance. The forms on the tables were hybrids, like the half-giants and demi-wolves she'd fought at Meadowfall, but thankfully none of them were alive. Each was hooked up to complicated equipment she could make no sense of, tangles of wires and tubes connecting the corpses to tall, malevolent-looking machines decorated with dials and buttons. Some of the creatures on the tables began to stir and wake, a blue glow lighting in their deep-set eyes.

Another high-pitched scream pierced the infirmary, and Sif found its source: halfway down the room on the right, a much smaller figure lay on a table with a hunched figure busy at her side. Coils of tubing were attached to her face and chest, her limbs restrained but thrashing.

Inge.

"No," she breathed, disbelief paralyzing her for one awful, endless moment. *How?*

Brunnhilde had no such hesitation. The Valkyrie cut her way through the figures between her and her lover, apparently oblivious to the fact that none of them were putting up any sort of a fight. An elf stepped forward, unarmed and his face curiously blank, and the Valkyrie ripped Dragonfang across his throat, almost severing his head. Blood misted into the air as he fell, and a troll stepped through it, hands outstretched to grab Brunnhilde's wrist.

"Stop," Sif bellowed as her mind caught up with what was happening. "Brunnhilde, stop. *They're not armed.*"

The Valkyrie paid her no attention, nor did she seem to notice the monstrously formed warriors rising from the tables she'd already passed, cutting her off from Sif and from the exit. She had eyes only for Inge, barely even paying attention to the workers who threw themselves at her. One, dying but not yet dead, clung to the Valkyrie's right leg, leaving a long slick of blood as he was dragged across the ground. Brunnhilde twitched, looked down, and then stomped mindlessly on the man's skull, crushing it beneath her boot. She kicked free of the corpse and continued.

Sif swore and leaped forward, following Brunnhilde's bloody path, using her fist and the flat of her sword to club her opponents unconscious.

A troll looked up from where they loomed over Inge's table, and despite its unfamiliar features, Sif couldn't see any fear in their face. None of them, she realized, looked afraid. They threw themselves at a raging Asgardian goddess, putting their bodies between her and Inge without hesitation, and they died without a change in expression.

The troll did something complicated to the panel into which the tubes and wires fitted. Inge's back arched up off the bed, every muscle standing out in stark relief. A scream burst from her, loud enough to make Sif's ears ring in the echoing room, and Brunnhilde went *berserk*.

Inge. Her lovely, musical voice raised in pain, loud with fear and bright with defiance. Strapped to a bed and surrounded by enemies, surrounded by the deathglows of dozens of einherjar, deathglows that were blanking, winking out, one after the other, and Brunnhilde didn't care, *couldn't care,* because it was Inge. Hurt and trapped and helpless in the way a fierce, capable warrior – her fierce, capable lover – should never be.

Inge, here, incomprehensibly here, so incongruous it had stopped Brunnhilde's heart when she first heard her voice. It was beating fast enough now, though. Hard and wild, pumping blood black with rage.

The Valkyrie wasn't sure what happened next. Everything was lost in a buzzing haze of fury and a fear stronger than anything she'd ever felt for herself, for anyone. A fear that could paralyze, a fear that could kill. Or a fear that she could transmute into fuel, into an unstoppable momentum that had a single, all-encompassing goal: save Inge. She didn't care how she did it, she didn't care who had to die to achieve it. Saving Inge was her sole purpose. Anyone standing between her and that purpose would be cut down without thought, hesitation or mercy. Mercy wouldn't save Inge. Mercy was for the weak, and Brunnhilde couldn't afford it and didn't want it.

A figure rose up before her, hands clutching at her arm, and Dragonfang cut them off. She kicked the figure out of her path and took another step. Someone else came forward and she jerked her sword through their throat, stabbed the next in the gut.

There were only a few people left between her and Inge on the metal table. So close. Seconds away. And then Inge screamed again, wild and unrestrained as if she was pouring every last ounce of herself into the sound.

Brunnhilde jolted under a new impact and looked down long enough to register the scalpel buried deep just above her hip. She pushed past, ripping the blade out of the person's hand and cut backwards, shearing her sword through the back of their skull without looking. She hadn't even seen their face. She didn't need to.

Inge was arched like a bow on the table. Her breath rushed out of her in one long, unstoppable expression of agony. There was a troll in shapeless gray robes bending over her lover, a taloned hand forcing a tube into the warrior's neck through a small cut. Brunnhilde reached across the table and punched her blade through their chest, twisted her wrist to burst their heart and then dragged it free. More tubes connected Inge's face and chest to some strange, ominous machine at the head of the bed, and there was something, some essence, being sucked from the warrior into it. Thick leather straps held her wrists and ankles to the table. The Valkyrie grabbed at the tangle and then hesitated; the troll was down, of no use, but she didn't know what to do. Could she just pull these free? Would that stop whatever was happening or kill Inge outright?

There was someone else behind her. She spun and grabbed them around the throat, held her red-clotted sword to their belly. "Turn it off," she snarled, her voice a death-rattle in her own ears. "Turn it off now."

"Brunnhilde? Brunnhilde, it's me. Let go."

They weren't doing as she commanded, so the Valkyrie began squeezing.

"It's me, it's Sif! I don't know how to…" The voice was a wheeze, almost lost beneath Inge's screams. "Aragorn! *Aragorn!*"

Inge's scream stuttered to a halt. Brunnhilde stabbed the nonsense-speaker, her sword grating over armor, but she didn't have time to finish them so instead hurled them into the wall and whirled back to the table. She wrenched at the tangle of tubes, ripping them all free from Inge's face and chest. Blood plumed up as they exited her flesh, and Inge twitched, twitched again and then stilled. Her skin was waxy and pale, her lips blue and her eyes glassy and unseeing. Motionless.

SIXTEEN
Life and Deathless

Dragonfang clattered to the stone, and Brunnhilde broke the restraints free from the table and gathered Inge into her arms, wrapping her senses around her, too. There was a spark of life still in her. Brunnhilde breathed air and love into her mouth through a throat almost entirely closed up from fear.

Terror stalked the room, and where before it had worn the Valkyrie's own shape, now it appeared as death, hovering on black wings over the best and brightest thing in Brunnhilde's life and trying to take her away. *Not today. Not ever. I will not lose this. Her.*

I will not.

She poured more air into the limp body in her arms, poured all of herself as well. Behind her, another deathglow blanked, a spark of light in her mind going out, a soul in torment and then not. Gone. Didn't matter. Nothing mattered but this.

And then Inge breathed in. And out. And in again, without aid. Brunnhilde's knees almost gave out as the woman's lashes flickered, her eyes moving beneath the lids, but she braced her hip against the edge of the table, jostling the blade still sunk into her flesh and feeling the pain of it for the first time. She didn't let go of Inge to remove it. She didn't look away from her.

There was an abrupt clatter from behind her, an explosion of movement and a loud grunt. "Brunnhilde? Brunnhilde, a little help?"

Metal carving flesh, grating against bone. The Valkyrie knew those sounds, knew what they meant, but she just ducked her head and trusted that her armor would hold against the coming attack. It had worked before; it would work now. She ripped the scalpel out of her hip, the metal scraping against the bottom of her breastplate, and then lifted Inge fully off the table and cradled her tight, leaving her sword somewhere among the bodies and the blood.

Inge opened bleary, dazed, green eyes, dull with incomprehension and hurt. Brunnhilde's knees did buckle this time and she slumped against the table and clutched her tighter.

There was a long, bewildered silence, and then: "Where am I?" Another silence, this one marred by a choking inhalation. "What have you done?" Inge croaked. "What have you…"

She wasn't looking at her, Brunnhilde realized. She was staring over her shoulder at the carnage. The Valkyrie pressed Inge's face against her breastplate. "Don't look, my heart," she said. "I'll get you out of here. You're safe, I promise you're safe now."

She glanced at what Inge had seen. There were corpses

everywhere. Unarmed, unarmored corpses. Hacked down and sliced open; the walls, floor and tables splattered with blood. Beyond them, moving faster than a hawk in flight, was Sif. The warrior was leaping and fighting, running up walls and over tables in order to evade the figures chasing her. Some were mortal workers, like the troll who'd hurt Inge – Brunnhilde clutched the woman tighter – but the rest were tall, twisted figures similar to the other few lying on the tables. Where had they all come from? Why couldn't she remember?

"Deathless," Inge croaked. "The einherjar..."

Instinctively, Brunnhilde prepared to Realm-jump with her girlfriend clutched against her chest. She had to get Inge somewhere safe before they tried to take her away again.

Keep her safe. Keep her safe. Keep her safe.

It was a litany in the Valkyrie's head, as insistent and pounding as her pulse, and it was only stopped by Inge's abrupt struggling in her arms, even weak as it was. "Stop! Brunnhilde, love, stop. *Don't jump!*"

The power coiled in Brunnhilde, the source of her ability, flickered and went out. Inge squirmed as if to get away from her, as if she didn't want to be touched by her.

"What?" the Valkyrie managed. "I have to save you, I have to–"

"*You have to help Sif!*" Inge scrabbled an arm free, the restraint still dangling from her wrist, and slapped Brunnhilde across the face. Hard.

The Valkyrie gasped, shock briefly overwhelming the fear and the strangling, crawling horror, and then it all drained out of her in an unstoppable flood. The terror winked out, and as if she could breathe clearly for the first time all day, she sucked in air foul with the stench of death.

Inge struggled again, and this time Brunnhilde put her back down on the table. The insistent pounding of *keep her safe keep her safe* cut off and she became aware of other sounds, shouts and grunts and the clash of metal on metal.

Inge shoved her in the chest. "Help her," she snarled weakly. Pain hovered in the tightness of her mouth and the corners of her eyes, and yet she was implacable. She was angry. Because there was Sif, backed up against one wall by four… things, four half-giant warriors that had faces of troll and animal. One, horrifyingly, had the head and feathers of a giant eagle, and hands instead of wings. Hands that clutched sharp metal. Sif was fighting a desperate losing battle. For every strike she deflected, it seemed another one made it through her defense. She was cursing steadily, face and armor streaked with blood. Brunnhilde could tell that not all of it belonged to her enemies.

There were overturned tables and a dozen corpses between them. There were other hybrid creatures lying dead or unconscious on tables or the floor where they'd fallen.

Brunnhilde bent and retrieved her sword, still dazed as the fog of fear cleared from her mind, leaving her confused, slow to understand. Dragonfang's hilt was sticky with blood, but she tightened her grip and then thrust the scalpel that had been in her hip into Inge's hand. "Defend yourself until I come back," she said.

"Go," Inge insisted. Brunnhilde went.

She leaped the chaos of tables and corpses and took the wolflike head off the closest warrior with a single sweep of her sword. Adrenaline brought clarity, and though combat brought fear, it was manageable this time. Normal. The headless body reached for her with furred, clawed hands. She jumped away and then back in, lopping off its limbs like she was chopping wood. More pieces of the puzzle clicked into place. She almost staggered under the realization, but then Sif gasped in pain and slumped against the wall.

Brunnhilde waded in, ducking and lunging, slashing and thrusting, until she reached Sif's side. She swept her free hand around the woman's arm, focused her power even as she parried, and then jumped to Inge.

The deathless shouted in surprise at their sudden disappearance and began to turn. Brunnhilde shoved Dragonfang into Inge's hand. "I need time," she shouted, even as her heart squeezed at the risk she was taking with her girlfriend's safety.

Sif straightened, and Inge pushed herself off the table and stood, a little wobbly, at her side. "You've got it," she said grimly. "Save them."

The deathless charged. The mortal workers followed them.

Brunnhilde took two steps away and focused on the deathglows. There were a dozen, perhaps, and they were… she took another few steps, over to one of the machines standing behind a metal table. There was a troll the size of a juvenile giant on it, unmoving, its chest still. Dead?

"Or just dormant." She sucked in a breath so deep her ribs pressed against her armor. "Odin's eye, let me be wrong." She plunged her dagger into the troll's chest to release the soul. Nothing. No deathglow. She felt the first stirrings of relief, but then hesitated again, concentrating. It was here, the einherjar was right here; she could still feel it.

Brunnhilde's eyes flickered from the unanimated body to the machine. She ran her hands over the wires and dials and, *there* – it was somehow *inside the device.* The Valkyrie blinked and drew it forth softer than breathing, her fingers gentle on the cold metal to create the link and beckon it to safety. The soul came to her, a rush of overwhelming emotions spilling from it, and Brunnhilde tucked it safely within her, shuddering as she felt what it did.

"Faster, Valkyrie," Sif yelled, and Brunnhilde became aware of clashing blades and shouts again. Inge was still groggy with whatever had been done to her, and Brunnhilde thought she knew what that was now, but if she dwelt on it, it would drive her insane. Sif was injured. They were outnumbered and these things were monsters, yes, but they were monsters filled with Asgardian souls. What in Odin's name was she supposed to do about that?

Brunnhilde concentrated on what she could do and ran to each machine in turn, hurdling tables and corpses, evading the reaching fingers of one of the deathless who'd pulled back from the attack to chase her down. She ripped souls from the machines as fast as she could, though many were empty – those einherjar had new, terrifying bodies and were busy using them to try and kill the three Asgardians. They were inside the deathless.

Something grabbed her hair, yanking back hard on the end of one of her braids. The Valkyrie lashed backwards with her heel, which connected with solid muscle. She drove through the kick and was rewarded with a grunt. Turned and kicked again, a roundhouse to the side of the creature's knee this time, low and fast. The joint snapped with a crunch and a pop, and he fell howling. Brunnhilde stepped back and then paused.

The einherjar were in the machines, and then somehow they were drawn into the empty bodies and brought to life. Which meant… The Valkyrie reached out and placed her palms on the warrior-hybrid's head. Even kneeling on a dislocated leg, its punch dented her breastplate and drove the air from her lungs, but she found what she needed. With a twist of her mind and a roar, Brunnhilde tore the soul out of the deathless warrior's body. It crumpled like a puppet with its strings cut. The einherjar rushed inside her, bewildered, confused and not entirely itself. Her innate ability to know a soul, its name and life and moment of death, failed her now. She knew nothing about this soul except its fear and confusion. Even the ones in the machines were more coherent than this.

And yet it was Asgardian. It was one of her people, and she would see it safe to Valhalla or die in the attempt.

Brunnhilde leaped away from the empty corpse and over to the next machine, ripping the soul from it, and then she staggered. She was full of them, weighed down by wisps of life and consciousness that had a heft and presence that filled her to the brim. She forced herself on. Two more machines. Potentially two more souls. And now, of course, the deathless warriors themselves.

"*Now, Valkyrie,*" Sif screamed, and there was warning in her voice. Warning and strain. They couldn't hold out much longer.

One machine was empty of einherjar. One machine remained.

She reached it and tore the soul from it, and Realm-jumped just as another deathless came for her, its clawed, troll-like hands skimming her armor before she disappeared. Perhaps she should have stayed and tried to rescue its soul, but Sif and Inge were backed into a corner, bloody, sweating and about to be overwhelmed.

By their own kin in monstrous form.

She couldn't save them all. The knowledge was like fire beneath her skin, scorching her very sense of self. Brunnhilde emerged in the center of the fight, grabbed Sif and Inge by the napes of their necks, the souls nestled deep within her, and Realm-jumped them all away.

SEVENTEEN
THE DEEPEST FEAR

They emerged into the bright, aching blue of a winter's morning. On a bare mountainside, a mile at least below the cave mouth.

Brunnhilde staggered as she brought them out of the between-space, the weight of more than a dozen souls and two Asgardians increasing the energy drain on top of everything they'd experienced in Jotunheim and before. On top of her emotional turmoil at finding her girlfriend being tortured. If she could have, she'd have jumped them straight to Asgard. She'd have taken Inge direct to an infirmary and then the souls on to Valhalla.

She didn't have the power for either right now. They were trapped in Jotunheim, at least for a while.

The three of them collapsed onto bare rock. Sif cursed loudly and inventively between the panting breaths of someone who an instant before had been battling for her life. Brunnhilde crawled straight for Inge, checking her over feverishly. Inge was utterly exhausted, retching weakly with the sudden onslaught of jump-sickness as well as what had been done to her. She was dazed, unfocused as if not entirely present, as if the clarity needed to fight had vanished now that they were out of danger and had taken her senses along with it.

Sif crawled in next to her and put her palm to Inge's brow. Gold light flared against the brightness of the day and streamed from Sif's chest down her arm and then into Inge.

"Thank you," Brunnhilde breathed, keeping her hands to herself with an effort. She wanted to hold and touch and examine Inge, but was afraid the contact might steal some of the Quellstone's binding power. It all needed to go into Inge. All of it.

The wounds from where the tubes had been pushed into her girlfriend's flesh sealed up under the onslaught of healing magic and Brunnhilde was able to take a full breath for the first time since she'd heard Inge's voice raised in fury and fear under the mountain.

"Inge, Inge my heart, talk to me. Tell me you're all right," she begged over Sif's rasping breaths next to her.

"We have to get her to Asgardia. To Frigga," Brunnhilde said when Inge didn't reply. She searched inside herself for the necessary strength to transport them all. She'd find it; somewhere, somehow, she'd find it.

"No." Inge's voice was thready but firm and Brunnhilde almost collapsed in shock and relief. "No, there are more einherjar there. A lot more. You must be able to sense them. And they'll be speeding up the, the conversion now, knowing they don't have a lot of time. You have to stop them.

You have to save them from the machines and save them from the deathless. I saw you during the fight," she added feebly, trying to bat away Sif's hand. "That's enough. Lady Sif, please, that's enough. You need that power more than me."

Sif lifted her hand away and Brunnhilde made an inarticulate sound of protest.

"Talk to me about the souls," Inge said, before she could do anything hasty like hold Dragonfang to Sif's throat until she poured more healing magic into her lover. "You freed one, didn't you?"

Brunnhilde nodded, teeth and fists clenched.

"You did what?" Sif demanded, pale and hoarse. She grabbed the Valkyrie by the shoulder. "Tell me how? Brunnhilde, focus and tell me how. Inge's alive, she's alive. Come on, focus."

"Right now, we need to save the ones we've got," the Valkyrie said grimly. "I have thirteen souls here, and Inge shouldn't be here at all. So, we're taking them home first. Then we can decide what to do about the rest."

There was a long silence. "That might actually be a good idea," Sif said slowly. She was staring off into the distance, her throat working as she swallowed. "It might be better if we had other help. Someone… else."

"What do you mean?" Inge asked. Gently, she took Brunnhilde's wrists in her hands and held her still.

Sif turned back and met their gazes one by one. Her eyes rested on Brunnhilde, but it was to Inge that she spoke. "I don't trust her. I'm sorry, but after that–" She cut herself off and gestured uphill, back towards the cave.

Brunnhilde gasped, and the dread clawing at her was replaced by anger when Inge nodded slowly. "What are you–" she began. She wrenched her hands away and sat back on her heels.

"Do you know how many people you killed in there, Brunnhilde?" Sif demanded, and now her voice was as cold and hard as the mountain itself. As implacable and immoveable as granite reaching to the sky. The warrior pushed up onto her knees, and her hand wasn't as far from her sword hilt as courtesy demanded.

Anger congealed into ice and slithered down the Valkyrie's back. She scowled. "I killed as many as I needed to, to save Inge. To save the souls."

"And how many of those that you killed were armed?"

"I..." she tried, and stopped. Replayed the events. Inge's voice, heard from the tunnel, Realm-jumping towards her without hesitation or thought. People, creatures, rushing towards her, and over it all, Inge's screams and the crippling, choking terror seeping through her like thick poison. "They were the enemy," she snapped. "They were torturing Inge. I had to–"

Sif's eyes were hard, but the hand – her sword hand – she put on Brunnhilde's shoulder was gentle. "You slaughtered more than a dozen unarmed civilians of various races. Cut them down without a thought. Without hesitation."

The Valkyrie wrenched back, wobbled and then stood up. She strode away, her back to them. "I didn't," she whispered, whether to herself or them didn't matter. "I'd never do something like that. That's not what happened. They were attacking me." She repeated it, louder for the others to hear, her voice bouncing from the stone as she whirled back to face them. "They were attacking me. *And Inge.* I did what I had to do. And besides, they weren't civilians. Look at what they were doing, at what they tried to do to her. The einherjar are in those monsters. Every deathless has an Asgardian soul, Sif. All of them."

Sif paled at the revelation. Her hand half-rose and then fell back into her lap. She didn't seem to know what to say.

"So don't accuse me of murdering innocents. You killed our own kin." A vicious delight surged through Brunnhilde at the stricken look on the warrior's face. "Cut them down without thought or hesitation. And you're accusing me of being a monster? You're no better than I am."

"Enough," Inge snapped and then she coughed. "You're changing the subject, my love, and assigning blame where no blame lies. Sif could not have known that about the deathless, but you knew that those workers were unarmed." Her tone was neutral, containing neither condemnation nor understanding. A simple statement of fact.

"I have a hole from a scalpel in my gut that says otherwise," she tried, but from the look on both warriors' faces, it wasn't enough. "I didn't – I couldn't – think straight. All I could see was you; all I could hear was you screaming." Brunnhilde clenched her jaw against more words, sharp breaths scouring through her lungs.

"Anyway, who cares if I killed them?" she demanded when the shield-maidens showed no signs of understanding. "They're murderers and thieves who steal not just life but souls. They steal the warriors we will need when Ragnarok comes. They steal the very promise that you will live again when the Last Battle comes and that until then you will feast and fight and be content. And you favor their lives over those of good Asgardian warriors? Perhaps they deserved to die, have you thought of that?"

Shame was a snake coiling in her belly despite her defiance, oily and slick and coating her insides until she wanted to shuck her skin and scrub clean her very bones. She was angry and defensive and that was proof of her guilt more than any admission would be. Behind her, Sif tutted but didn't speak, which was for the best, or Brunnhilde would not be able to answer for her temper. She stared down at her shaking, blood-splattered hands. Despite her protests, she couldn't remember it, not clearly. The veil of fear had lifted once she'd seen Inge was alive, and the single deathless she'd killed after that had been armed and trying to kill Sif. She'd saved Sif's life and somehow it wasn't enough.

"They were under someone's control," she tried, but her voice was weak.

"Yes," Sif said in a voice of ice. "And so their actions were not their own. They were forced. They were innocent."

Brunnhilde took a threatening step forward, and the raven-haired warrior stood to meet her. "Then what's your solution, *Lady Sif?*" she demanded, angry and mocking. She shoved the shield-maiden in the shoulder, hard enough that she stumbled backwards on the uneven ground. Defiance and justification were a poorly woven cloak, ragged and full of holes, that she was attempting to pull over her shame and guilt. Sif knew it, and that just made Brunnhilde angrier.

"Shall I give you my ability to sense deathglows? Shall I make you a Valkyrie and send you in there, righteous and alone, to do my duty for me? You think yourself better than me, is that it? Think your hatred of Loki is some impenetrable armor against his schemes, against *making mistakes*?"

Sif shoved her back, and before it could devolve into a brawl, she dragged at the collar of the jerkin she wore beneath her armor and revealed a neck ringed with bruises. "You did this," the shield-maiden hissed in a voice black with venom. "As I yelled our failsafe word in your face to try to make you see sense, you throttled me and tried to stab me. There's a scar on my armor to prove it, so don't stand there and pretend you're in any way equipped to deal with whatever is down there. You're no better than me, no matter what you believe!"

"What I believe? I'll tell you what I believe–"

"Hammer and lightning, shut up, both of you!"

Inge was between them, horribly pale and waxy with sweat, but vibrating with utter, implacable disgust. She shoved them apart, her hands braced against their breastplates. She lashed them in turn with an emerald-hard glare.

"Is this what Lord Thor expected when he sent you here? When he trusted you with a mission so critical we've had to keep it secret from *the entire Realm?* Is this how you, Lady Sif, protect your fellow warriors? Is it how you, Chooser of the Slain, perform your duty? Who the Hel do you think you are? Asgard's mightiest heroines or spoilt, bickering children? To think I ever looked up to either of you."

The anger that was threatening to strangle Brunnhilde withered under her lover's fury. She glanced at Sif and then away; the other woman looked equally mortified.

"Brunnhilde, tell me again how many einherjar you saved." Inge's voice was a little quieter, but no less implacable.

"Thirteen." And just like that, all the fight was gone from her. Thirteen out of dozens, perhaps scores. No, more even than that. With the numbers at Meadowfall and what had been happening at the Great Northern Wall, plus however many are there, She feared it was hundreds. She shuddered all over and unclenched her fists and then forced the words past the thorns in her throat. "The blanking of the souls I mentioned? That's when they're put into the deathless creatures. I can sense them up until that moment, and then they lose themselves and their ability to feel and think. They're still there, living in the deathless, but everything that makes them who they are is gone."

Brunnhilde took a deep breath and watched as one sort of tension left Sif and was replaced with another.

"When I realized what the blanking must be, I had to see if I could save one. I drew the soul out of the deathless. I didn't kill it because the soul didn't belong to it in the first place. You can't kill something that's never really been alive. That said, I definitely stopped it. But touching is the only reason I could harvest it, I think."

"That's possibly the most awful thing I've ever heard," Sif whispered, flinching as the wind moaned across the mountainside.

Brunnhilde let herself feel the sorrow and horror of it. She rubbed her arms, chilled to her core. "It is. And although I saved one today, what about all those who died at Meadowfall? There is no deathglow from a deathless, so none of my sisters will have shepherded those freed souls to Valhalla. They're gone, lost possibly forever."

"Hush, my love. It's more likely that they are wandering the battlefield waiting to be found," Inge said soothingly. "When we get back home, we can devise a way to check."

"But first we need a plan to save the rest under that Hel-cursed mountain." Sif's face was hard with determination and righteous fury. "We are not leaving a single one down there, I can promise you that. So that means you need to tell me how best I can help you. Can I draw the souls forth myself?"

Brunnhilde was already shaking her head. "I don't believe it's that simple. I think I have to strip them from the living deathless with my own hands. A Valkyrie's hands. Meaning, I have to be touching them. Removing the soul will stop the body, but if you kill them and release that soul, there's no guarantee I'll be able to locate it again."

Sif barked a harsh laugh. "You're telling me I can't kill the creatures bent on killing us? Is there even any point in me coming with you?"

Brunnhilde rubbed her hand over the nape of her neck. "You can… distract them."

"Well, that sounds like something that's definitely going to get me killed," Sif said, kicking a scatter of pebbles down the hillside with something almost like resignation, but at least she didn't look at Brunnhilde as though they were enemies anymore. Or as if the Valkyrie was something she needed to scrape off the sole of her boot.

Inge sat suddenly, her legs crumpling and dumping her on the bare rocks with a grunt. "Remember how Sif speculated they were snatching the souls of the best and brightest warriors? She was right, but their insertion into these creatures steals their memories and abilities. They can follow orders and fight, but they can't strategize or plan or adapt. They're mindless drones, like worker bees. Like the people in the laboratory."

Brunnhilde put her fingers over Inge's lips. There was only one question, the question that was so big she'd trembled under its weight ever since she'd first laid eyes on Inge under the mountain, that she needed the answer to now. Everything from before – her actions, Sif's disgust, their argument – all faded into insignificance.

"Please, my heart, before I lose my mind: how are you here?"

Inge kissed the fingertips against her mouth and then took the Valkyrie's hand so she could talk. "I'm getting to that, I promise. It's related to what they're doing." She paused to cough again, and Brunnhilde snatched her cloak off her pack and wrapped the warrior in it.

"The person in charge has been experimenting, trying to find some way to keep the souls' knowledge but strip out their independence," she went on, her voice a distant monotone. "From what I understood, nothing they tried worked, so they returned to Meadowfall and took us – took me. An ambush at the portal – emerging, kidnapping warriors, and fleeing again before they could be stopped. Most of the raiders were killed, but enough made it back with us. They're trying to move the souls of living

Asgardians directly into deathless to see if that will give them the Asgardian abilities needed while ensuring their obedience."

Nausea surged in Brunnhilde's throat, and she couldn't prevent herself from reaching out to pull the woman against her. "I should have destroyed that portal," she grated out.

"How many of you did they bring?" Sif asked, interrupting the spiral of Brunnhilde's thoughts.

"Ten, I think. I don't know where the others are, if any are still alive. I heard… things."

Brunnhilde kissed Inge's temple and hair, the high arch of her cheekbone, wanting to press her through her armor and into her skin where it was safe. Carefully, she controlled her strength so as not to hurt her any further. "My love, my heart," she whispered. "I'm so sorry."

"You said the person in charge. Did you meet them?" Sif asked.

Inge shivered again, violently. Brunnhilde shifted until she was between her and the wind. "I think so. I couldn't identify them. Just a figure, hooded and cloaked, with a low masculine voice that made me anxious. He was amused when he told me what they were going to do. Amused and… expectant. As if I should be grateful. As if I should thank them for tearing me out of my body and putting me into a monster."

They sat with that for a moment, and then Sif clapped her hands on her knees. "Alright, practicalities," she said, and the Valkyrie tensed. She both hated and loved the raven-haired warrior's pragmatism. She herself was still reeling with everything that had happened and all they'd learned. "This one's on you, Bright-Battle. Can you get Inge to Asgard and the souls to Valhalla and then get back to me so we can go in there and find our people, living or dead?"

"No," the Valkyrie said quietly. "Or at least, not yet. But Inge can't stay here."

"Inge can," Inge said firmly. "I'll find somewhere secluded to hunker down and wait for you to come back. I'm not going back in there, I'm sorry," she added, blushing as if they might make her, as if Brunnhilde wanted her anywhere near that place. "I just can't."

"Of course you're not," Sif said briskly. "We wouldn't let you, anyway." She looked at Brunnhilde. "You and me, my old friend," she said softly. "Let's finish this."

"You trust me? After… that? After everything you just said?" the Valkyrie asked, unable to stop herself.

Sif grinned and punched her shoulder. "Always."

Sif didn't trust her, which made her gut churn, because Brunnhilde was her friend. But they didn't have any other choice. She just had to hope she could keep the Valkyrie under control long enough to free the einherjar and get back to Inge. *And then home.*

Sick and shaking from channeling the Quellstone – Thor certainly hadn't mentioned the side-effects when he gave it to her – they wrapped the exhausted Asgardian in both of their cloaks and then ensconced her in a small rocky overhang with their packs, and they made their way back to the cave. And the deathless. And the dead.

As they crept, the sun bright in a clear sky above them, the wind bitter but the stone of the mountain itself still strangely warm, Sif worried at the other information they'd gleaned from Inge.

The hooded figure was Loki, of course. It had to be. Only he could invent something so abhorrent and despicable, so uncaring of others' lives and wishes.

She'd questioned Inge on his appearance, not that it had done much good. The figure had been tall and broad in the shoulder; all else was hidden. But even if not for the expansive cloak hiding his features, Loki was a master of disguise. He could have appeared as the All-Father himself – he'd done it before, after all. Her heart kicked in her chest at the thought of facing him, somewhere down there in the dark.

Souls first, justice second, she reminded herself sternly, the same words she'd spoken to Brunnhilde the last time they were here. *And look where that got us.*

The Valkyrie had killed, recklessly, with abandon and without thought. Because the failsafe word had failed to break Loki's grip on her mind. Sif couldn't fix the corpses Brunnhilde had created, nor would she even if she had the skill. She would not delve into such atrocities and make herself another Trickster God. But the failsafe… could she fix that?

She halted a quarter of a mile from the cave mouth. The Valkyrie looked shamefaced and a little apprehensive, as if now that they were away from Inge, she was expecting the raven-haired warrior to take her to task. Sif didn't have time to allay that particular concern.

"Every time either of us has been manipulated by Loki's magic, it's found one of the deepest fears in us and used it to force us into poor decisions," she said without preamble. Sif didn't like admitting to vulnerability, but she couldn't see that they had any other choice. She fiddled with a strap on her armor for a moment and then pushed on through her reluctance.

"I think, in light of the fact that me screaming 'Aragorn' in your face didn't work, that if we are… aware of each other's deepest fears, that might enable us to talk the other woman down if we suspect she's being manipulated."

Brunnhilde blinked and then blew out her cheeks. "You want us to sit here, almost in the enemy's lair, and confess what we're most afraid of like children braiding each other's hair and trading secrets?"

"I absolutely do not want to," Sif disagreed, "because just the thought of it makes me itchy, but I think *we need to*. Our own emotions are being used against us and we have no other way to counter them. Unless you have a plan?" she interrupted herself, suddenly hopeful, but Brunnhilde scowled away the question.

Sif sighed and gave herself a moment's grace to check their surroundings – nothing but black, shattered rock around them, the snowline far below, and gray clouds massing overhead. Brunnhilde's hair was the brightest thing in the entire landscape. Brunnhilde's, not Sif's. She blinked and refocused.

"You heard Inge's voice and panicked. That fear was twisted and heightened in you by Loki's power. Earlier, when I wanted to run in and kill everyone, it was because I was seized with the fear that we would fail if we didn't. So, if we know what each other is afraid of, we can fight it."

Despite her words, Sif really, really didn't want to have this conversation. No one knew her deepest fears. She rarely even acknowledged them to herself, and now she was going to mutter them on a windswept mountainside in Jotunheim? But she knew, too, that the Valkyrie had been targeted more than she had so far. It was only fair that she be willing to confess her own fears in the face of the ones she already knew about Brunnhilde.

And more than fair. It might be crucial to their survival and the success of their mission.

"So," she began, determined, "if you're suddenly convinced that you've heard Inge's voice, and I haven't, for example, then that's an indication you're being drawn into danger. If I…" she paused as humiliation squirmed in her gut, then threw back her shoulders and met Brunnhilde's skeptical gaze. "If I suddenly start screaming about losing my hair – and please, don't tell me how vain I am, that's not going to help either of us right now – then you'll know I'm being manipulated and I'm not paying attention to my surroundings."

Brunnhilde had looked exactly like she was going to tease Sif, but then her expression softened. She half reached out, but let her hand fall before making contact. Perhaps she knew Sif didn't want empty platitudes. "It was never vanity, my friend," she said instead. "It was a violation. That it is still something you are afraid of proves how traumatic that violation was."

Sif exhaled hard, more comforted than she wanted to admit. She even managed a small smile. "It does seem silly," she acknowledged, tugging at the loose strands that had fallen from her braid. "But it's… always there. It was so long ago and yet he took something so personal from me. And replaced it with this." The warrior glanced down at the ebony plait hanging over her shoulder. "Forever different from how I was. Forever marked as, *as his*."

One corner of Brunnhilde's mouth lifted. "Beautiful," she said.

Sif slapped at her arm. "No flirting or I'll tell Inge," she threatened, but it shook a little more tension out of her. "Alright, so. My hair. Being maimed, I suppose, or losing a limb. Those are fairly standard for all warriors. Losing Heimdall or Thor, the people I love the most."

You, she wanted to add, but didn't.

"Failing my duty. Those are my fears. And being soul-snatched. That one is very intense right now." It was the newest of her fears, still bright and shiny with just-forged edges, sharp enough to cut. To be taken from her body and forced into one of those hideous, half-giant monstrosities. To *blank,* as Brunnhilde had called it. To be under the control of another.

"And… Loki."

The Valkyrie's eyebrows rose. "You hate Loki."

"I am terrified of Loki," Sif corrected in a small voice, swallowing against the bird-fast fluttering of her heart at the base of her throat. "I hate him, yes, because of what he's done to me and countless others, but deep down, right in the core of me, I'm frightened of him too. Of his power and his mercilessness. Of the fact that he will enjoy his vengeance against me if he catches me."

She concentrated on drumming a steady rhythm on her breastplate with her fingertips. "He knows me, Brunnhilde, the good and the bad, my strengths and weaknesses. He'll turn them all against me if he gets the chance. He can take me apart better than anyone and he'll do it just for fun."

They were silent for a few seconds, absorbing that. Sif was both pleased and disappointed that her friend didn't try to correct her. She wondered, in the brief silence, whether Loki was down there, waiting for her. Whether he knew it was Sif coming for him.

"Alright, then," Brunnhilde said slowly. "First of all, I just want to say this is horrible."

Sif snorted in fervent agreement.

"Second, in many ways we're not so different. For me, my two biggest fears are losing Inge and failing the All-Father. Being forced to abandon the remaining souls or otherwise failing in my duty to retrieve them. Losing other people, too – Thor, my shield-sisters. But mostly Inge and failure. Being helpless. And… I'm frightened of being so frightened that I turn and run."

Sif exhaled hard at that last. "Yes," she said quietly. "Me too."

Brunnhilde gnawed at her thumbnail. "There's one more," she said quietly. "I'm afraid… I'm afraid I will come to enjoy taking life. There was something about stripping that soul from that deathless warrior that I liked, and it was more than just freeing one of our own. I know that I'm a warrior first and foremost, but these days I do believe that my ultimate duty is as a Valkyrie. And that means far more to me than anything else. It's not that I don't want to be a warrior anymore – it's in my blood after all – but I've never lusted after battle. What if this changes me?"

Sif was silent for a long time, her gaze roaming across the landscape, flickering towards the Valkyrie and then away. "That is a fear that every warrior has," she said eventually. "That it becomes about the fight, the struggle. That eventually you only ever feel alive amid death. But it won't happen to you, Brunnhilde," she added in a firm voice. "You are leader of the Valkyrior, the most honorable of all your sisters. You will never let bloodlust overtake you. I'm here to stop you if that ever becomes a concern. Which it won't. Trust, remember?"

Brunnhilde forced a smile. "Alright, so now we know each other's darkest secrets, the next most important thing is that we are going to have to trust each other implicitly. Turn our fears – our weaknesses – into strengths. So not just trust the way we fight together, we've always been good at that, but trust in what we're seeing and feeling. If you're suddenly convinced Heimdall's in danger and you need to go and save him, abandoning your mission here, when I tell you that isn't true, you're going to have to do all you can to believe me."

The Valkyrie stared down at the backs of her hands, chapped from the cold and thick with muscle. "We're dealing with something new and unknown, and we're not going to get through it alone. We keep talking; we stay alive; we stay on mission."

Sif blew out her breath, a long white plume in the chilly air. "Faster we do this, faster we get Inge home and the souls to Valhalla."

"Faster we never have to have conversations like this again," Brunnhilde added.

"Gods be good," Sif prayed fervently, eliciting a forced chuckle. There was no more putting off the inevitable. She tried to still the nervous fluttering in her chest and failed. "Let's go."

EIGHTEEN
THE FATE OF THE MISSING

They took the left-hand tunnel this time, towards the remaining deathglows and that strange, unlikely familiarity Brunnhilde had sensed before. Loki was no fool, so the fact the einherjar appeared to still be in the same place as before meant they were surely walking into a trap.

Inge had said there were perhaps as many as ten kidnapped warriors to find as well as the missing souls, though the odds weren't good for their survival. Brunnhilde already had thirteen einherjar packed small and quiescent within her, brushing delicately against her own soul in a way unfamiliar but not unpleasant. Valkyrior did not normally transport the glorious dead in so intimate a manner. If necessary, though, she could take dozens more, each a tiny, energy-draining burden that would fill her and slow her. Make her weaker at the very time that she needed to be stronger.

I am Chooser of the Slain. It is my duty. I will not fail. My strength will be equal to whatever the task.

"Do you think Inge is alright?" she whispered just as they crossed into the shadow of the cave mouth.

"She's fine, Brunnhilde," Sif said absently, her eyes scanning the terrain ahead, but then she reached blindly back and gripped the fingers the Valkyrie stretched towards her. "She's fine, I promise. Come on, let's keep going. Left, is it?"

"Left," Brunnhilde confirmed, though a part of her attention was back in the hollow with her lover. Inge was resting in that dazed twilight that only the most exhausted ever visited. She was barely awake.

Reassured, she followed Sif in, both of them silent as ghosts as the gloom deepened. They'd both chosen thick, dark clothing to wear beneath their armor before leaving Meadowfall, knowing Jotunheim's climate and long nights all too well. With Sif's ebony hair she was a shadow amongst shadows as they stole into the cave. Again, like before, the left-hand tunnel held the promise of light at its end.

Sif had pulled a few paces ahead and the cave opening was far behind them. "Sif? Do you think Inge's all right?" Brunnhilde hissed.

Sif frowned at her and then came back. This time, she seized both of Brunnhilde's hands. "Listen to me," she said with quiet intensity. "Inge is a fine warrior, part of Asgardia's own shieldwall. She is strong, resourceful, fierce and independent. She has our packs, our supplies, and our spare knives. Inge is well, Brunnhilde. Do you hear me?" Brunnhilde couldn't answer and Sif shifted her grip to cup her face. "Do you *trust* me?"

"I…" Some of the chaos in the Valkyrie's mind subsided and she choked in a full breath, her first in several minutes.

She put her hands on Sif's wrists but not to push her away: she pressed her face into those calloused palms. "Yes. But hammer and lightning, I hate this. I hate that it keeps on being me he torments," she added without thinking, and then grimaced. "Sorry."

A muscle flickered in Sif's jaw, but she didn't let go of Brunnhilde's face. "It's because you're stronger than I am," she said, evenly and without hesitation. Brunnhilde startled. "You're more of a threat. You can sense the einherjar and you can get them straight to Valhalla, where they can't be snatched again. So of course Loki will concentrate his influence on you more than me. Which means that you," she added in a stern whisper, shaking the Valkyrie by the head, "need to listen to what I tell you. Inge is fine. And we have to carry on."

She hesitated, as if to say more, and Brunnhilde stepped out of her embrace and past her, taking point so that the warrior could make sure she didn't double back. Acid stung the back of her throat. When or if they finally confronted whoever was doing this, she'd be pleased to have words with them, spoken with blades if necessary. She was sick of dancing to another's tune. She was in control of herself, and she was going to stay that way.

The tunnel was wide and tall, adorned with geometric carvings typical to mountain giant clans. Smoky torches burned high above their heads. A scuffle of noise from ahead had them both melting into the shadows, crouched low against the wall on their left. A booming voice shouted something that bounced from the stone and was lost in its own echo before it reached them – and a soul went blank.

Brunnhilde jammed her fist between her teeth to prevent the cry of anguish from breaking free. It was the waking of a deathless warrior, another monster they would need to face. But worse, it was the torment of another Asgardian soul. Even though Loki knew it didn't work the way he wanted it to, he was still trying. Torturing einherjar with all the abandon of a child with a set of fragile toys, smashing them just to see what would happen. It was abhorrent. It was *enraging.* It was another living creature from whom she was going to have to strip a soul.

A hand reached forward to pat her thigh. "Easy," Sif murmured, the word more breath than sound. She couldn't have felt the loss of the soul, but something had alerted her to the Valkyrie's state of mind. Brunnhilde pressed her eyes shut for a long second, breathing slowly, and then nodded. They couldn't rush in this time. No matter what.

When the suggestion of movement from ahead faded, they rose again, creeping forward in tandem. The harsh white light from the doorway mingled with the unsteady orange flicker from above until they were horribly, mercilessly exposed.

"Fast?" she breathed over her shoulder, despite having just told herself not to rush. Sif's hand gripped her biceps and pulled her back. *Slow.* Brunnhilde obeyed, trusting the warrior's instincts. It was hard to acquiesce, but if it had been anyone else, with the exception of the God of Thunder or the All-Father himself, it would have been impossible.

The entrance was fifty yards, then forty, then thirty. The sounds became clearer from within: shuffling, a low, toneless murmur and the clatter of metal. No more clear voices, nothing raised in triumph or despair. Brunnhilde slid Dragonfang from its scabbard, the blade hissing softly against the leather. Behind, Sif did the same. Her free hand itched for a shield, but she only had a knife. She'd make it count.

Twenty yards.

"Who are you? Stop there!" A voice boomed around them.

"Go, go, go!" Sif snarled. They ran.

Brunnhilde skidded through the doorway, in and to her left, scanning the scene. Sif piled in a heartbeat later and went right, the pair of them flanking the opening with their backs firmly pressed to stone.

The scene was hideously familiar: metal tables, machines, the empty bodies of malformed warriors waiting to be filled with einherjar. Each table had an attendant, and they turned as one at the pair's entrance and the bellowing shout from back in the passageway.

This time, the Valkyrie wasn't panicked beyond all reason. She was very cold and very precise. The room was packed with trolls and elves and Midgardians. Even a couple of dwarves. Their eyes were blank, incurious, and they moved as one towards the Asgardians.

"No killing," Sif shouted.

Brunnhilde lifted a hand in acknowledgment. She wanted nothing more than to get past the workers and collect the souls while inflicting as little damage as possible. The thought of raising her sword to any of them made her feel sick. Two of the figures on the metal tables sat up and swung their legs down, the husks of their flesh newly inhabited with Asgardian souls. They stood and picked up the weapons that had lain beside them. These deathless weren't ugly. Their features were delicate and familiar, although painted across a canvas twice as tall as Brunnhilde. Too familiar. Enough to give her pause.

"I don't like this," Sif muttered as she slid away from Brunnhilde, her movement drawing the creatures' attention. "Valkyrie, do your thing, but do it fast. Why do they look…" She trailed off and then shook her head. "Go, go. I'll keep them off you."

"They're us," Brunnhilde said as one of the blonde deathless warriors shoved between the crowding workers and headed for Sif. "By the Norn, *they're Asgardian!*"

Nausea surged against the back of her throat. They'd fought twisted hybrids of giant and troll, giant and elf, even giant and predator. Now… now they were confronted with giant and Asgardian.

She couldn't even begin to speculate how it had been done, or the sheer amount of torment they had suffered to become what they were now. But if they truly were those warriors seized alongside Inge – and who else could they be? – then they weren't like the other deathless she and Sif had fought and killed. Or like the one whose soul she had retrieved. Because they must still contain their own souls. Loki hadn't pulled out their souls and put them in different bodies – he'd *combined the bodies* of Asgardians and giants. And if these were people with their own souls, rather than empty husks with a soul trapped inside, then how could Brunnhilde tear them free? Wouldn't that be murder?

Sif was being loud and fast, drawing the attention of every living thing in the room, including the two newly awoken deathless. Doing what she had promised and giving Brunnhilde time to harvest the einherjar trapped in the machines who were waiting to be fed into other, non-Asgardian deathless. She shook her head and followed the black-haired warrior's last piece of advice: be fast. She shoved between two blank-eyed workers and crossed to the nearest machine. It was unattended, a dormant deathless lying on the attached table. Quickly, she drew forth the soul and tucked it away.

Sif let out an inarticulate cry that had the Valkyrie's heart jumping into her throat. She spun so fast that her elbow cracked into the machine and knocked it down with a clatter that drew all eyes. Sif backed steadily away from the two deathless, her sword trembling in her fist.

"Brunnhilde? Brunnhilde, I know her. It's Sigrun and she wasn't stationed in Meadowfall. She's from south of Asgardia. She's… she's deathless. How can she be deathless?" The shield-maiden's voice was high and raw with shock. She wasn't even trying to defend herself, just backing away faster now. Her backplate clattered into a metal table, and the deathless lying on it twitched.

"Behind you," Brunnhilde shouted.

"What do I do?" Sif shouted again. "*She's my friend.*"

The creature on the table grabbed around Sif's waist, and she let out a squawk of shock. The shield-maiden tried to twist away, but both its arms were firmly wrapped around her. Its head was pressed against her hip as it scrabbled to clear the table. As soon its feet hit the stone it picked her up and hurled her directly into the wall. Her cry of pain was almost lost beneath the scraping clatter of armor on rock.

Brunnhilde felt two more souls blank and, seconds later, a fourth and then a fifth deathless warrior sat up on their respective tables and picked up weapons. These were both half-elven, and through the chaos of bodies moving, she saw more workers fiddling with the machines connected to the others awaiting their new, enslaved lives.

"Sif?" she screamed. "Sif, you bloody idiot, get up and fight!"

"*Kill them!*" The new voice was so deep and loud that Brunnhilde felt it in her ribs, the very air shivering and the stone and metal in the room bouncing the echoes back at her in a clanging cacophony. Instinct told her to flee the source of the sound, but she made herself move towards it – towards the door… and saw the mountain giant who'd bellowed at them from the corridor now ducking into the laboratory. He carried a spear the shaft of which was thicker than Brunnhilde's thigh.

A worker clutched at the Valkyrie. She reacted without thought, flinging the Midgardian directly at the giant, who responded by setting his spear and impaling the hapless man as he flailed through the air. Not what Brunnhilde had intended at all, but nothing she could do about it now. She spared an instant to offer a silent apology to him and then ran to the next table. She caught a glimpse of Sif, up on her knees and fighting her way to her feet as three deathless hacked through the workers to reach her.

"Giant at the door," she bellowed, and ripped the soul out of the machine and then Realm-jumped away. The table she emerged next to this time was further down the room and had two workers feverishly connecting wires to the empty husk of another deathless.

Brunnhilde was deeply glad they hadn't come here first on their rescue mission, because now she knew what that strange, edge-of-her-senses familiarity had been: kin. Home. Her people.

Commander Olafson in Greenside had said his warriors were convinced they knew some of their enemies. They'd thought it was because the deathless had blue eyes, like most Asgardians. But maybe they really had been fighting their own. What they were facing now was evil on a scale she couldn't comprehend.

Across the room, the giant's enormous spear smashed down onto the spot where Sif had just been standing. She weaved and dodged, defending desperately against five deathless and one giant jostling each other to get to her. This had been the plan, for Sif to distract them so Brunnhilde could harvest the einherjar, but against such odds, the warrior wouldn't last long. The Valkyrie could help her. Probably should help her.

"Keep going," Sif yelled, as if she'd read her mind, and Brunnhilde set her jaw and did as ordered. Half of the workers were scrambling to reach her now, while the rest worked on the machines and the empty deathless. There were just enough of them to hamper Sif's enemies as she flowed around them like water, their efforts to slow her actually keeping her alive as they lumbered between her and the deathless. But Brunnhilde could hear the harsh rasp of Sif's breath; she had to move faster.

The Valkyrie seized the soul in the next machine, punching both workers as they tried to stop her, and then Realm-jumped away. She flitted between the tables that had workers around them, doing her best to snatch the souls before they could be poured into the dormant deathless. Each soul in her was one fewer deathless trying to kill Sif.

Brunnhilde's erratic movements and sudden appearances attracted the mountain giant's attention. He gave up his pursuit of Sif to try and chase her down. Although he was clearly acting under orders, he wasn't controlled the way the workers were. His thoughts and understanding were very much his own and he saw the pattern to the Valkyrie's movements and began to anticipate where she would appear next. It became a race, and despite her ability to Realm-jump, he could cross the room with deceptive speed.

Brunnhilde managed to retrieve two more einherjar and received four long scratches down her cheek from a troll worker's claws before the giant closed in on her, flinging a table out of his path. It smashed into the back of the tallest of the deathless warriors trying to herd Sif against the wall. The deathless stumbled, dropping to one knee and knocking another foe off balance. Sif reacted on instinct, ducking the table as it spun past and slicing her sword through his throat.

Horrified – he had once been Asgardian; was still Asgardian, on some level – her blade dipped, and she stared open-mouthed at the kneeling deathless and the flood of crimson pouring from his neck.

"They don't die that easy," Brunnhilde screamed at her, ducking behind a tangle of machinery. The mountain giant was two steps away. "Sword up, Sif." No response. "Hey, Reckless! Fight!"

Sif shook herself out of her shock and began to defend

again. Brunnhilde moved, pausing just long enough to harvest each soul before jumping again. She could feel the drain on her energy like someone had their fist clenched around her heart, but there were only eight or so machines left before she could turn her attention to the awoken deathless. She could do this.

Sif screamed.

The Valkyrie's jump energy flickered out and she turned. There were dazed or dead workers scattered around Sif, and she was cornered, pressed against the stone wall and hemmed in on both sides by upended tables and smashed machines. The five deathless warriors were crowding in, shoving the tables aside and kicking workers from their path in their eagerness to reach her. Blood had turned her face into a crimson mask. She was on her knees, her sword above her head blocking a long, hooked knife. The half-Asgardian she had called Sigrun was behind the knife-wielder, leaning past to stab at Sif with a spear. At such close quarters, there was no way her armor could withstand such a blow. The spear was going to punch through Sif's chest and out her back and there was nothing she could do to prevent it.

The Valkyrie Realm-jumped straight into the spear's path. The impact knocked her into Sif, and she grabbed the warrior's face, the skin to skin contact necessary for her magic to sweep up others with her, and she jumped them away to the other end of the room.

Sif had been staring at her own death one moment and was huddled at the opposite end of the laboratory the next, the imprint of the Valkyrie's hand still on her cheek. The

Valkyrie who was collapsed on the stone next to her with a spear rammed through her backplate.

"Hold still," Sif snapped and wrenched the huge weapon free. Brunnhilde let out a wordless cry and shuddered, curling onto her side. Blood pumped from beneath her armor, and Sif ripped the sleeve from beneath her vambrace and wadded it up, sliding it underneath the backplate. It would do little to staunch the bleeding, but it would at least provide a barrier between the wound and the torn metal where the spear had punched through it.

"You stupid idiot, save the einherjar, not me. Never mind, can you walk?" Sif was panting from the battle and her own disbelieving anger. She swiped sweat and blood from her face, but the cut at her hairline sent a fresh trickle down her brow.

The giant had spotted them and was charging down the length of the room, well ahead of the deathless warriors. Sif slid in front of the downed Valkyrie, her sword sheathed and the spear ready in both hands. All she had to do was kill the giant and disable the five deathless so that the Valkyrie could save the Asgardian souls trapped within them. Easy. She blinked more blood out of her eyes and drew in a deep, deep breath.

"How much time can you buy me?" Brunnhilde asked, her voice thready with pain.

"Not much," she said truthfully.

The mountain giant had picked up a sword from one of the tables. Although the weapon was too short for him, the length of his arms more than made up for it. They came together in a clash of steel and fury and will, Sif's greater agility allowing her to dart around the giant's bone-crushing strikes. She sensed Brunnhilde moving and shifted to keep herself between the Valkyrie and their enemy, who picked up a metal table in one hand and hurled it. Sif brought up both forearms in front of her face and braced, planting her boots against the stone. The table hit her head on, driving her back a step and screeching down her armor to gash open her thigh just above her knee. The giant followed up as she had expected, and Sif jammed the butt of the spear against the stone and angled the tip, letting him impale himself through the gut as he ran onto the weapon.

Roaring, she shoved it deeper to cleave liver and lung. The giant coughed blood, his fingers clutching at the spear and at her as he stumbled, his face slack with surprise. Blood glistened in the tangle of beard decorating his chin. Sif let go, danced backwards, and then leaped up onto a nearby table and from there onto the giant's back, where she stabbed her knife into the side of his neck.

He went down hard, the spear snapping as he fell, and Sif rolled off him and bounced back up onto her feet. She dragged her sword free and prepared, again, to face the deathless. In the few seconds' grace she had, she looked for the Valkyrie. Brunnhilde was at the machine on the left-hand side of the room, determination and agony tightening the muscles of her face. A trail of blood followed her shuffling footsteps. She was too slow, and they were too outnumbered.

The first of the half-Asgardian deathless reached Sif: it was Sigrun. Something twisted painfully in her chest at the dark, hungry expression on her former friend's face. Sif slid beneath the first overhand blow and chopped her sword into Sigrun's knee, shattering the bone. The deathless howled and lunged clumsily for her, but Sif was already past and cutting into the second. She fought like a whirlwind, pouring every last bit of strength and speed into her movements. It took her long, dizzying seconds to realize she was only fighting three deathless. The mortal workers had finally fled, but the other two monsters were closing in on the Valkyrie.

"Behind you!"

The raven-haired warrior didn't have time to see whether Brunnhilde could defend herself. She picked up one of the machines, praying it was empty of soul, and hurled it at Sigrun who limped towards her. It hit her in the face and sent her tumbling backwards into the other two. Sif sprinted straight for Brunnhilde, her blades slicing deep into the deathless that were threatening her as she pushed between them.

The Valkyrie could barely lift her sword, and so Sif did the only thing that she could: sheathed her blades and dragged the other woman onto her back. "Save your jump energy. Guide me," she panted.

"Three on the right," Brunnhilde gasped in her ear, pointing with Dragonfang. Sif ran for the waiting machines, skirting the bleeding, angry deathless and scrambling over broken tables and corpses.

She skidded to a halt at the first machine. The Valkyrie grabbed it and ripped the soul free. "Go!" Brunnhilde cried.

Sif went. They managed two more before the five deathless had formed a ring around them and were closing in. The Valkyrie was a dead weight on her back, sword hanging limply from her hand. Sweat and blood blurred Sif's vision and her chest heaved with ragged breaths. She couldn't fight like this. Brunnhilde was barely clinging to her as it was, let alone if she began moving any faster.

"We can't," Sif gasped. "I'm sorry, but we need to go." The words tasted of blood and defeat, but Brunnhilde didn't protest. Instead, she felt the gathering of the Valkyrie's magic and then the shattered, blood-soaked laboratory was replaced with the nothingness of the between-space. A second later they were out, blinking in bright afternoon sunlight and the silent safety of the mountain.

Nineteen
Blood and Healing

Sif staggered on wobbling legs towards where they'd left Inge. She could hear the Valkyrie's teeth grinding, and something wet was pattering onto her calves as she walked: blood.

"Inge?" Sif called, her voice hoarse. "Inge, we need you."

She got another dozen paces before the shield-maiden appeared, a knife in each hand and a pack on her back ready to flee. The blood drained from her face when she saw Sif, bloody and sweating, and Brunnhilde draped over her.

"No!" she cried, dropping the weapons and rushing forward.

"Hush," Sif hissed. "She's alive, but none of us will be for long if you keep shouting! Help me lie her down, on her side. We need to get her armor off and bind the wound."

"Is she dying? What happened?"

"She's not dying if we help her. Quickly now. Focus," she added as Inge knelt beside them, horrorstruck at the

Valkyrie's pallor. Sif began unbuckling Brunnhilde's armor. "Get needle, thread, salve and bandages from the pack. *Now*, girl."

The crack of command in her voice woke her and Inge hurried to comply. She let out a whimper when Sif tossed the breastplate and backplate aside and yanked up Brunnhilde's jerkin and tunic to reveal the jagged, red-mouthed wound in her back. Blood leaked from it steadily.

"Treat and bind it," Sif ordered and then dug out the Quellstone from her shirt. It had taken on a pale, almost cracked-eggshell appearance within its silver filigree. It was running out of power, but she placed her hands on the Valkyrie's brow and throat and sent a trickle, a stream, a flood of golden healing magic into her anyway, scouring her own body to fix Brunnhilde's. "Don't die on me, you stupid, beautiful idiot," she breathed, sweat standing out on her brow. "Don't you bloody dare."

Inge worked quickly and carefully despite her trembling fingers, not interrupting Sif's transfer of energy. "Hold on, my heart," she whispered as she slid the needle and thread through Brunnhilde's flesh, closing the slit. She smeared it with healing salve and then bandaged her, wrapping linen tight around her waist. The pale material slowly bloomed with pink roses, then red, as she bled through.

Inge murmured reassurance and dribbled water between Brunnhilde's dry lips. Sif grunted and kept going. The golden light was paler, and exhaustion caused black motes to dance before her eyes before the Valkyrie stabilized. Shuddering, her breath high and tight in her chest, Sif removed her hands from Brunnhilde's skin and slumped back on her heels. She rubbed sour sweat from her face and stared at her friend. Her eyes were closed but her chest rose and fell rhythmically and there was a soft blush of color to her cheeks.

"She'll be all right. Her own energy will replenish and speed any more healing she needs. I shouldn't use any more of this unless there's no other choice, though, I'm sorry."

Inge's eyes were shiny with tears. "I understand. Thank you for doing this much for her."

Sif nodded wearily and then used the hilt of her knife to hammer flat the rent in Brunnhilde's backplate.

They were silent for a few minutes, both watching the Valkyrie sleep.

"Did you get all the einherjar? Where are the other warriors from Meadowfall?" Inge asked eventually, smoothing Brunnhilde's hair back from her damp brow.

If Sif needed any further reason as to why Brunnhilde cared for this woman so deeply, the fact she could still think of the mission while her lover was desperately weak was it. Still, the questions hurt to think about, let alone answer. "We got as many souls as we could. Not all of them. The others, the living warriors…" she cut herself off and pressed the back of her hand to her lips, and then wrenched it away. It tasted, smelled, of blood. "Some of the deathless are half-Asgardian. I don't know if–"

"*What?*" Inge stopped running her fingers through the Valkyrie's hair and stared at Sif as if she'd suddenly revealed herself to be the Trickster God in disguise. Sif hushed her and they sat in tense silence, waiting to be discovered. No one came.

Sif let out a slow breath. "One of them was my friend Sigrun. She wasn't at Meadowfall, which means Loki has been taking them for longer and from further than we thought. I didn't recognize any others from Meadowfall in these new deathless, but I think it's likely that that's who they are." *First Gyda and now Sigrun.* As if Loki was taking the people closest to her. Making it personal. She didn't know if that was guilt or fear talking, or even hubris.

Inge's green eyes were wide with shock and disbelief.

"We got most of the einherjar, though," Sif said awkwardly, trying to reassure her.

"Most," Inge echoed hollowly. A tear slipped down her cheek. "Most won't be good enough for her, you know that. This is going to eat at her, Sif. She'll count it a failure, and on top of her injury…"

"Then it's a good job she has us, isn't it?" Sif said with a hint of steel in her tone. "This isn't over yet, Inge. Now, I'm going to sleep to restore some strength, so I need you to guard us. Can you do that?"

Inge licked her lips, but she nodded. "I can. I won't let you down."

Sif forced one side of her mouth to curl up. "I know you won't," she said softly. Now that she was ready to let go, fatigue slipped its oily embrace around her. Sif cast a final look uphill before lying down next to Brunnhilde and pulling her cloak over them both. Her eyelids fluttered as she watched Inge draw Dragonfang and then sit next to them, focused and alert.

Sif rubbed her tingling fingertips together, legacy of the Quellstone's magic, and had one final, hazy thought before sleep took her: *did we manage to save Gyda? Was she one of the ones Brunnhilde managed to steal back?*

It wasn't the point. It hadn't been since they understood the scale of the atrocity Loki was committing. Every soul saved was a soul to be treasured and every soul lost deserved equal mourning.

No matter how sternly Sif told herself that, deep in her secret heart she wanted to wake Brunnhilde and demand to know who she had saved. Sigrun was lost, perhaps forever: a twisted, evil remnant of her former glory. The need for Gyda to be safe was as sharp as daggers in her heart. Resolutely, Sif closed her eyes and slept.

The sun was dropping when a hand on her shoulder startled Sif out of her sleep. She came up to sitting while reaching for a blade, but her knife sheath was empty. Then she recognized the figure crouching over her. Inge was pressing her finger to her lips, and when she saw she had Sif's attention, it moved to point uphill. She made a walking gesture, cupped her ear to indicate voices, and then held up four fingers.

Oh, that's not good.

Sif eased onto her knees, then crawled sideways further into the boulder field before risking a look. Inge might have heard four voices, but there were more than that searching. Three mountain giants, whose height would give them an advantage on finding the group huddled among the rocks, and a mix of those workers from before. Again, they seemed oddly blank, as if without a will of their own. Whatever Loki had done to them, she suspected it was permanent.

With Brunnhilde deep in a healing sleep, and Sif herself

drained of much of her energy despite her rest, she wasn't sure they would emerge victorious if it came to a fight this time.

She crept back and put her mouth to Inge's ear. "We need to wake Brunnhilde and Realm-jump." She didn't wait for the warrior's inevitable protest, just shook the Valkyrie's shoulder gently, and then harder when there was no response. She hissed her name and then, with a whispered apology, ground her knuckle into the delicate flesh over her clavicle.

Brunnhilde flinched and jerked away, her hands coming up in instinctive defense and grabbing Sif by the throat. Sif didn't bother shifting her grip, just took Inge's hand and croaked, "Giants. Get us out of here."

The haze was clearing from the Valkyrie's eyes, and she let go of Sif's throat with a blinked apology. "How long?"

"Two minutes," Inge said.

"That should be long enough."

"For what?" demanded Sif as she massaged her throat. Brunnhilde's fingers had dug in over the bruises from last time. "We really don't–" she began, but the Valkyrie wasn't paying attention.

Instead, she met Inge's eyes and gave her a wan smile. "We're not done here, and you can't stay," she murmured, her voice thready. "Inge, my heart, I need you to take the souls."

"What?" she began and then shook her head. "Doesn't matter. Of course, whatever you need. I'll keep them safe here."

Brunnhilde winced. "This is going to hurt, love. I'm so sorry."

Inge gritted her teeth but nodded, and Brunnhilde pressed her palm against her stomach. Sif felt the tingle of magic in the air, and then Inge stiffened and clapped both hands over her mouth. "Hold her steady," the Valkyrie grated.

The blood drained from Inge's face, but she shook her head and gestured towards the advancing party instead. Her fingertips were white where they dug into her own cheeks. Sif risked another look: they were close now, too close. By the time she looked back, it was done. Inge was breathing hard, her lip bitten raw, and Brunnhilde kissed her briefly.

"I've given you the souls we saved, and a one-time-only ability to reach Valhalla. The route is implanted in your mind. You'll emerge by Odin's Hall and one of my sisters will help you from there. She'll take you back to Asgard afterwards. Send a message to Thor that we're going to finish this."

Sif blanched, but Inge interrupted before she could begin to argue. "Absolutely not. I'll hold the souls so you have more strength, but I'm not leaving you here. Just–"

Brunnhilde cut her off with a kiss and used the contact to send her through the between-space to Valhalla.

"You b–" Inge began, and then vanished.

Brunnhilde's hand hovered in the air where Inge had been, and then she blinked once and lifted her armor over her head. Automatically, Sif began to buckle her into it, her fingers moving on their own as she stared into the growing gloom of another dusk. The icy wind burned in the cuts and injuries painting her skin in blood and bruising.

Sif was as empty as the landscape, and they were going back in. She didn't want to go back in. She was going to have to hurt Sigrun and the other half-Asgardians so badly they couldn't fight, and then watch Brunnhilde tear their souls out. If that was the actual plan. Perhaps the Valkyrie could fix them, or they could take them back to Asgardia and find a cure. Surely that was a better solution…

Take a group of half-giant mind-controlled killers back to the heart of our Realm? Parade them around in front of our people and their kin? Bring the enemy into our homes?

The brief candle-flicker of hope she'd had guttered and went out. Sif concentrated on the buckles beneath her fingers and on the steady, slow breaths in and out of her lungs. They couldn't do that. The warriors themselves wouldn't want that, most likely. What if there was some spark in them that knew what was happening but couldn't fight it, and they ended up in Asgard compelled to kill everyone they met? Sif and Brunnhilde would have visited that torment upon them on top of all the others they had already suffered. Still…

"The half-Asgardians," she breathed. "Plan?"

"Free the trapped souls," the Valkyrie said after the barest pause. She understood, then. She agreed. They would bear the responsibility for these actions together, for the rest of their lives. The two of them, alone. *No, the two of us together.*

"Inge's going to be furious you sent her away," she murmured instead when she had her voice under control.

Brunnhilde arched a blonde eyebrow. "Think we'll be alive for me to make it up to her?"

The raven-haired warrior chanced another look. "Not if we don't get a move on. They're nearly here. How are we doing this?"

The Valkyrie curled her lip in disdain. "Leave this lot stumbling around outside and jump all the way in."

The warrior eyed Brunnhilde. She didn't ask if the Valkyrie was strong enough – she had at least half the Quellstone's magic swirling through her veins. "It's a terrible plan and I hate it. But I don't have an alternative."

They exchanged a grin, all teeth and determination. Sif took Brunnhilde's hand again and they jumped through space.

Into the heart of the mountain.

Brunnhilde's back was a constant low throb of agony, duller than it had been before, but still enough it would slow her. Just a little, but a little was often the difference between life and death. And this was a war. A quiet one, fought in the shadows and the ice, but one they had to win. The alternative didn't bear thinking about, because it was an army of deathless warriors and snatched Asgardian souls. It was an army of their own turned against them. It was Ragnarok as civil war. It was, perhaps, the end of the Nine Realms themselves.

Brunnhilde brought them straight to the junction of the two tunnels leading from the main entrance. There were three Midgardians there, and while Sif staggered and retched from the after-effects of the jump, the Valkyrie clubbed them unconscious and hid their bodies in the shadows. Loki was finally taking his security seriously, it seemed. The thought didn't reassure her.

She felt lighter without the souls inside her, even as she worried about how Inge would deal with the Realm-jump and everything that would come afterwards, but she knew she had made the right decision. Those einherjar were now safe, no matter what happened to Sif, Brunnhilde, and the others still trapped here. Inge was safe.

The sun was dying behind them, and turning away from it felt symbolic, as if the next time it rose, they would either be victorious or they would be souls in other bodies, destined never to see it shine on Valhalla. The Valkyrie wanted to refuse to be afraid. She discovered it didn't work like that.

Brunnhilde could still sense the deathglows, but they were few and they were weak. Worse, they didn't come from either direction they'd already explored, but from below, deeper within. There had to be a third tunnel somewhere. She twitched, turning left and then right, seeking that elusive strengthening of the deathglow that would tell her which way to move.

"Hurry," Sif breathed from behind. "I can hear movement."

Brunnhilde chose right and hoped. She had a grim mental image of them stumbling around for hours until they were discovered and captured or killed. The idea did its best to make her more afraid, and she fought against it.

Sif let her lead, sword in hand, trusting her to find the souls that needed their help in the same way that she trusted the warrior to watch her back. They encountered nothing on the long route towards the room where they had found Inge, the reminder of her lover's scream sending a prickle down her spine. This time the chamber was dark, quiet and still. Brunnhilde peered in when they reached it, but there was nothing to see. No workers. The machines that had contained the souls were quiet and unoccupied. The room was a chaos of overturned tables and splashes of blood, but no empty deathless or corpses could be seen. Echoing and eerie.

"Wasn't there another exit at the back of the room?" Sif asked, squinting past the Valkyrie's taller form.

Brunnhilde blushed. "I don't remember much about the layout," she muttered. "Bifrost itself might have opened on that side of the room and I wouldn't have known about it."

"It might lead in the direction that we need to go," Sif said easily. "We should check it out."

Brunnhilde grunted and peered back into the tunnel down which they'd come. It stretched on into the darkness past the room, but she could see nothing, sense nothing in that direction. They picked their way between the tables and shattered or overturned machinery, their eyes adjusting to the deeper darkness. There was, indeed, another door. This one was far too small to fit mountain giants. Why would a mountain giant-built fortress contain doors they couldn't fit through? And if they didn't make it, then who did? Who had been sharing this place with them long enough to have customized it?

"Well, this is worrying," Sif muttered, clearly coming to the same conclusion. She moved to flank the door when Brunnhilde stepped towards it.

Taking a deep breath, the Valkyrie waited for Sif's nod and then heaved at the door. It ground open with a low noise of stone on stone. The passageway beyond was utterly dark. Immediately, her sense of the deathglow increased, just a little, but enough to encourage her. "This is it," she breathed. "They're somewhere in here."

"Then somewhere in here is Loki, too," Sif muttered, and her words resonated with a tightly controlled, grim satisfaction.

Brunnhilde wondered how much more blood would be spilled before this was over.

Twenty
The True Enemy

Brunnhilde led off again, quicker this time, her left hand trailing along the wall for a point of reference within the blackness. Sif was behind her, a solid, comforting, lethal presence at her back. There was no sound other than the soft scuff of boot leather on stone.

The tunnel began to curve to the right and slope downwards. The Valkyrie reached out with her senses, trying to feel whether it opened up ahead. Were they coming to another room? Was the tunnel full of enemies creeping to meet them? Her imagination populated the darkness with a hundred types of monster, each more dangerous than the last. Brunnhilde's breathing roughened and sweat dampened her palms. She tried to calm herself, but panic tightened her throat despite her best efforts. Behind her, she heard Sif breathe a curse. A second later, the shield-maiden reached out and grabbed her from behind. Brunnhilde had to suppress a shriek.

"There's something in here with us," Sif said. "I can feel it. We need light."

The edges of her voice were scraped raw with panic, which only heightened Brunnhilde's own anxiety. She turned in the darkness and reached out for her friend, gripping Sif by the shoulders. "Take a deep breath, Sif," she said softly, low enough that the tightness in her voice was hopefully inaudible. She tried to let the soothing of her friend soothe her, too. "We are the only things in here. Whatever you can hear is in your head."

"No," the warrior said in a gasp. "I can feel it. I can feel something behind me." She shifted under Brunnhilde's grasp, tensing as if to spin and attack. "I've got a torch in my pack. Let me–"

Brunnhilde tightened her grip. "Listen to me," she hissed in a fierce whisper. "You have to trust me now, Sif. When I tell you there is nothing behind you, you have to believe me."

She waited, but Sif was silent.

"Do you believe me?" she insisted. She didn't know what else she could say to convince Sif otherwise.

Still there was silence. Then, just on the edge of hearing, a sigh. "If you say there's nothing behind me," the shield-maiden said in a tiny voice, "then I trust you. I mean, I can still hear it, but I trust you."

"Do you want me to take the rear?" Brunnhilde asked her. "I don't mind being a barrier if it will make you feel better."

There was another pause, long enough that the Valkyrie was about to repeat herself, and then a whispered, "No, but thank you."

"Alright then," Brunnhilde said, trying to inject authority

and even a little humor into her tone. She squeezed Sif's arms and then paused in order to listen once more, just in case. The tunnel was silent. They set off again, and Brunnhilde didn't comment on the finger Sif hooked into her swordbelt to keep her close.

The downward slope became more pronounced as they traveled deeper into the heart of the mountain. The air, already warm compared with the snow and ice and bitter gales of the outside world, grew even warmer, until the sweat slicking her brow was from the temperature as well as her steadily growing, impossible-to-calm anxiety.

Sif's conviction there was something behind them meant that Brunnhilde spent more time than she should with her awareness trained backwards. She was supposed to leave securing their retreat to the shield-maiden but found she couldn't. It wasn't that she didn't trust Sif… or maybe it was. That was an uncomfortable thought, but once the seed was planted it grew swift and strong in the rich soil of her worries.

There was nothing to see in the darkness, no point on which to rest her eyes, and she found the lack of sight only exacerbated her nerves. What would they find at the bottom of this tunnel? She knew it would be more than just the missing souls, whether trapped in machinery or in deathless half-giants. In her heart and in her gut, she knew that they would face the architect of this atrocity. Would she be strong enough to face someone who treated life with such callous disregard?

Who was she after all but a Valkyrie, more used to dealing with the dead than the living? She knew death in all its forms; she knew the exquisite agony of onrushing oblivion and that a person's mortal life was over. But did she know how to really live? Who was she to say that these hybrid creatures, these half-giant, half-Asgardian constructs, were not happy? What right did she have to take life consciously when her duty was merely to reap it when taken by others?

Brunnhilde clenched her fist around her sword hilt until her knuckles creaked. *Discipline your mind,* she told herself. *Don't let these lies take over.* As she walked, she practiced some of the meditation exercises that had formed a part of her training back when she was a girl. They seemed overly simple in the current circumstances, a paltry barrier against the insidious voice that whispered of her lack of worth, but they were just enough to quiet the frantic whirling of her mind and allow her senses to examine the tunnel.

Ahead, the space opened up, and warm air currents drifted to them. The scent they carried was at once both familiar and unpleasant. She knew it, but she didn't know why.

"Hammer and lightning," Sif suddenly swore, the fingers clutching Brunnhilde's belt dragging her to a halt hard enough to make her stumble. "I know this smell. Brunnhilde, we have been *so stupid*."

She had made no effort to lower her voice, and dread coiled in the pit of Brunnhilde's stomach. She shoved Sif back against the wall. "Quietly," she hissed.

"Sorry, sorry," Sif muttered. "But I know who's doing this." Her voice cracked. "We've been so stupid," she said again, shaking Brunnhilde by her breastplate until she rattled gently. "It's been right in front of us this whole time. Fear, Brunnhilde. Fear. Why would *Loki,* out of all of Asgard's enemies, use fear? Does that really seem like something he would do? With his mastery of tricks and illusions, why would he stoop to making us afraid?"

The dread in Brunnhilde's stomach writhed faster. "You mean–?"

"Yes," Sif said, and dragged her into an embrace, their armor clanging softly in the darkness. "It's the Serpent," she murmured into her ear, close and low like a lover, although the words were the worst sort of pillow talk. "I know the stink of his magic."

Cul. The God of Fear himself. Brunnhilde shuddered in her friend's arms and gripped her in turn. On the very edge of hearing, on the breath of the warm air rising from below, she detected the hint of a laugh. As if the Serpent was pleased that they had finally discovered him.

Sif must have heard it too, for she stiffened, then let go and stepped away. There was the low hum of her sword cutting air, restless. As if she needed the reminder that she was armed, that she was not helpless.

"He knew we'd come back," Brunnhilde said. "That's why he's put the souls somewhere secret, somewhere warm. The Serpent has ever loved the heat."

"Secret and warm?" Sif demanded with a touch of hysteria. "He's leading us into a trap."

"Yes," Brunnhilde said heavily. She could feel the words piling up behind the shield-maiden's teeth, the soft-voiced suggestion that perhaps they should go back and find reinforcements. She spoke before Sif had a chance to, unwilling to test her resolve if the question was put to her. Unwilling, too, to hear those words fall from Sif's lips. They would disrespect them both. "We push on."

The black-haired warrior was quiet for a long, endless moment, the pair of them simply breathing together in the darkness, and then she gave a small grunt. "We push on," she agreed. "We'll make him pay one way or another for everything he's done here and back on Asgard, and across who knows how many other Realms," she promised in a voice that had lost its vulnerability and was now as cold and vicious as a Jotunheim winter. They were both drawing on the very heart of their courage, and the years of life and combat that had forged them into weapons as well as women. Brunnhilde knew it was the only thing allowing them to walk forward into the Serpent's den instead of running back screaming the way they had come.

"He'll know we're coming," Sif added. "He knows everything that goes on in his lair. There's no point in stealth anymore. Speed is our friend now." She laughed bitterly. "Never before have I thought I would prefer to face Loki. And yet it is true. The Trickster God is a far preferable foe than the God of Fear. I know where I stand with that Jotunn. With this, with him, everything has changed."

Brunnhilde took a deep breath and projected strength and confidence she didn't feel, before setting out again, faster than before. Sif dogged her steps, if anything urging her faster until they were striding forwards in the darkness, every sense straining.

The heat in the air and the scent of the Serpent's magic thickened as they followed the tunnel down and around in a slow spiral. Brunnhilde couldn't help the crawling of her skin as they marched ever deeper into the trap.

"Do you think he's baiting us?" asked Brunnhilde, after they had walked perhaps a mile.

"Yes," Sif said immediately, and then paused. "In what way?"

Brunnhilde scrubbed sweat from her face before answering. The pain in her back was a constant irritant and she could feel it shortening her temper. Sif's thoughtless response before she asked for clarification grated at her; they couldn't afford such recklessness once they found Cul. She strove for patience. "Well, he doesn't seem to be putting the einherjar into the deathless warriors anymore. I can still sense them. If he knows we are coming, why isn't he increasing the size of his army to fight against us?"

Sif was silent and then she groaned. "I really, really wish you hadn't said that, Brunnhilde," she said quietly. "As much as I would like to believe he's leaving them trapped as a beacon to draw us to him, I'd say it's more likely that the only reason he wouldn't be increasing the number of warriors who'll face us is because he believes he's already got more than enough to do the job."

"Oh," Brunnhilde said. "You're right. I really wish I hadn't said that."

There was the faintest snort of amusement from behind her. Brunnhilde couldn't help a wry smile crossing her face. Then she slowed and held out her sword to stop the warrior from passing her. "Hush," she whispered. "Open space ahead, and movement. Get ready."

A low, guttural growl echoed towards them, deep enough that it had to come from a mountain giant. *Which means,*

Brunnhilde thought grimly, *that there is another way in after all, and one large enough to admit the true inhabitants of this place.* The odds against them had just grown worse. She swallowed a sudden urge to laugh and concentrated on moving forwards swiftly and quietly. At first, she thought her eyes were playing tricks on her, but then she realized she could see the tunnel walls to either side. Looking down, she was able to make out her hand and sword. In the distance, the tunnel opened into a space barely lit with flickering orange torches. Their destination. The Serpent's lair.

Wordlessly, the Valkyrie glanced back, feeling unaccountably relieved when she could observe Sif for the first time in what might have been an hour and found her still whole and healthy and armed. The warrior licked her lips and then nodded once: *Go, I'm with you.*

Taking a deep breath, Brunnhilde flexed her fingers on Dragonfang's hilt and then strode forward into the brightening tunnel.

The air itself was hot now, and overlaying it, the dark, particular scent of the Serpent himself. Musk and magic and old, dry hate. She slowed as they came to the tunnel's end and saw what lay beyond: a vast cavern that opened to either side of their position. The Asgardians crouched in a patch of shadow as close to the opening as they could get without being in full view. Brunnhilde felt Sif press against her back, the tiniest kiss of armor ringing through the hot air.

The Valkyrie counted at least twenty hybrid deathless warriors, only a few of them half-Asgardian, and a few mountain giants, but their monstrous forms did not hold her attention. The cavern was at least three hundred feet wide, painstakingly carved out of the very bones of the mountain. Towards the rear, a long, low platform was raised above the rest of the floor. Its edges were beautifully chiseled with representations of giants, gods, and monsters. Scenes of mountain giant victories against their many enemies, including others of their kind on Jotunheim.

Brunnhilde knew that if she looked closely enough, she would find depictions of wars against Asgard and the very few victories the giants had won over the centuries. But even that was not what drew her eye. Atop the platform, which was at least eighty feet in length, and coiled upon himself, lay Cul in his true, hideous serpent form. His head lay upon his own length, and wide, lidless eyes stared down at his creations. Dotted amongst the deathless and the giants were thirty or more workers from different Realms. Again, they appeared to have no will of their own. They stood unspeaking in clumps and groups, waiting vacantly for their next order.

The God of Fear. Magic and malice rose from him in equal measure, and the deathless milling below him seemed as mindless as the workers themselves. Sif squeezed her elbow, pulling gently backwards, and Brunnhilde went with her willingly. They moved fifty feet down the passageway and then crouched again.

"I take your orders in this," Sif breathed. She was so close that Brunnhilde could see the thin sheen of sweat on her brow. Her pupils were wide and black – from fear as well as the low light.

"I have to face the deathless warriors to free the souls, and I need to find the other trapped einherjar," she whispered softly and then paused to lick her lips. "But that means you have to confront the giants and the Serpent. Maybe, if you can distract him, it will break his hold on the deathless. And the workers will hamper us as before, I expect."

Sif blew out her cheeks, a look of consternation flickering across her features before they hardened into determination. "That's a big ask, Valkyrie," she said, staring down the tunnel without seeing it.

"I know, my friend," Brunnhilde said softly. "But I trust you. Can you do it?"

Sif scowled. "If it was anyone else asking and it was under any other circumstances, I'd be offended by that. As it is," she added in a slightly more strangled tone, "the answer is yes. Or at least, I'll do my best."

"As will I, and Odin watch over us." They studied each other for a few seconds, looking for, and finding, the reassurance that they both needed. "I'll be as fast as I can," the Valkyrie promised. She put her hand over Sif's heart, the metal of her breastplate cool under her fingertips. "Trust me as I trust you. If you see anything or anyone that can't be here, call. Let me know and I promise I'll do the same."

Sif put her own hand over Brunnhilde's where it rested against her armor. She took a deep breath, but she met the Valkyrie's eyes without flinching. "I didn't trust you," she said and there was a faint blush across her cheeks, visible even in the gloom. "After the first time. After we saved Inge and we were coming back here for the rest of the souls and those kidnapped in Meadowfall, I told you that I trusted you to have my back. I didn't, not then anyway. I was worried you'd snap again. But I want you to know that I do now. I do trust you, Brunnhilde, for this and for everything. Forever."

The Valkyrie felt tears pricking at her eyes, both in shame at the remembered loss of control, and in unexpected gratitude, not just for Sif's trust but also for her honesty. She felt strangely pleased that Sif had confided in her. The rivalry of their sparring bout on the way here seemed ridiculous now – Brunnhilde didn't need to fight against Sif to prove her worth. She just needed to be good enough to fight alongside her. She swallowed hard and gave a light shove of the warrior's breastplate.

"Thank you," she whispered, "and I'm sorry. I won't let you down again."

Sif grinned. "I know you won't, that's why I'm here with you and not anyone else. Now, are you ready? We've crept around in here for long enough. I'll go straight for the Serpent; I expect the mountain giants are his guards, so that should draw them to me. If you could distract everyone else, that'd be great."

Brunnhilde gasped in mock outrage. "*Everyone* else?" she queried, even as a small smile tugged at the corner of her mouth. "I see I have the harder of the tasks before us."

Sif grinned again, as if there was nowhere else she would rather be. It made affection and courage pool in Brunnhilde's gut. "Well, you're so much bigger and stronger than I am, it's only fair you have more enemies to fight."

Brunnhilde shook her head and stood, checking she had freedom of movement within her armor one last time. "We will discuss the matter further once this mission is complete," she said severely. "Perhaps even a test of that strength you mentioned."

Sif mirrored her actions, ducking her head to hide her

expression. "Valkyrie," she said and looked up with a wink. "It would be my genuine pleasure. You go left, I'll go right."

There was nothing left to say and nothing left to check. Brunnhilde stretched out her hand and took Sif's in the warrior's grip. They stared at each other for one final moment and then, at the same time, they let go, turned and ran straight for the cavern.

Twenty-One
The Serpent

The echoing vastness was awash in the low murmur of giants' voices, and the light grew steadily until Sif could clearly see the ground and the walls and Brunnhilde a single stride ahead.

The Valkyrie took a deep breath, her shoulders rising and then falling in the instant before she rounded the corner to the cavern. A war cry ripped from her throat. Sif heard the responding roar as their enemies moved under the God of Fear's command to oppose her.

She skidded onto her knees at the cavern's entrance and shot a quick look in. Brunnhilde had immediately ducked to the left as promised, clearing the entrance and drawing all attention to her. Everyone, bar the Serpent himself, was charging the Valkyrie.

Brunnhilde was twenty feet from the entrance and moving fast when Sif followed her in. She clung to the edge of the wall, running right and doing her best not to be noticed. She had got fifty feet or so when the Serpent's head rose on his long, sinuous neck. His gleaming eyes fixed on her. In the next second, the four mountain giants had changed direction, two retreating to the Serpent's side while the other two ran directly at Sif.

Sif left the protection of the wall and ran a wide, arcing loop around the main cavern floor, away from the heart of the fight and the Valkyrie spinning, slashing, and harvesting souls in its center. The God of Fear watched her come, radiating cool amusement and malevolent curiosity. His guards stood at the base of the platform between her and him, while the other two ran at an angle to cut her off. The Serpent's scales rustled as he shifted on his coils, the sound as crisp as fallen leaves and as deadly as the ring of a blade even over the echoing sounds of combat. It sent a trickle of primal fear along the warrior's spine. It sounded like death itself.

Sif didn't know exactly what she was going to do when she got to Cul, because the size of the Serpent was only just being revealed to her as he began to glide towards the edge of the platform, lethal and unstoppable. *I fought Hakurei,* she reminded herself. *Fought and defeated a dragon.*

She was a hundred feet from the platform when the two mountain giants reached her. Sif had all the momentum of her run behind her, and she used it to her advantage, leaping above the strike from the leftmost giant and then running up his spear to plunge her sword through his eye. She vaulted off the collapsing form onto his companion, taking a blow from his enormous fist against her side that would have caved in her ribs if she'd been without her armor. She narrowly avoided being thrown clear by the force of the punch.

Instead, she clung with her free hand and stabbed the giant in the armpit as he tried to drag her off him. The giant coughed and shuddered as her blade bit deep, severing nerves and muscles. His other hand came up, and she sliced across his palm and fingers, but not deeply enough to prevent being grabbed by the back of the neck; this time he succeeded in prying her off him and flinging her across the stone.

Sif's fingers loosened on her weapon as she hit the ground, and she almost lost her sword as she tumbled over and over. Groggy and hurting, she rose to her knees to discover she had been thrown directly into the path of the giants guarding the God of Fear. She grinned without mirth, tasting blood, and spat it at them.

Brunnhilde did ask me to keep you busy.

It was hard to breathe: the right-hand side of her breastplate had been caved in by the giant's fist. It hadn't buckled the steel completely, but it was just enough to restrict the movement of her ribs. She rolled onto her feet regardless.

Behind her, the sounds of combat were unrelenting, clattering steel and bellowing war cries and shrieks of pain. There were workers dotted around the cavern, advancing slowly on the Asgardians with their blank, incurious gazes that made Sif's scalp prickle with unease.

She wondered whether the God of Fear would simply recline on the platform and watch them be cut down, and grimaced. Of course he would. Their lives meant nothing to him; he wouldn't need to be controlling them if they were here willingly.

The remaining mountain giants came at her, one from each side, and Sif was reminded that this was a terrible plan.

She wondered if it was possible to outrun them and just as quickly dismissed the notion. Sif was fast, but she couldn't beat anything with legs longer than she was tall.

"Come on then," she growled, beckoning with her free hand. The giants indulged her, closing at the same time from either side, weapons outstretched to fence her in. Despite their control of the space around her, these two were wary, perhaps having learned from how quickly she had killed their companions. They were fast despite their size, shifting away when she tried to close to a distance that would benefit her and disadvantage them. Sif darted and dashed, her sword flickering in the yellow torchlight like a fish underwater, the blade shuddering as it deflected the axe and sword of her opponents. Their weapons were big enough to split her in two without effort, and she could feel them herding her where they wanted her, towards the platform.

No doubt Cul was waiting to lunge down from above and bite her in half. Or maybe swallow her whole or crush her to death. Maybe he simply wanted to hold her still in his coils until the workers could extract her soul from her living body, the way they had planned on doing with Inge.

The torchlight glimmering behind the platform suddenly darkened as the Serpent rose up on his coils above them all. Sif's heart stuttered at the size and strength of him, the richness of ancient magic rolling from his dry scales. She flinched backwards, unable to prevent it, and was immediately seized from behind. The mountain giant wrapped one huge arm around her shoulders and chest and lifted her easily into the air. The shield-maiden thrashed and shouted, kicking backwards with all her might and trying to slash with her sword, but none of her blows had enough strength to do any damage. The giant began to squeeze as he stepped forward, offering Sif to the Serpent.

Her armor creaked under the strain and was the only thing preventing her ribs from snapping like twigs in his grip. The fourth giant, this one female, crowded close with a wide, toothy grin on her slab-like face.

"Bring her here." The God of Fear's voice was a dry rustle, filled with cool amusement and bottomless malice.

Fear ran its clammy fingers down her spine. "Let me go," Sif wheezed, kicking ineffectually backwards. "Put me down right now." She felt the rumble of the giant's laughter through her backplate.

The giant stepped onto the platform on which lay the Serpent, his companion flanking him. The God of Fear loomed over them all, and Sif could not suppress the shudder that ran through her from scalp to toes.

The Serpent's head lowered out of the air towards her. "You are Lady Sif," he said. "Why are you here, slaughtering my people?"

Sif muttered something under her breath. The mountain giant holding her gave her a shake. "What was that?" Cul asked in an angry hiss.

Sif looked up into one jewel-like eye. "I said come closer," she said and drew on the Quellstone's ability to break.

The golden blast erupted from her whole body and threw the two giants backwards. Sif tumbled from the male's grip as he convulsed. Even the Serpent was rocked by the expulsion of energy, writhing away in a profusion of coils.

She crawled to her feet, reeling and almost blinded by the force of the magic and feeling as if she'd turned her skin inside out.

Dizzy but determined, she stumbled to the male giant and hacked her blade through his throat as he tried to roll onto his hands and knees. The female was already standing, albeit wobbly. She saw Sif coming and looked for a weapon. The warrior didn't give her chance, dodging between her legs and hamstringing her as she went.

The giant screeched and hopped sideways. Sif hacked at the back of her ankle until she went to her knees and then sliced the wicked edge of her blade through the giant's sword-belt. She caught the thick leather in her free hand and leaped upwards, discarding her sword on the platform below.

The warrior slipped the wide belt over the giant's head from behind, braced her feet against her shoulder-blades, and began to pull.

Cul was still thrashing, furious hisses escaping his throat as he battered his head against the stone as if the blast had deafened him. The giant tried in vain to reach far enough behind herself to grab hold of Sif, but with her boots planted against her enemy's spine, Sif leaned backwards to evade the grasping hands. The giant's grunts soon turned to wheezing chokes. Sif wrapped the leather around one fist in order to drag her dagger from its sheath at the small of her back. Pulling backwards, she strained every muscle and sinew until the giant's scrabbling fingers lost their strength, and then she placed the tip of the knife at the back of the thick neck and punched it in. The enormous form beneath her twitched and collapsed.

Sif rode the body down onto the stone and staggered off it. She scrabbled with numb fingers for her sword and then, when she saw the Serpent still some distance away, she allowed herself to sag onto her knees and take several deep breaths. *Four giants down, one god to go.*

A hysterical laugh bubbled through her chest, and she swallowed it with only a squeak. She wasn't dead, and the giants were. She called that a win, even though she could feel the Quellstone rough against her skin where before it had been smooth with power. Yes, she had to face the Serpent while on the very edge of exhaustion, but her job was purely to distract him long enough for Brunnhilde to harvest the souls. It didn't matter what happened to her as long as she kept his attention.

Sif concentrated on blinking away the black dots dancing in her vision and sucking air into her lungs. They felt bruised, raw, as if she inhaled water instead of oxygen. The shadows shifted around her again, warning her, and the warrior pushed herself up onto her feet. She looked up to find the Serpent's broad, blunt head hanging above her like an evil sun. He was immense and timeless and all-powerful. Despair washed through her chest.

The sword in her hand seemed a pitiful weapon against something so huge. Sif knew with a sudden lurch of sickness that her blade wouldn't even penetrate his scales.

A low, sibilant hiss echoed from the high stone vault of the cavern. Sif's eyes narrowed; the God of Fear was laughing at her. Anger blossomed within her, burning away her doubt and despair. The shield-maiden embraced it and held it close, allowing it to warm her blood and thaw her muscles. She snarled up into his hideous face, and the Serpent's tongue flicked out towards her. She ducked.

The sounds of combat were loud and frantic, but she didn't look back. The Serpent was her target, and nothing would stop her from killing him and being famous, more famous than her brother, more famous than the God of Thunder himself.

"Your evil ends here today," Sif shrieked. "Your disloyalty to the All-Father will no longer go unpunished!"

The Serpent's tail lashed back and forth in fury, catching one of the dead mountain giants and flinging the corpse towards Sif. "*I am* the All-Father, the only true All-Father," Cul hissed. Rage seemed to boil from his scales, and the torchlight flashed in his glittering eyes. He struck, his great head lunging down out of the shadows above, faster than Thor's lightning. Sif threw herself out of the way, narrowly avoiding the gaping mouth and flashing fangs.

She both heard and felt the impact of his head against the stone of the platform. A loud, mocking laugh broke from her chest. "Is that the best you can do?" she jeered as she bounced back up onto her feet, giddy with adrenaline. The God of Fear had already withdrawn, resettling with his neck pulled back into a sinuous curve to strike again. Cool superiority radiated from his expressionless face.

"You should know better than to provoke me, little sister," he said. His voice was the rasp of scale against scale, a sound that had inspired terror since the dawn of the Nine Realms. All it provoked in Sif was righteous fury.

"You're not one to talk when you are down here, in a Realm not even your own, creating monsters out of good einherjar." She brandished her sword, daring him to attack again. The Serpent swayed but didn't take the bait. "And not only Asgardians," she continued in a shrill voice. "Mountain giants, trolls, the inhabitants of Alfheim and Svartalfheim. Enchanted Midgardians to carry out your vile experiments, even. Who are you to think to rule over so many, or to twist and destroy them in such a manner?"

The Serpent lowered his great head until it was level with Sif's. "Who are you amongst Asgard's pantheon to decide what I, Cul, can and cannot do?" His head lowered further until it rested on the stone a single jump away. Sif's fingers tightened around the hilt of her sword before she made them relax again. He was taunting her, she knew, and yet the urge to close that gap between them and plunge her blade through one glittering eye was almost overwhelming. She was more likely to run straight down his throat.

"You think to challenge me, little sister," the Serpent mused, condescending. "You think you could, without Heimdall or Thor or the Warriors Three to back you up?"

Sif narrowed her eyes. "You list so many people," she said in a cold voice. "So many *men*. Why do you think I would need their help when I have Brunnhilde, leader of the Choosers of the Slain? Between us, we are more than enough to face you. To beat you."

"And is that why you are here, little sister? To beat me?" That dry, dead laugh echoed around her again, even though the Serpent's mouth never moved.

Sif didn't waste her breath on further talk. The God of Fear was stalling for time, and a single glance behind her told the shield-maiden why. Three of the deathless warriors that had been jostling to attack the Valkyrie were making their stealthy way towards her, intent on a surprise attack.

Sif decided on a surprise of her own. Carefully, she stepped sideways so that she could keep both the Serpent and the advancing deathless in view. As expected, the God of Fear was amused, his head turning to follow her movements. He shifted more of his bulk towards her as she retreated. As he began to settle, Sif sprang directly at him. She landed next to the Serpent's body, and before he could lift himself back up or even start to whip his coils away from her, her sword flashed in the gloom and the torchlight, and she carved a rip in his side.

Cul vanished in a blinding flash of light, bright enough and loud enough to throw Sif from her feet and off the platform itself. She landed hard, the impact on her shoulders and the back of her head leaving her dazed and breathless, but she scrambled back to her feet before the deathless reached her.

The God of Fear's laughter came from somewhere above on the platform, but Sif didn't have time to respond to the mockery. The first of the hybrid warriors reached her, a howl tearing from its throat as it attacked with a two-handed axe. Sif ducked the flashing blade and brought up her sword as the creature reversed its blow. This time steel kissed steel in a shower of sparks. Sif's sword juddered in her hand as the half-giant, half-elf tried to force her back. Its strength was a match for hers, possibly a little more, but nothing she couldn't handle – at her best. Sif parried the axe and lashed out with her foot, crunching it into the deathless warrior's knee and snapping it the wrong way. It fell with a scream, and she sheared her blade through the side of its neck.

"Kill you!" Sif screamed, hacking at its neck again. A red haze descended over her vision, part rage and part the onrush of fatigue. "I'm going to kill you. I'm going to kill all of you!"

From above there came a low chuckle. "Yes, little sister, yes. *Kill them all.*"

Distantly, echoing across the width of the cavern and somehow rising above the sounds of battle, there came another voice. A different voice. One that Sif thought she knew. "You're being controlled, Sif," the voice shouted, strained and desperate. "We're here to save them, not kill them. Do you trust me, shield-maiden? Do you trust Brunnhilde?"

The words didn't make sense at first, mere noise in the way that the God of Fear's were not. It would have been easy to ignore them, but the name meant something. *Brunnhilde,* Sif thought to herself, *Brunnhilde is important. Listen to Brunnhilde. Must listen.*

"Brunnhilde?" she yelled, and there were a few seconds of shouts and the clang of steel and then, breathless, a response: "Yes, Sif, it's Brunnhilde. Don't kill the deathless."

"Hela's teeth," Sif swore as understanding crashed through her, hard enough to almost distract her from the second monster's attack. She had been guarding against fear, but of course Cul had other weapons at his disposal.

Focused again, the warrior swung at the second deathless' leg, shattering the thighbone. It fell with a shout, and she left it there, leaping past its grabbing hands to confront the third and final creature.

It was Sigrun. Sif's former friend and sister-in-arms attacked without hesitation. No light of recognition burned in her eyes. Her lips peeled back from her teeth in a snarl of concentration and of hate. She had never looked like this, not even in the heat of battle. The hate infusing her now was not hers.

Nausea washed through Sif. It was no easier to face her this time than it had been the first. She parried the sword arcing for her head with a speed born of instinct, biting back a cry of Sigrun's name. She knew what she needed to do, but the thought of plunging her blade into her friend was abhorrent. She leaped up onto the platform instead.

Sigrun followed her, and Sif was once more confronted with two enemies, for Cul stood to her right. He was clad in the skin of an Asgardian god now, a couple of feet taller than her but otherwise appearing as a man, older even than Odin and yet broad through the shoulders and chest. She had no doubt of his prowess with the spear in his hand. He leant it against his chest in order to give her a slow round of applause. Sigrun halted at some invisible, unheard signal.

"My my, you are fun," Cul said. "Such a small, easily led mind you have, Lady Sif. I really had expected you to put up more of a fight." He snapped his fingers and Sigrun attacked again, without recognition or mercy. Sif met her blade to blade, a grunt escaping her chest as their swords clashed in a lethal, furious dance.

Sif fought defensively for long moments, backing steadily across the platform away from both the deathless and Cul. There had to be a way out of this that didn't involve her disabling the thing that had once been her friend. She was so fixated on this goal that her sword moved almost on its own, Sif putting in only the barest amount of concentration.

It wasn't until Sigrun's blade tore a chunk out of her upper arm that she realized she was out of choices.

"I'm so sorry, my friend," she said and blocked the next attack before twisting her wrist and bringing her blade inside the other's guard. She punched her sword through Sigrun's chest, and the half-giant, half-Asgardian fell to her knees with a bubbling cry, dropping her weapon to clutch at the blade buried inside her. Sif wrenched it free, the edges slicing into Sigrun's fingers. It wouldn't kill her but might buy Sif enough time. She stumbled back a pace, tears pricking at her eyes, and then swallowed hard and turned to confront the Serpent.

He wasn't there.

Sif's sword drooped in her hand, and she gaped in incomprehension. "L-Lord? What are you doing here?"

"When I realized it was the God of Fear you were facing and not my brother, I knew you would be unable to prevail. I've come to help."

Thor smiled as bright as lightning and held out a hand. "Let me help."

Twenty-Two
Faith and Truth

Sif panted out a laugh and then bent over, bracing her hands against her knees as she sucked in air. "I can't believe you came," she said to the stone between her feet.

Opposite her, Thor rumbled a laugh. "Of course I came," he said, and she could hear the humor in his voice. "Couldn't let you and that Valkyrie have all the fun now, could I?"

Sif straightened and wiped the sweat out of her eyes with the back of her hand. "What about the other incursions into Asgard, though?"

The God of Thunder waved a hand in dismissal. "All under control. Want to tell me what's going on here?"

Sif's brow creased in puzzlement. "What do you mean, what's going on here? It's pretty obvious, isn't it?"

Thor's face darkened and he swung Mjolnir idly beside his thigh. "And yet I am asking," he said. Sif flinched, waiting for the smell of lightning to drift to her nostrils; it didn't come.

She looked beyond him at the rest of the platform. Sigrun had fallen to the ground below, near her companions. None of the deathless were dead, of course. Even as she watched, the blood stopped flowing from their wounds and bones straightened to knit back together. They'd be up and fighting again soon. Too soon.

"I asked you a question, warrior," Thor grunted, irritation clear in his voice.

Sif's eyes flicked back to the Thunder God, assessing. "Forgive me, my lord. The situation is that we need to disable but not kill the deathless, so that Brunnhilde can collect the einherjar trapped within them. And the God of Fear is here, too. As you said, it's not Loki who's doing this."

"So, you were wrong? Such a pretty tale you spun me, and you had it all wrong."

Sif scraped blood and sweat and strands of hair out of her face before answering. Then she gave an elaborate shrug. "We can't all be right all the time, can we, my lord?"

"Loki, Loki, Loki," the Thunder God said and chuckled low in his throat, ignoring her. "Is it really hatred that drives you regarding my brother? Perhaps it is actually envy, or unrequited love."

Whatever expression was on her face, it caused vast amusement within Thor. He threw back his blond head and laughed.

Sif took her chance. She didn't scream a war cry; she didn't make a sound. Instead, she sprinted across the gap between them and punched her sword straight through his chest. Thor's eyes widened in shock at the last second, but he made no move to defend himself. He didn't even raise Mjolnir from where it hung at his side. Blood burst from the wound and then from his mouth. She wrenched her blade free with a stricken sound and a flare of panic brighter than the sun winking from steel. *What have I done? Oh gods, what have I done?*

Thor fell to his knees and his hammer dropped from nerveless fingers so he could clutch at the hole in his chest.

"Please, please, please, please," Sif babbled, dread writhing within her. She circled him, her sword in guard even though her fingers opened and closed on the hilt in helpless little spasms. *What have I done?*

"My lord? My lord, forgive–"

Thor threw back his head and laughed, the sound wet and bubbling and alien. His form shivered and wavered and for an instant a man-sized snake coiled before her, gone even as Sif struck at it. Her sword whistled harmlessly through the air. Heimdall, her brother, materialized in its place. There was no blood on him, no wound in his chest, but the expression he turned upon her was one of utter betrayal.

Sif snorted even as relief flooded her. As if pretending to be her brother now would make any difference. She knew this trick and she wouldn't fall for it again. The Serpent was wasting his time and his energy, which could only benefit her and Brunnhilde. Heimdall – *no, Cul, it's Cul, remember* – let out a roar and sprang at her, a sword appearing in his grip. There was nothing fake about his attack or the rage twisting those beloved features.

Sif met Heimdall's blade with her own in a viper-quick exchange and was reminded of when they had been youngsters, training on the fields outside of Asgardia. She grinned in delight as she felt her brother's sword dip beneath hers, the angle of his blade wrong and weakening his parry.

She knew exactly what his next move would have to be if he was to regain control of the bout. She also knew the counter that would overcome it. They were evenly matched today, and Heimdall was annoyed by it.

Both warriors danced around each other, exchanging blow for blow, parry for riposte for deflection, Asgard's grass springy beneath their feet and its sun warm in the sky above.

"Is that the best you can do?" Heimdall taunted, his breathing easy despite the effort of keeping her out of range.

"Oh no, I can do much better," she said and responded with the counter he himself had taught her, twisting her wrist at the perfect moment to slip inside his guard. She poked him lightly in the chest with the tip of her sword. "You lose," she said with a laugh.

Heimdall grunted, scowling, and then stepped forward, hooked his foot behind hers and shoved her in the shoulder. She tripped and sprawled into the grass, her thick blonde plait smacking her in the face. Sif lay in the grass and giggled.

"Such a poor loser," she sighed in mock pity. "How does it feel to know I can beat you in a fight? What will the other boys say?"

Storm clouds raced in across Heimdall's features, the genuine anger he so rarely turned on her darkening his eyes. His lips drew back from his teeth, and he loomed over her with the Asgardian sun winking along the length of his blade. Deliberately, her brother angled his sword so that it blinded her. Sif screwed up her eyes before raising her free hand to shield them.

"That's cheating," she protested and rolled out of range before coming back up onto her feet again. The breeze was light and playful, teasing at the loose strands of yellow hair that had come out of her plaits. She shoved them irritably behind her ears.

"Your opponents will not all be as honorable as you, little sister," Heimdall told her. "You can't just complain and ask them to stop if they do something you don't like in the middle of a battle."

"I know that," Sif said sulkily. "I'm not stupid, you know."

Distantly, as if it came all the way from the depths of the city itself, she heard someone calling her name: "Lady Sif, wake up. Hel's teeth, woman, *open your eyes!*"

Sif frowned, but Heimdall sniggered and reached out to smack her arm with the flat of his sword. "*Lady* Sif?" he asked, mocking. "Which one of your friends did you bully into calling you that, little sister?"

Sif stumbled away in the grass, a frown tugging at her forehead. "Lady Sif," she mumbled to herself. The voice was familiar, and not because it belonged to one of her friends. It sounded the way Sif had always hoped she would sound when she was a grown-up. Authoritative and commanding and supremely self-assured. The plea came again and this time the voice – her own voice? – sounded desperate. Panicked, even. But why would she be telling herself to wake up when she was here in the fields outside Asgardia, practicing her sword forms with her brother?

"Little sister wants to grow up to be a great warrior lady, does she?" Heimdall asked with a sly smile. He'd sheathed his sword and now crossed his arms over his chest and raised one eyebrow, using his superior height to stare down his nose at her in disbelief. "My little sister aims too high. My little sister will never be so great. But if you take my hand, I can craft you into something truly special."

Unaccountably, Sif felt tears burn her eyes. Heimdall was rarely mean to her, his teasing usually good-natured. Almost without volition, she raised her hand and stepped forward, ready to take her brother's. Her voice – her own future voice – screamed at her again, laden with curses and spitting with anger.

Sif looked down at herself, at her boots planted in Asgard's green grass. Small breasts barely in need of support and small hands wrapped around the hilt of the practice sword that had been her prized possession when she was a child. Above, the wide blue sky and the bright gold sun of her home.

With numb fingers, she dragged one of her plaits over her shoulder and stared at it. Blonde.

"This isn't real," she whispered. She stared around the fields again and then over to the distant glitter of white and gold stone that was the city. It was perfect; too perfect. It was a memory taken straight from her mind, one of the most cherished of her childhood, and now it was being used against her. Its purity was being eroded every second she relived it here, in this place. Heimdall had not mocked her that day. He had been delighted when she disarmed him, the technique clumsy but strong enough to tear the blade from his hand. She clearly remembered his whoop of joy and the way his sword had spun end over end over end in the air before coming to rest several feet away. How tightly he had hugged her after her victory. That wasn't what was happening now.

Now, there was an edge to Heimdall's humor that spoke of anger and a curl to his lip that was malice, not approval.

Sif still wasn't entirely sure where she should be, but she knew with increasing confidence that it wasn't here. That she wasn't, in fact, physically here despite the evidence of her senses. Nor was she still a clumsy child.

"I'm not in Asgard. This is not real. Get out of my head." The words were spoken in a young, high voice, but they were threaded through with steel.

Her brother's taunts dried up and he watched her in wary surprise. "Don't be silly, little sister. Take my hand now and everything will make sense."

Little sister. She had heard that before, but not from his lips, because Heimdall almost never referred to her that way.

Little sister, little sister.

"Get out of my head," she repeated, and now her voice had the whipcrack of command. There was another flash of sunlight on steel, bright enough to blind, and then Sif was in a dark, echoing stone vault.

The reality of her surroundings returned just as the God of Fear's spear entered her left shoulder, tearing flesh and muscle and punching all the way through and out the back. Steel grated on bone and then rasped past the edge of her breastplate.

A wail exploded past her teeth. Sif kicked, entirely on instinct. Cul vanished before she could make contact, pulling the spear back out of her body as he fled. The warrior staggered forwards three paces as the weapon exited her flesh, and by the time she had steadied herself, the platform on which she stood was empty.

"Sif? Sif, I need you. Please, Sif."

Sif's head turned slowly in the direction of the call. She moved to the edge of the platform, sword hand clutching at her torn shoulder and blood leaking steadily between her fingers. Her blade was held shakily in her left hand. Two deathless warriors lay at the platform's base, along with Brunnhilde. The Valkyrie's face was covered in blood, and she was stretching a hand up towards the black-haired warrior.

"Please," she cried, "you have to help me." Sif looked away from the Valkyrie and found the fight in the center of the cavern was over. There were bodies littered here and there and more deathless running towards them, their expressions intent and murderous and triumphant. Howls rose from their throats. They were coming for Brunnhilde and, when they'd finished with her, they'd come for Sif. She scanned the platform behind; it was still clear. Cul was gone.

"Sif." Brunnhilde's voice this time was weak and choking.

This could be him. It might be him.

A spear shattered against the side of the platform a foot to the left of Brunnhilde's head, splinters and the steel tip flying in all directions and flaying the Valkyrie's scalp open. Blood began soaking her hair.

Brunnhilde slumped backwards and her eyes rolled up into her head. From where she stood above her, Sif could see the ugly tears in her breastplate and the blood leaking through from within. Panic flooded her. The Valkyrie was the only one of them who could save the einherjar. She was the only one who could get them out of here afterwards. If Brunnhilde fell, it was over.

Sif threw herself off the platform. She landed next to the unconscious Valkyrie in a crouch. Before she could even put one hand on Brunnhilde's brow to call on the Quellstone's healing magic, the woman's eyes opened and she lunged upwards, a knife clasped in her hand. "You should be more careful… little sister."

Sif howled in pure frustration at being fooled yet again. She scrambled backwards, but the deathless wearing Brunnhilde's form followed until they were both on their knees facing each other. Sif caught Brunnhilde's wrist in her hands and they wrestled for control of the blade.

The shield-maiden groaned, straining against her enemy's strength. The knife wavered between them, but the wound in Sif's left shoulder had weakened her arm and slowly – and yet all too fast – the blade inched its way towards her face. This felt different from what she'd faced with Thor and with Heimdall. Those had seemed like hallucinations, terrifying and real but lacking in solidity, in weight. Not this. The pain and the blood were too real for this to be a hallucination. The uneven stone scraped across her knees, and her greaves squealed and slid as she pushed, seeking some form of leverage to shove Brunnhilde – no, the deathless – away.

She needed to watch for trickery, but the pain was blinding her, and it was all she could do to keep the knife away from the hollow between her clavicles where her pulse jumped like a frightened rabbit. They were caught in a stalemate, but the deathless wearing Brunnhilde's skin could just wait for reinforcements or for Sif's arms to fail, whichever came first.

Sif looked wildly left and right in the vain hope something or someone might come to her aid. The deathless whose leg she had shattered had dropped their axe, and the handle was possibly just within reach. Only Sif would need to let go of Brunnhilde's wrist in order to reach for it.

Her shaking hands were slick with sweat and blood. Brunnhilde – *no, the deathless,* she told herself again – sensed it. She let out a guttural cry of triumph and shoved harder on the hilt of the knife and Sif, out of options, pushed her foe's wrists right and threw herself left. She rolled desperately and felt the shock of the blade shattering stone just behind her. She reached the axe. Her own sword was behind the fake Brunnhilde; as good as lost, at least for now.

She scooped up the axe, dove into a forward tumble that saved her from another knife attack, and then came up swinging. "Show me your real face, you coward," she snarled, as the deathless leaned backwards away from the axe and then stabbed with the knife. Sif skipped out of range. "Let me see exactly what monster I'm about to kill."

It – or perhaps the Serpent – didn't drop the glamour. It was still wearing the Valkyrie's face when it attacked again.

"Sif, I need you."

Brunnhilde's voice, but not from this creature's mouth. This cry was thin and high across the distance. Perhaps it really was Brunnhilde but, if so, Sif was in no position to go to her aid. The knife scraped across her breastplate, and she jerked sideways and flung out the axe in reply.

Beneath the glamour, the creature wore only scraps of armor. Thick padding and boiled leather protected its lower abdomen, and neither were a match for the speed and force of the strike that opened up its gut in a great, red-lipped smile.

Brunnhilde – *it isn't, it can't be* – fell to her knees, clutching at her middle and emitting a series of blubbering howls, and Sif stepped out of range and looked over her head, wincing. At the rear of the cavern, back near the entrance they'd come through what seemed like a lifetime ago, a knot of deathless half-giants struggled around a lone, desperate, yellow-headed figure. *That* was Brunnhilde. That was the friend who'd screamed that she needed her.

And to whose aid she had to go. Sif retrieved her sword, hurled the axe as far across the width of the platform as she could, and began to run.

Twenty-Three
Glamours and Lies

There were too many of them.

Brunnhilde had been almost lethally distracted at the blinding flash of the Quellstone's blast, staggered that the shield-maiden had been forced to take such desperate measures at the very start of another fight. Only the Valkyrie's lightning-quick reactions prevented her being cut in half by a deathless warrior wielding a great-axe.

The mindless workers were as much a hindrance here as they had been in the laboratory, until a second blinding flash of light, this one oily and unpleasant, had seemed to bring them to their senses. As one. the elves, trolls and Midgardians had fallen still in shock, staring wide-eyed at the flurry of battle around them, before screaming and fleeing. Several were cut down by the deathless warriors as they ran.

Brunnhilde didn't understand it, but whatever Sif had done, she had broken the God of Fear's hold on his mindless workers. She dared to hope the same might be true for the deathless, but it seemed that whatever was powering them ran deeper than mere mind control. The workers had been uncaring of what happened around them, whereas the deathless seemed motivated specifically by hatred of Asgardians. It was a particularly cruel trick on Cul's part to corrupt einherjar so much that they could hate their own living kin enough to want to slaughter them.

The Valkyrie didn't know how long she'd been fighting, but she was bleeding from at least a dozen cuts. Her arms and shoulders were beginning to burn with strain. The swirl and crimp of battle had torn her away from the cavern wall, allowing her enemies to get behind her yet again.

Brunnhilde blinked away sweat and kicked one attacker in the chest, tumbling it into the deathless behind it. An attack to the back of her leg sent her onto both knees on the stone and immediately she was swarmed. She thrashed wildly, punching, clubbing and slashing, wide sweeping blows to keep the deathless back. A half-elf lunged for her with a long, serrated knife glinting wickedly in his hand. With a speed born of desperation, Brunnhilde blocked the knife and lurched forward, grabbing him by the wrist. Her little finger just grazed the creature's skin, but it was enough: the Valkyrie tore the soul out of him without warning or finesse.

The creature collapsed, eyes rolling up in his head. He made no effort to save himself, thumping onto the stone as a lifeless husk. Brunnhilde lurched back onto her feet and back into the fight. She leaped over the empty deathless and out of the closing ring of enemies, catching a second by the nape of her neck as she passed before racing towards the cavern wall. She could jump but running cost her less in energy.

A cold, analytical part of her mind told her there were fifteen more. Despair trickled in around the edges of her resolve and she forced it away with grim determination. The deathglows from the remaining einherjar who hadn't been forced into deathless constructs were rising from around the platform. A single instant of reprieve early on in the battle had allowed her to look over and spot the tall glass amphorae clustered in the shadows with Asgardian souls bumping within like trapped fireflies. Once she had defeated the deathless, she would have to save those too.

Brunnhilde reached the wall and turned to face her pursuers, only a pace behind. The closest was a half-troll, and an eager one at that, their need for violence outweighing any martial lessons they – or even the soul within them – may once have known. They let out a coughing bellow somewhere between the guttural shout of a giant and the wail of an animal in pain and attacked. It was easy enough to block the spear swinging clumsily for her and grab the creature's face as they stumbled past. The soul fled into her safety and nestled close.

Brunnhilde eyed the shadows in the distance and above; they were still empty, and she finally understood the wrongness that had been taunting her since their arrival. There were no archers. It would have been so easy for three or four workers or giants, let alone deathless, to pick off both Brunnhilde and Sif from a distance, either killing them outright or wounding them in order for the Serpent to harvest their souls. The fact ranged weapons were missing had to be by design. Cul was testing his inventions against talented and vicious warriors. Ascertaining whether his monsters were enough to overcome the mightiest of the Nine Realms.

The deathless in Meadowfall and Greenside had been hard to kill but not hard to defeat. Their clumsiness and predictability had meant that sufficient numbers of Asgardian warriors could bring them down. These must be the next generation, those containing souls stripped from living warriors and others forged from Inge's kidnapped companions. The Serpent was eager to see for himself how they performed.

A grim smile tugged at the corners of Brunnhilde's mouth. If he wanted to see how pathetic these creatures were, she was more than happy to show him. If he realized that nothing he could build from flesh and stolen soul could ever defeat good Asgardians, it might be enough to make him stop. And if not? Well, the Valkyrie was happy to do whatever was necessary to bring an end to this horror. If that meant ending an Asgardian god at the same time, so be it.

Brunnhilde braced to meet the attack of the warrior running at her from the side and then hesitated. They were shorter than she was but moving with intent – neither a deathless nor a worker. She squinted in the gloom and then sucked in a gasp. The figure wasn't running at her; it was fleeing the deathless that were chasing it. And its features were heartbreakingly familiar.

"Inge?" Brunnhilde screeched as her heart leaped into her throat. "What in Hel's name are you doing here? How–"

"Save me!" her girlfriend screamed. "Brunnhilde! Save me!"

She had a sword strapped across her back but made no

attempt to draw it, concentrating instead on fleeing from the monsters at her heels. Brunnhilde took two steps away from the wall before remembering herself and retreating again. She held out her empty hand and beckoned before losing sight of Inge behind a deathless half-elf. She ducked, lashing out with her foot even as her blade was engaged by a second. Her kick caught the elf in the thigh, arresting her charge and sending her skidding backwards.

"Hurry," she shouted as she parried another blow. "Inge, hurry!"

"Valkyrie, that is not Inge. *Defend yourself.*"

Brunnhilde couldn't see Inge because of the deathless warriors clamoring to reach her flesh with their weapons. She blocked again and, for one insane moment, contemplated Realm-jumping to Inge and sweeping her up and away from Jotunheim.

"Brunnhilde," Sif's voice came again, thin with distance yet throbbing with command. "Trust Sif! That is not Inge."

"But," Brunnhilde whispered, parrying on instinct and striking back. "But it is. I'd know her anywhere." The Valkyrie's sword tip dropped as she got her first look at Inge's terrified face before she was forced to defend against a half-Asgardian armed with a spear. Lank yellow hair hung around his face, silvery and braided at the temples. His long mustaches were similarly plaited and beaded, and one was clenched between his teeth. A memory tugged at her. Shouting, Brunnhilde brought Dragonfang down on the spear haft and snapped it in two, the return strike flicking out and into the deathless' chest. He fell to his knees, clutching at the wound, and Brunnhilde knew him.

"Commander Olafson?" she gasped and then slapped her palm against his brow and ripped his soul free.

"Brunnhilde!" Inge screamed again.

Distant and this time laced with strain, Sif shouted again. "Reach out with your senses, Valkyrie, and tell me whether that's your girlfriend's soul in there–" her voice cut off in a flurry of shouting for a few seconds "–the one you kept awareness of back in Meadowfall."

Inge was only strides away now, but Brunnhilde did as she was told. A second later she let out a scream of pure fury and Realm-jumped, not towards Inge but out into the center of the cavern. Space and a few moments to breathe through the rage and fear and grief.

The Serpent had given one of his deathless Inge's face. The thing that was not her lover snarled and changed direction. The glamour covering Brunnhilde's eyes – or perhaps that covered the creature itself – fell away. This deathless was a hideous mix of mountain giant and light elf, pale blue skin stretched tight over too-big bones until it looked almost ready to split. Its moonlit hair fell in lank greasy coils behind its head and its face was contorted with empty malice.

How had she ever considered this monster to be Inge? She met his blade with Dragonfang, the steel clanging and echoing from the high stone roof. The other deathless, still far too many, were a few seconds away, and although she tried not to look, Brunnhilde couldn't help but notice how each of them wore a familiar face. Thor. Frigga. Baldur. Odin. The Valkyrie Eira, and more.

She focused back on the half-elf, accepting a cut to the side of her neck in order to get close enough to make contact with his skin. She took a vicious, visceral pleasure in ending the existence of the deathless that had worn Inge's face like a trophy. She laughed as he collapsed and then hauled up his empty body in her arms and hurled it at the advancing creatures masquerading as her friends and gods.

Two went down in a tangle of limbs, buying her an instant's reprieve in which to settle her feet and bring her sword back to bear.

She used the moment of distraction to full effect, kicking out at what her brain stubbornly insisted was the All-Father himself but which she knew – hoped, prayed – was her enemy. Or no, not her enemy, but merely a vessel made of flesh filled with both the God of Fear's malice and a tormented Asgardian soul. Brunnhilde's kick sent it staggering, but three more closed in and took its place, and she Realm-jumped back to the wall.

She harvested another soul as she fled, but even her vast strength and speed were being worn away by the sheer number of her opponents and the awful magic animating them. She couldn't keep this up indefinitely. She was outmatched and she knew it. She needed help.

"Sif! Sif, I need you."

Sif, warrior and friend, wasn't coming.

Brunnhilde's voice was hoarse from screaming and still Sif was nowhere to be seen. In the brief glimpses she could afford between attacks and Realm-jumps, the Valkyrie had noted her absence from the platform and the area around it, but she didn't know where she'd gone. If she had known, she would have transported straight to her.

The Valkyrie was so tired she could barely raise Dragonfang, and the blade itself was getting heavier by the minute. She'd tried to become invisible for a moment's reprieve and found the power unavailable to her. Their plan to distract Cul in the hopes that he might lose his grip on the deathless had failed, and so there was no point in being separated from the shield-maiden. If Sif was here, guarding her back, Brunnhilde could take greater risks to rescue the einherjar, which was their only objective. But Sif wasn't here; the warrior was nowhere to be seen. And she wasn't the only one.

The Serpent was gone, too. There was no one in this cavern anymore except for the Valkyrie and a seemingly endless number of near-immortal enemies. She had no idea how much time had passed – minutes, hours, even days. This far underground the sun was a distant memory and only the number of wounds and the black gnawing exhaustion within her spoke to how long she had been fighting.

There were still twelve deathless warriors opposing her. The souls of the others were tucked within her, their fear and confusion bleeding through to slow her reactions and tangle her emotions. The ground before and below her was liberally splattered with blood. Too much of it was her own.

Twelve was too many. She Realm-jumped fifty feet along the cavern wall. When she flickered out of the between-space, she let herself press back against it for just a few seconds. Her legs shook in gratitude at the support and her arms and shoulders were on fire as she looked once more for Sif's distinctive hair and armor. Nothing.

A half-troll was the first to reach her this time. Usually

it was the elves, their lightness making them the fastest of those bent on her destruction. This one had been at the rear of the pack and begun moving before the rest had relocated her. Whatever intelligence Cul had hoped for by snatching Asgardian warriors still wasn't manifesting: instead of waiting for the rest to back them up, this one leaped straight into the attack. They carried a spear that was hatched and splintered below the head where Dragonfang had parried it a dozen times already. They'd been fighting for so long that even her enchanted blade was nicked in places, its long, sun-bright length a distant memory. Now it was crusted with filth, each particle of which added immeasurably to the sword's weight. The Valkyrie disarmed the troll, caught their spear as they dropped it and threw it at the oncoming pack. Her aim was true, and the weapon punched a half-elf off her feet. She slapped a hand against the troll-giant's face and tore the soul from within them. The deathless didn't even twitch, simply ceasing to exist, their body collapsing in a limp heap.

Something threw itself onto Brunnhilde's back and she fell flat beneath its weight, the side of her face cracking into the stone. A bright, hot pain erupted through her cheek and upper teeth, and she felt the sting of parted flesh and the hot bloom of blood below her eye. She was face down, scrabbling beneath the creature's bulk and Dragonfang no longer in her grip.

A sharp, sour wash of dread flooded her, leaving her shivering in its wake. The deathless' weight was supported by the strength of her backplate, but it didn't stop her feeling as if she was being crushed. The Valkyrie planted both hands beneath her shoulders and tried to push upwards, only for the creature to rake at her with its claws, shredding her sleeves and the skin of her upper arms as it tried to pin them to the stone.

Brunnhilde wriggled and shoved, bucking wildly until she felt her attacker's weight slide to one side. She threw herself in the same direction and her legs slipped free. She was about to roll away when another deathless stamped on her sword arm. Brunnhilde screamed and instinctively snatched her arm back – her hand and fingers still worked. It wasn't broken.

I'm not that easy to kill, or to stop, she thought with a wild, misplaced burst of confidence.

But now, at the worst possible time, it seemed the deathless were learning. Some of them, at least. The one that had been on top of her had scrambled out of the way as soon as she freed herself, as if it knew that her touch would end its existence. Was this what the Serpent had hoped would happen, that it would learn to avoid skin-to-skin contact with the Valkyrie? Or had Cul told them so?

Brunnhilde rolled onto her feet and discovered the half-Asgardian Sif had named as Sigrun clutching Dragonfang in one huge hand. The deathless was pale, scraps of armor and the shirt beneath hanging in tatters and a thick fresh scar bisecting her gut, another, smaller, in the middle of her chest. The sight of her blade in the hands of an enemy drove everything but white-hot rage from her mind.

The Valkyrie did the only sensible thing in the circumstances: she leaped at Sigrun, narrowly avoiding being spitted on her own sword, and crashed into her chest.

The blade rattled her teeth as it smacked into her backplate, but in the next second she had a hand on Sigrun's face. Sif's friend toppled with her still clinging to her and she wrestled Dragonfang out of her hand, tumbled into a forward roll to get out from amongst the others, and came up on the balls of her feet behind two deathless warriors who had been fashioned from dark elves. She slapped them both across the ears and sucked the life from them.

"Sif?" Brunnhilde shrieked. "Hel's teeth, Reckless, where are you?"

She ducked a sword swing, hacked back with Dragonfang but missed, and Realm-jumped, back to her spot near the exit. "Sif, come back," she begged one last time, the words so soft that they barely echoed from the cavern walls. Again, she leaned against the wall for a few precious seconds, letting the fresh souls settle within her, adding their negligible and yet enormous weight to her limbs. A flicker of movement and she braced and then, despite herself and every innumerable hour of training that had taught her otherwise, she allowed herself to be distracted on the battlefield. Because there behind her enemies and clad in gleaming armor, with long ebony plaits hanging down her back, stood Lady Sif. She was grinning.

Brunnhilde's heart gave a lurch of relief, but it was short-lived. There were a dozen deathless between them, all intent on ending the Valkyrie's life. She lost sight of Sif for a few moments during the next frenzied wave of battle, and when next she saw her, she'd somehow threaded her way between the deathless and was within arm's reach.

"Sif!" Brunnhilde began, her voice strangled with too

much emotion, and the warrior launched a cut at her neck that would take off the Valkyrie's head. Brunnhilde parried clumsily, shock and disbelief slowing her reactions. Their blades clashed in a shower of sparks.

Roaring, the Valkyrie lashed out, kicking Sif in the belly and throwing her backwards, but moments later she advanced again, somehow from Brunnhilde's right this time, moving as fast as fire behind and through their enemies, but there was a deathless dark elf coming from her left, too. Without hesitation, she scythed the half-elf's legs from under her. The deathless screeched and went over backwards, and Brunnhilde followed her down, reaching for the creature's face in order to collect her soul.

A fast-moving, heavy weight drove into her back and sent her tumbling over the prone creature's form and into the stone beyond with a clatter of armor. She didn't let go of her sword this time, but by the time she was back up onto her feet she saw that the entire pack of deathless were wearing the face and form of Lady Sif.

Each one had lips peeled back and murderous intent in her eyes, armed with swords, axes, knives, and one with a spear. There was something eerie and utterly alien about them, despite the perfection of the glamour and the silky-smooth prowl that was Sif's signature when she stalked her enemies. They absolutely were, and yet definitively were not, her friend. Was the real Sif still up and fighting, or was she a bloody corpse somewhere in the dark of the cavern?

Brunnhilde reached yet again for her Realm-jump ability and found it was weak, barely there as if trapped behind a glass wall. She could see it and almost touch it, but there wasn't enough for her to do what she needed it to do. She was trapped for real this time, no way out and no help coming. Nine deathless warriors animated by einherjar, intent on ending her life.

She couldn't jump and they were too close for her to run. Brunnhilde was going to die.

Twenty-Four
The Trickster God

Lady Sif was almost within reach of the frantic battle between Valkyrie and deathless when a flicker of movement brought her skidding to a halt. Two figures battled in a shadowed corner where the stone wall was rough and unfinished. It was hard to identify them as they darted, ducked and spun, but their stature was neither that of giant nor half-giant. The shorter of the figures hacked into the other and, as it fell, spun and charged towards her with a triumphant screech.

It was Loki.

Adrenaline flashed like a bolt of lightning through her spine, swiftly followed by a bitter triumph. Here was her enemy, her true and eternal foe. And, of course, he would be here, taking advantage of any chaos he could find to turn to his benefit. A chance to meddle in the affairs of Asgard? How could he resist.

Sif screamed her battle-cry and leaped to meet the Trickster God. He was clad in his usual long green robes and the sword he wielded was bright and long and slightly curved. How intimately Sif knew that blade. How many thousands of hours had she spent stealing the power of its attacks and turning it against its wielder when they were young, back when they'd been allies, even friends? And, in turn, how many hours had she spent being beaten by him, learning his every trick and tactic until they were as ingrained in her mind as the face of her brother, as her own secret hopes and wants?

A grin split Loki's face when he saw her coming and he took one hand from his sword hilt long enough to beckon her on. "At last we come to it," he said with wry amusement, sharp enough to make a muscle jump in Sif's jaw. "Time to see whether your pathetic need for vengeance is stronger than my desire to live."

"It will be. It already is." She shouted the words before she even had to think them, but she also took the time to glance past Loki to identify who he'd been fighting. She blinked and almost faltered: it was Cul. Loki had been dueling Cul. Even as she watched, he flickered out of existence and was gone, his face drawn tight with pain. The distinctive odor of his magic lingered in the air and then she faced Loki blade to blade and hate to hate.

Their weapons met in a shatter of sparks and a clang that echoed from the walls. They parted, circled and clashed again, stepping in time with each other, moving almost as one, as if they were dancing.

As if they were lovers.

They attacked at the same instant, and Loki let go with his rear hand in order to catch Sif's wrist as she slashed. She responded in kind, grabbing his wrist until they were pressed together with their swords forced up above their own shoulders. Loki was taller than her, just, and she felt an uncomfortable flutter in her belly as she looked up into those cat-green eyes and that sensuous mouth with its sardonic twist.

"Having fun yet?" he whispered, and she felt the brush of his breath against her mouth. Shuddering, she tried to wrench her wrist free, but Loki refused to let go. Sif jerked up one knee and he fell for the ruse, flinching away to protect his groin, and she seized on the instant of inattention and drove the heel of her boot sideways down his shin and onto his instep with all her strength.

Loki howled and his grip on her wrist faltered. She twisted it free and at the same moment let go of his arm and shoved him hard in the chest. They both stepped back out of range, the Trickster God with a distinct limp.

Sif took the short reprieve to look past him again. There had been… something, or possibly someone, else in the shadows where he'd been fighting the Serpent. Now, her eyes more used to the extra gloom out here at the edge of the cavern, she saw it. Rather, she saw him. Again, she felt a flood of adrenaline course through her limbs. Slumped in a depression and half-hidden by an unfinished outcrop, the All-Father lay against the rock wall clutching the bleeding wound in his neck.

"What have you done?" she demanded, all the strength stolen from her voice so that it came out in a horrified whisper.

"Of course, of course you think it would be me hurting him," he said, but there was a strange vulnerability in the set of Loki's shoulders. "I've wanted a lot of things in my life, Lady Sif, but I've never wanted Asgard's destruction, and that is what Cul is promising."

"Liar!" she spat. "Everything that comes out of your mouth is a lie. You've tried to destroy Asgard yourself more than once, so don't pretend you're suddenly on our side now." She ran at Loki with her blade raised in both hands above her head. Shock slackened Loki's features, and he parried her attacks with desperate speed, but still she forced him back a step, and then two and then three, the breath whistling from her throat along with grunts of exertion and fury. She had to end this now so that she could go to Odin and check his wound. Pour every last trickle of healing magic from the orb into him. *Save him.*

"I'm going to kill you and feed your liver to the eagles," she grated out between gritted teeth.

"So be it." Loki had withstood her initial frantic attack and now his expression seemed almost bored as he deflected with minimal effort, until she was panting for breath and he was as calm and unruffled as a placid lake under the summer sun.

A sudden clever twist and triangle step brought Loki behind her, scoring a cut to the back of Sif's thigh. He swept back in front of her and grinned again.

"I will kill you," Sif snarled again, almost choking on her need for vengeance and the constricting fear for the All-Father. "I will. You can't stop me."

"Can't I?" Loki asked with a knowing glint in his eyes. "When I just cut you with a poisoned blade?"

Sif barked a harsh laugh as she leaped out of range, and she tried to inspect his blade in the inconstant light: there was nothing that might indicate he was telling the truth. Surely her healing ability would negate any poison he could invent, but even as she told herself that, her injured leg began to burn and then to buckle. With a startled cry, Sif fell to one knee on the stone. Her gaze slid past Loki towards the All-Father. She found him looking back at her, waxy and pale with the blood pumping from his neck black in the distant firelight.

He reached for her, fingers curled upwards in what was probably supposed to be a beckoning gesture but which reminded her of nothing more than the weakly waving legs of a dying spider. Sif stared at Odin, unable to move, until his hand dropped into his lap and his head tilted down onto his chest.

"Help him," she breathed through a tight throat. "Please, Loki, please help him."

Loki's cat-green eyes widened in comical surprise. "But you think I'm the one who hurt him. Don't you?"

Sif sobbed as she forced herself onto her feet, her leg shuddering beneath her. She pointed her sword at Loki's face. "I said help him."

The Trickster God glanced casually back. His shoulders tensed and then slumped, but when he faced her again, there was nothing to see but that smiling mask. "No."

The shield-maiden screamed curses at him, but they bounced off him like raindrops on armor. She tried to rush past, but her cut leg was weak and slow to respond and he easily herded her back. "All-Father," she shouted. "All-Father, go home. Go back to Asgard. Go now!"

Odin did not stir.

Fear and fury blossomed into a perfect storm within her breast. Even though she was going to die, she swore to take Loki with her. It was a vow inviolable. If Sif had to give up her place in Valhalla to see him bleed out upon the stone, then that was a sacrifice she was willing to make. She didn't need an eternity of feasting; one moment watching him choke and gasp his way into death would be the sweetest reward she could ask for. For Odin, for Asgard and for all the Nine Realms, Lady Sif would end this scourge that plagued them.

In your name, All-Father, I swear it.

The warrior wiped a trembling hand across her mouth, tasting sweat and blood and defeat and the hot metal tang of vengeance. Loki watched her from three paces away, his head tilted to one side like an inquisitive bird.

"How could you?" she choked, her voice little more than a hoarse croak. She was so thirsty. "He's your father."

Loki's face twisted with sudden rage, and he spat deliberately on the stone. "He is *not* my father. He never was and he never will be, in the same way that that hammer-wielding idiot is not my brother. I spit on all their promises of glory and eternity, all of which are denied me. Every breath I take, every accomplishment of mine, is overlooked. And I *will not* stand for it anymore."

Slowly and deliberately, the Trickster God put down his sword and stepped away from it. Stepped towards Sif and opened his hands in supplication. She twitched and readied herself.

"I came here for you and the Valkyrie," he said, the words so unexpected that she caught her breath. "I came here because even I would not stoop to this. Even I am disgusted by what is happening here. It was not I who attacked the All-Father." He laughed, the sound low and tinged with mockery. "Not that you will believe me, of course. No one ever does."

He made an abortive gesture, as if wiping away all he had just said. "Doesn't matter. I came here to help; I came here for you, Sif. You too are an Asgardian god. You too are overlooked by those in charge." He didn't wheedle; he didn't beg. He simply stated the facts and laid bare the truth. Sif felt something within her respond.

"You are nothing more than a blade to be held to the throats of their enemies, and one who is denied the right to choose at whom you are pointed. Aren't you tired of that? Aren't you *so tired* of being a weapon?"

Sif tried to deny it, but he hushed her with such sympathy in his expression that the words died in her throat. It was true; she *was* a blade, honed and kept sheathed until Thor or Odin needed her. Never allowed into the sun unless she must spill blood beneath its watchful gaze.

Loki stepped forward until they were almost touching. Sif's sword hung loose at her side. She tried with every fiber of her being to strike at him, but the weight of the entire mountain seemed to be concentrated in the tip of the blade and she could not lift it. As if it had become Mjolnir. Instead, she went to her knees again, but this time softly, with a sigh that might have been acceptance.

And Loki – unarmed Loki – knelt too. There was such compassion in his face that it transported her back in time to when they'd been children and none of them had understood the fates that awaited them. Back to when they'd been friends and almost closer than blood. Both dwelling in the shadows of their more famous brothers. Misunderstood.

Carefully and without threat, Loki laid both his hands on Sif's shoulders. His handsome face was so open. "Join me, Sif," he murmured in his soft, melodious voice. "Loki and Lady Sif, the forgotten gods of Asgard. Overlooked and underestimated. Lifelong friends; perhaps even more. I've never met my equal before, my lady. Think of all we could accomplish together. Beginning with bringing the Serpent's reign of terror to a halt. United, he cannot stand against us."

The words echoed, thrilled, pounded in Sif's head. All we can accomplish. The overlooked and underestimated.

All we can accomplish.

Sif could see it, the other Asgardian gods giving her the respect that was the only thing she'd ever wanted. An acknowledgment of her worth to Odin and Asgard, to all the Nine Realms. A worth that had been forever underrated and discarded.

"Smile for me, Sif. Smile and say yes."

"Odin," she managed.

Loki grimaced, his mouth turning down. "Ah, you're so good, so loyal to those who may not deserve it." Sif flinched, and his fingers pressed gently against her shoulders, so gentle on the wounded one. "Forgive me; that was unkind. He has been like a father to you, as he was to me – so kind on the surface. So generous where other people could see it. But behind closed doors, in private, that's where the 'No, Sif, not today' and 'No Sif, you can't' comes into play, isn't it? He seems to give you everything; the reality is so different. Don't you think?"

Loki paused, intent, and when she didn't answer immediately, he went on, "But of course, as a show of good faith, I will take him back to Asgardia for treatment. How's that?"

Sif nodded. She was thirsty and tired – gods, so very tired – and she hurt all over. And no one had come for her. No one but him. She took Loki's hand off her wounded shoulder and pressed it to her cheek. She leant into the caress, his palm warm and sticky with blood, and she smiled.

Smiled and stabbed her knife through his chest. Loki coughed, his eyes opening very wide. A thin whine slipped out on a ragged exhalation.

"Smile for me, Loki," Sif said with sweet malice. "You're prettier when you smile."

She wrenched the blade free and sliced it through his throat. Loki coughed again and then collapsed in on himself and vanished. When Sif looked over into the shadows at the edge of the cavern, Odin, of course, was also gone.

She pressed her hands to her face and began to weep.

Brunnhilde was fighting a multitude of battles. The first, of course, was against the deathless warriors wearing her friend's face. They pressed in close, stumbling over their empty companions and snarling and cutting and slicing. The second was against the cresting wave of fear, defeat and grief that choked her lungs and wound thorns around her throat. The third was against the glass wall between her and her ability to Realm-jump. And that one, finally, blessedly, she defeated.

Without hesitation, she threw herself into the between-space and back out by the platform where she had last seen Sif – the real Sif – so very long ago. She'd been moving and fighting and jumping without cease for a day and a night and however far they were into the next day now, so the jump itself was harder than normal. Although she knew all the pathways of the between-space, there was an instant of disorientation and when she emerged, it was in the center of the platform, not quite where she'd meant to be.

Still, she could at least verify that the God of Fear definitely wasn't on this side of the cavern. That it was, in fact, empty of all life. Including Sif. Brunnhilde searched desperately for her and finally found her – or someone wearing her skin – far across the cavern and back towards where she herself had been fighting. Her friend was kneeling alone in the shadows. The deathless were closer to Sif than to Brunnhilde now, a clear threat. Groaning, she Realm-jumped to her and emerged to find the shield-maiden sobbing.

"Sif? Sif, what's wrong?"

The warrior gave no sign that she had heard Brunnhilde's words, so she grabbed Sif's arm and shook it hard. Still nothing. "Come back to me; I need you."

She might as well have been talking to a statue for all the reaction she got, so with a mumbled apology that the warrior probably couldn't hear, she let go of her hand and then slapped her hard across the cheek. Sif's head snapped to the side and when it came back to center, her eyes were clear and filled with murderous intent.

"Finally," Brunnhilde grunted before she could say anything. She hauled the other woman to her feet and pointed. Instinctively, Sif looked that way and the Valkyrie heard her small intake of breath. "They're… me," she said.

"Yep. Horrible, isn't it?" The deathless were already charging towards them. "You knock them down, I'll free the souls. Where's Cul?"

"Cul?" Sif said. She sounded confused. "It wasn't Cul who said… or was it?" She stared around them wildly, her fists clenching and unclenching by her sides. She was pale beneath the sweat, grime, and blood, but her eyes glittered with a strange intensity.

Brunnhilde bent down and retrieved Sif's sword and shoved it into her hand. "Ready?" she asked instead of puzzling over Sif's disjointed words.

"It doesn't matter," Sif muttered to herself. Her fingers closed reflexively around the blade. "Truth or lies, none of it matters. If all I am is a weapon, then at least I can be a sharp one."

Sif gave her a level, neutral glare, warning her not to ask, and pushed past to face the monstrous versions of herself. She paused and then asked Brunnhilde, "What about your glamour? If you need a break, can't you just–"

Brunnhilde shook her head. "There's something in here stopping me." She gestured angrily. "They can glamour – or be glamoured by the Serpent – but I can't. Believe me, I've tried."

The Valkyrie shook out her arms and legs and then cracked her neck, settling into stance at Sif's side, two paces out from the wall. The warrior's presence next to her was more comfort than she would have thought possible. It was as if Sif was a source of energy; Brunnhilde could feel it pouring into her limbs and strengthening her on a cresting wave of confidence. Nine deathless warriors. They could do this.

The deathless came in hard and fast, spaced out in a skirmish line to cut off any avenue of escape that wasn't Realm-jumping. Brunnhilde and Sif stayed close, but soon enough the swirl and dance of battle pulled them apart. Just a pace at first, and then another.

"Backs to the wall," she heard Sif shout. Brunnhilde disengaged and threw herself backwards against the stone. She found Sif only inches from her side once more. The black-haired warrior spared her a single, wild grin, as if there was nowhere she would rather be. The Valkyrie felt both an answering smile tug at her mouth and reckless ferocity rising in her breast.

Once again, the faces in front of Brunnhilde began to change and Dragonfang now bit deep into Inge's shoulder. The Valkyrie cried out.

"Glamour!" Sif bellowed. "Not real."

Brunnhilde cursed, but her flicker of hesitation had lasted long enough for a deathless looking like the God of Thunder to slice a great-axe down between them. The Asgardians had no choice but to dive in separate directions. The axe split the ground where they had been standing.

The Valkyrie regained her balance and was immediately attacked by a deathless wearing Odin's skin and wielding a huge, black-edged sword. She parried, grunting at the strength of the blow, and riposted, only for her blade to be intercepted. The deathless stepped inside her guard, his free hand shoving her back. She stumbled a step, cutting his forearm with her sword and then flicking it down to slice into his thigh. The creature squealed, and Brunnhilde dragged the blade downwards, opening him up all the way to the knee. He clubbed her with the pommel of his sword, splitting the crown of her head.

Lightning flashed in Brunnhilde's skull, and they separated, the Valkyrie bleary from the blow and blood creeping through her hair. The Odin-deathless was bleeding and limping. She couldn't give him time to heal. The Valkyrie lunged for him again despite her heavy arms and was nearly in range when someone grabbed her wrist and spun her backwards into the cavern wall. Their other hand clamped around her throat and began to squeeze, and Brunnhilde was looking into the face of her sister Eira. She grabbed the hand attempting to suffocate the life out of her and used the contact to draw forth the soul.

She shoved the now-limp deathless off her. Sif appeared at her side, steadying her with one hand in her armpit.

Or at least, it looked like Sif.

The Valkyrie slapped her palm instinctively against Sif's hand and reached out with her senses: it really was her. The corner of Sif's mouth quirked up and then she turned away to engage the Heimdall-deathless trying to sneak up on her blind side.

Brunnhilde steadied at that – she had a way to identify Sif from among the glamoured deathless. As long as she could touch her, she'd know she was real. Something unclenched in her chest at the realization that she wasn't alone anymore, and then Sif was throwing a broken deathless at her. Instinctively, she braced and caught the flying figure. Her bare hands touched face and arm. She ripped out another einherjar and packed it away inside, but when she went to throw the empty husk at her attackers, her strength gave out. The body dropped in front of her with a meaty smack.

A wave of nausea flowed through her, swiftly followed by dizziness. Her first thought was that the new soul was somehow poisoned, but the truth was she was reaching the end of her abilities. She had too many inside her and she had Realm-jumped too much, fought too long and lost too much blood. If they didn't end this very soon, they weren't getting out alive.

Sif ran at her, howling. "Sif?" Brunnhilde shouted.

"On your left!" Sif shouted back.

Brunnhilde let the Sif-deathless come on, and then dodged at the last instant. The hybrid ran straight onto Dragonfang, impaling herself. "Ha!" the Valkyrie shouted in triumph, and then nearly swallowed her tongue as the deathless proceeded to ignore the sword rammed through her belly and tried to stab her with a wickedly curved knife instead, her hand coming up and around in a blur.

The Valkyrie swayed back out of reach, the blade a whisper from her skin. She grabbed her opponent's wrist as it flashed past her face and jerked so that the creature's temple came into range of a roundhouse elbow strike. The blow snapped the deathless' head sideways and she fell, boneless, on top of the other. Brunnhilde took that soul, too.

Another coil of nausea spiked through her gut. The einherjar was uneasy within her. It felt as if it had sharp edges and was scraping her raw from the inside. Brunnhilde staggered and put her sword hand up against the stone wall behind them. Seven more deathless was six too many.

"I'm nearly done, Sif," she called, too tired and too desperate to feel embarrassed.

Sif appeared in front of her, settling herself between Brunnhilde and the remaining deathless. Her arms were visibly shaking as she raised her sword into guard. "I'll knock them down, you take the souls," she shouted and there was nothing but determination in her voice.

Brunnhilde was about to agree, relief surging within her, when the between-space opened up and a hand reached out and dragged Sif into it. She let out a surprised squawk and began to resist, but the hand was implacable. The between-space closed.

Sif was gone.

Twenty-Five
The Last Stand

"We were so rudely interrupted earlier. I wanted to make sure you were alright," Loki murmured once he had pulled her, struggling, into the disorienting, mind-bending between-space. He tutted when she tried to pull her hand from his. "Do you really want to let go? You don't know the way. One wrong step and you'll be cast off the path forever. Even if that big Valkyrie came looking, she'd never find you."

"You're not really here. You're not Loki. It doesn't matter whose face you wear or what promises you make, it doesn't matter how much you think you know me. I'm going to end your evil, and if it ends my life at the same time, so be it."

Sif raised her chin in defiance. In truth, she didn't know whether it really was Loki, but it didn't matter. God of Tricks or God of Fear made no difference in the end. Evil was evil and Sif was a weapon designed to end evil.

Loki ran his tongue across his upper teeth as he considered her. "Very well. If it's death you're looking for, I won't stop you." He let go of her hand and shoved her hard. Instantly the between-space rose all around her in confusing, twisting chaos.

Sif raised her sword and stalked him through the eye-watering changing dimensions, knowing she was getting further and further from where she had entered the between-space and knowing, too, that she had failed Brunnhilde at the very second the Valkyrie had most needed her.

Because Sif wasn't just a blade. She was a shield too, and she was supposed to preserve Brunnhilde's life so that she could complete the mission and get the einherjar home.

"Come on, Cul," she snapped, her temper fraying. Her head pounded from the shifting planes of the between-space, but she brought all her focus to bear on the figure grinning lazily before her. "How about you end this farce and show me your true self? I tire of such petty tricks."

Loki's face and form shifted, melting into something monstrous and then back into that of a tall Asgardian with white-blond hair falling straight as an arrow down his back. He wasn't old this time; he was beautiful. "My true self?" the God of Fear asked. He tapped his fingers against his chin as if in thought, humming. "Are you sure you could bear to see it again?"

Sif snorted and took another step forward. "I'd like to sink my blade into your hide again, yes. Slice you right open so that you flee like last time."

Cul looked down at himself and then shrugged. "I didn't flee, little sister. Merely… shed my skin, you might say. And besides, you can see I am uninjured." He gave a theatrical sigh. "What a pity you didn't listen to my dear brother Loki's advice."

Sif stilled, a little thrill of fear racing up her spine. "He… no, Loki wasn't here. That was you."

Cul let one side of his mouth curl up. "Was it?"

"Yes," she insisted, with a little more confidence. "It was. Not that it matters," she added, a beat too late.

The Serpent laughed, a hollow rasp like a rattlesnake's tail. "Of course it matters. How can you live with yourself knowing he was here, and you did nothing but let him weave his schemes and stab you? How are the wounds, by the way?"

As though the words were the blade itself, reopening the slice in the back of her thigh and through her shoulder, pain arced through her again. Sif grunted and flexed carefully. There was a lot of blood.

"I'm fine," she managed, convincing neither of them.

Cul attacked. One moment an Asgardian stood before her and the next he was the snake. His head was longer than she was tall, and it shot out faster than a lightning strike, his gaping mouth exposing long, recurved fangs.

The shield-maiden leaped straight up into the air, allowing the Serpent to pass beneath her. She landed astride his back facing towards his tail and scored a deep cut through iridescent scales.

Cul hissed in outrage and whipped his head back along his own length, but Sif had already thrown herself clear. Or so she thought. A huge, muscular coil appeared out of nowhere and wrapped itself around her, crushing one arm against her chest. She just managed to lift her sword arm high enough to avoid the constriction, but her blade was too long to get a decent downward stabbing angle as she was wrapped chest to knees in Cul's body.

She made the best of it as he began to squeeze, sawing the blade back and forth over the tough, plate-like scales. The sword wasn't made for such abuse, but she could feel her armor beginning to creak under the immense pressure. The arm that was pressed to her breastplate was fizzing with pain as it was crushed, and her feet left the floor as the Serpent shifted his grip.

It would take hours for a non-serrated blade to saw through the God of Fear's body, but Sif kept going. At the same time, she closed her eyes and focused on the cracked and fading Quellstone. It was sorely depleted, but she thought there was enough to do what it needed to do, albeit probably for the last time.

Gathering it all beneath her skin, Sif channeled the energy into a single blow directed through the edge of her blade. Screaming, she brought her sword down upon the Serpent's back. There was an explosion of golden light and the distinct sensation of her blade biting deep into flesh. The between-space reverberated with her power, flexing and tearing and absorbing. Cul shrieked, the sound an unholy mix of voices, and thrashed wildly.

Sif was thrown free, arcing through the air before slamming into cold stone. Weakened from the expulsion of power, she had to blink several times to recognize that she was back in the gloom and normal dimensions of the cavern within the mountain. She was back on Jotunheim.

Less than a hundred feet from her was Brunnhilde, surrounded and coated in blood. By the way the Valkyrie swayed and the laborious slowness of her ripostes, she was done.

Sif's use of the Quellstone within the between-space had somehow ejected her back to the last place she'd been, but how, she had no idea. Right now, she didn't care. Retching, she rolled onto her hands and knees, biting back a sob of pure exhaustion, and then planted one foot and forced herself to stand.

"Brunnhilde," she tried, but her voice was little more than a croak. She cleared her throat, wishing for water to wet her parched mouth. "Brunnhilde." Only a little louder. She broke into a shambling run towards the Valkyrie.

She was nearly there when the between-space opened up again and a hand reached out and tried to drag her back in. This time, she planted her boots, struck with her blade, and dragged him out into the cave instead.

Sif scored a deep cut down Cul's face and neck, and he roared and punched her. She hit the ground again. When she stood, Heimdall was in front of her and even as she brought up her sword, he raked a knife across her vambrace and opened up the inside of her elbow. Sif struck back, praying he hadn't hit the artery.

Cul-Heimdall dodged back out of range and then ran his finger across the cut in his face. "You really are fast," he said in the condescending tones of an adult to a precocious child. "That mewling, hammer-wielding pup you still moon after must be pleased."

Sif's lips peeled back from her teeth, but she didn't waste her breath responding. She threw herself into the fray again. Cul neither raised his knife nor sidestepped; instead, his form melted and collapsed in on itself so that her sword whistled through the empty air where he had stood. She reversed the strike, bringing the sword up and around and down in a whining arc towards the shifting, amorphous mass of the god, but a hand formed and caught her blade, stopping its descent.

Cul reformed into the face and figure of the All-Father. His knife shifted too, taking on the familiar and awe-inspiring appearance of Gungnir.

It's not him. It's not him. It's not him.

Odin-Cul punched Gungnir into her thigh, just above her right knee. She screamed.

Abandoning her sword in his grip, she flung herself into a clumsy backflip, but when the world was the right side up again, she found the Serpent was already before her.

Gungnir came in hard and fast. The shield-maiden blocked with her vambrace, the spear-tip scoring deep into the leather and cutting a groove through the steel plating. Sif wrapped her hands around the spear just beneath the head, set her feet, and pulled with all her strength. Odin-Cul grunted in surprise, but before she could feel even the first stirrings of triumph, he released the weapon and she stumbled back a pace.

By the time she regained her balance, the Serpent was transforming again, his form melting away from her blows, shimmering as if about to vanish and then reforming, once more the giant Serpent.

His enormous body formed a complete ring around her, trapping her inside. Sif's vision was narrowing, exhaustion and bloodlust and energy expenditure combining until it was sheer stubbornness keeping her on her feet and in the fight. She took three hobbling strides, planted the butt of the spear, and vaulted over the Serpent's back. She neither halted nor looked behind at Cul's furious hiss, instead drawing desperately on the orb's golden flickers of energy. She pictured the Valkyrie and *pushed.*

Brunnhilde coughed blood, but no matter how much she spat, she couldn't draw a full breath. Couldn't draw a half-breath. Couldn't do anything but sip at the air, her lungs and ribs, chest and back a litany, *a symphony,* of pain. Her latest enemy's axe hadn't penetrated her armor the first time, but the blow had lifted her off her feet and thrown her into the wall. The back of her head hit so hard she saw stars. Before she could shake off the daze, the axe had come in again and again, each clanging hammer-blow adding to the dent.

The third cracked her breastplate, and the deathless wielding it yelled in triumph. A spear jabbed at her from the right as she brought up Dragonfang to deflect the next blow, but it still ripped open her arm – tore free of the flesh and sleeve and somehow slid in through the sculpted armhole of her breastplate. Into her chest.

Brunnhilde grunted. The sound was breathy and wet. She stabbed at the deathless wielding the axe, forcing it back a step, and tried to tug the spear out of herself. The monster it belonged to – what had once been a light elf – snarled something and shoved it deeper instead. Brunnhilde was pushed sideways, and her backplate squealed horribly against the wall, giving voice to her pain in a way the Valkyrie herself could not.

The half-elf twisted the spear inside Brunnhilde. She gasped – tried to gasp – but it was obscured by more blood in her throat. The deathless wrenched the spear out and the Valkyrie fell forwards onto her hands and knees, Dragonfang skittering away from her grip. She was dizzy, her lung torn and filling with blood, not air. Agony consumed her.

Something cold and bitter pressed against the back of her neck: the axe blade. The souls within broke into a clamor, a riot of sensations and emotions, conflicting advice and orders and pleas. She couldn't make sense of it, of anything but that icy steel pressed to her skin and the fire and blood in her chest. And the knowledge she had failed – Odin, the einherjar, Sif, Inge.

Inge.

Brunnhilde watched the blood dripping from her mouth spatter against the stone. Inge's face floated in her mind, Inge's voice telling her to *get up right now* ringing in her ears. The deathless hadn't killed her yet, the axe resting just below the curve of her skull. Perhaps they were waiting for the Serpent; no doubt he would enjoy watching her die.

Brunnhilde sat back on her heels, both arms extended as if in welcome. They were shaking and her vision was narrowing. The deathless shifted back out of reach and the axe parted skin on the back of her neck. She was the leader of the Choosers of the Slain, entrusted by the All-Father himself in her sacred duty, and nothing would stop her performing it.

Brunnhilde extended her senses, her power and her will. She was frantic, and probably dying, and the einherjar needed her. "*Come to me!*" she screamed, the words tangling with the blood in her throat. With the very last of her strength and consciousness, she tore open her mind and her ability and reached out. Pain exploded through her head, sharper even than that in her chest, but she ripped the souls out of the remaining deathless all at once, without touching any of them. The einherjar trapped in the amphorae came too, a number she couldn't even begin to guess at. They slammed into her with the force of arrows and buried themselves in her bleeding flesh.

She didn't know what she'd done, or how. She was fire and agony, raw nerve endings, a shattered mind. She was broken.

Inge, she thought, and her girlfriend's lovely, dimpled face was the last thing she saw. Darkness overwhelmed her.

Someone was shaking her. Hard.

Brunnhilde let out a long, heartfelt groan and tried to turn away, her entire body one dull throb of hurt almost lost against the bright sweep of pain in her chest. The hands were insistent, annoying her into cracking open one eyelid.

Awareness flooded back – a deathless wearing Sif's face was looming over her. She grabbed its shoulder with her left hand, slammed her right into its armored waist, and flipped it over her head to crash down on the stone with a startled squawk.

The Valkyrie staggered onto her feet and then fell back to her knees, the world spinning crazily around her and her insides sloshing. No… not her insides. Brunnhilde was full, crammed with souls. Packed so tightly that they rubbed up against her own, against her consciousness and bones and the inside of her skin, jagged and prickling. The soul-snatched. But that meant…

"Sif?"

"If I say yes, are you going to throw me around again?" came the muffled reply. Brunnhilde looked over. The shield-maiden was facedown on the stone. Somehow, they appeared to be in the shadows behind the platform. Brunnhilde didn't know how they'd got there. "Where is… Sif?" she asked again, unable to really believe it. The warrior grunted. "What the bloody Hel happened?"

Sif groaned and pushed herself up onto her knees. The Valkyrie gasped when she saw how ashen she looked.

"Did you heal me?" she demanded.

Sif lifted one shoulder in a half-shrug. "You were dying, I think. And you have the einherjar."

"How much energy did you use?"

Sif swayed and she blinked owlishly at Brunnhilde and then gave her a lopsided smile. "Enough. Now help me up, because I don't think he's going to give us much longer."

Even as she spoke, the air split open and the Serpent appeared in his huge, sinuous snake form, iridescent scales glittering and his eyes bright with malice and amusement.

"Oh," Sif said faintly. "Bloody Hel."

Brunnhilde leaped to Sif's side and grabbed her hand, dragging her onto her feet and preparing to Realm-jump.

"He'll follow us in," the warrior said, pulling free. "We can't win in there. Trust me."

There wasn't time for more: the Serpent struck. The Asgardians both leaped up onto the platform and he followed, whipping his body around and sending the Valkyrie sprawling. Gods, but he was fast! How had Sif survived against him by herself?

"Pincer attack," Sif called from somewhere on the other

side of the Serpent's huge form. Brunnhilde broke into a run. Cul's attention was on Sif, at least for now, and the Valkyrie closed the gap between them and thrust her blade through his scales all the way to the hilt and began working it side to side, widening the wound.

The enormous snake thrashed wildly. It was all Brunnhilde could do to keep hold of her sword as she was whipped through the air, her feet flying out behind her from the violence of his motions. Her many wounds were sealed, but her body remembered the pain and weakness and shied away from enduring any more.

Cul seemed determined to throw her clear, and she couldn't do anything more like this anyway, so Brunnhilde judged her moment and as the curve of his body reached its apex, she pulled her sword free and tumbled backwards across the stone and almost over the edge of the platform. The Valkyrie rolled to her feet and ran back in. This time she leaped high, her body an arc in the air and her sword gleaming silver and a bloody, clotted red. She landed across the Serpent's back, sword tip first. Momentum and her body weight drove the blade deep within the God of Fear's body. The bitter edge sank in, and more blood welled up from the wound and sprayed high as he writhed.

Sif was flung out of his coils by the force of his reaction, sliding over the platform's edge forty feet away. She made no sound as she hit the rock, limbs flopping bonelessly. She disappeared from view.

"Sif!" Brunnhilde screamed. She ripped her sword free once more, but this time dug her left hand deep into the wound she'd carved, anchoring herself upon the Serpent's broad, blood-slick back. She stabbed Dragonfang back in and this time felt the grating scrape of steel on bone before the blade pressed in between two vertebrae. The length of Cul's body behind her blade stilled, and Brunnhilde let a wild grin spread across her face.

A shadow fell over her.

She looked up into the Serpent's eyes. Fear seized her by the throat, cutting off her air, and her fingers slackened on the sword.

"You are bold, Valkyrie," Cul said, writhing gently as he assessed the extent of the damage. He hissed, part annoyance, part amusement. "But you are foolish."

The God of Fear vanished from beneath her and she fell to the ground. Panting, Brunnhilde forced herself to stand again, weapon in hand, and turned in a slow circle, waiting for Cul's inevitable reappearance. Was Sif still alive?

Of course she was; *of course*. She had to be, because the Valkyrie was exhausted again despite the borrowed energy from the Quellstone's healing, weighed down with too many souls and their accompanying confusion and burdens of grief and horror. Each was a tiny knife stabbing her and slowing her. *Where were they? What had happened? Why were they not worthy enough to join the glorious dead in Valhalla?*

Their quiet, forlorn babble was like a grindstone against her nerve endings, wearing them down until she was nothing but hurt. Cul reappeared, not out of the between-space as she had expected, but simply materializing in front of her. This time he was tall, old, and stooped, propped up on a spear that looked blunt. Cul, wearing the face and form of the original All-Father.

Dragonfang came up of its own volition, biting deep into the God of Fear's thigh before his spear batted it away. "Traitor," she spat at him. "Thief of lives and souls. Maker of monsters. Why are the mountain giants helping you when they see what you do to their kin?"

Despite his apparent frailty, the God of Fear moved with a lithe, reptilian grace even in his Asgardian body. Seeming not to feel the cut she'd made in his leg, he whirled around her, his spear darting in to crack against her elbows and the back of her head as he toyed with her.

The Valkyrie's legs wobbled beneath her like those of a day-old foal. Her vision began to narrow into a long tunnel. She gritted her teeth and parried the next blow of the spear, refusing to look into the Serpent's face and see his brows raised high in amusement. Brunnhilde struck back, but the blow was weak and would have done little damage even if Cul had allowed it to make contact with his body.

I could leave. I've probably got just enough energy to Realm-jump close to a portal. I could leave.

She had completed her task. She had done what the God of Thunder had instructed her to do. And Sif was a warrior: she understood the risks of a mission like this. She could just leave.

"Yes," Cul whispered.

Brunnhilde sidestepped, forcing the Serpent to turn with her so that she could get the edge of the platform in her eyeline. Relief washed through her when she saw the black-haired warrior appear over the lip. She looked as if she'd bathed in blood, but she was alive.

The Valkyrie met Cul's eyes and grinned. "I think not."

Despite her bravado, she was consistently half a movement behind as the fight became a twisting, leaping, lethal dance. She ducked to avoid a whining lateral blow that would have broken her jaw. Still in the crouch, she lashed out with Dragonfang and felt the God of Fear's shinbone splinter under her blow. Cul shouted in pain, and his spear – up to now acting as both weapon and defense – faltered. He took a limping pace backwards, one hand falling from the spear to grip above his knee, and Brunnhilde seized on the opening.

She feinted left, drawing him into a parry, and then struck out right. The tip of her blade tore into his belly as a long shallow slice that immediately began pouring blood, and then Sif was somehow, impossibly, stepping out of the between-space behind him. Cul didn't even know she was there until she drove her blade up beneath his ribs far enough that the tip punched out of the top of his chest.

The Serpent tried to cry out but only blood misted from his mouth. His form shifted and wavered as he strove to heal and change his skin, and the goddesses both cleaved through him again even as he collapsed into a form part Asgardian, part reptile. He made a high keening sound and opened the air to Realm-jump. Sif and Brunnhilde grabbed him – his flesh twisting and changing under their fingers – and with a scream of exhausted rage, Sif drove her sword through him and into the stone beneath.

There was a crack as the blade plunged deep into the bedrock, trapping him.

Brunnhilde's knees began to buckle. She wanted nothing more than to sink to the stone next to the trapped and twisted god. "Jump," she gasped. "Need to… jump."

Sif's face was a crimson mask. "No," she croaked. "We need to bring down the mountain."

The Valkyrie gaped at her. "Bring down the mountain?"

The warrior gestured vaguely at the high stone vault of the cavern. "Imprison him here," she added, as if she was making any sense. Dizziness assailed Brunnhilde and all she could do was stare in incomprehension.

Sif grabbed her, one hand on her shoulder and the other on her cheek, forcing her to make eye contact. "I'll do it. You just get ready to jump us, alright? As far as you can get us." She gave her a little shake. "Far away, Valkyrie, yes? *Far away.*"

Brunnhilde sucked in a slow, deep breath. She nodded, even as she wondered *how.* Sif gave her a manic, wild-eyed grin and let her go.

"This is really going to hurt," Sif muttered to herself, but shook her head when Brunnhilde instinctively reached for her.

The Valkyrie stood guard over Cul, who writhed between two or more forms, attempting to shift away from the blade pinning him to the stone.

Sif stared up into the vaulted roof of the cavern. "Alright. Ready?" she asked, and drew forth the Quellstone. It resembled nothing more than an ancient, sea-washed rock now, dull and pitted and cracked all the way through within its silver filigree cage. A bare moment's inattention away from shattering.

Brunnhilde nodded and put her hand on the nape of Sif's neck. Her palm tingled with a sudden concentration of power, and then a brilliant flash of gold light erupted from the warrior's hand and arm and exploded the cavern's arched roof. A series of deafening booms resounded and were lost within their own echoes, the sound building to a painful crescendo. The orb's power streamed from Sif in a series of gold lances, driving up into cracks above them, each smaller and weaker than the last but just enough, until the first massive blocks of stone began to fall. One, then another, then three and then all of them at once – the entire roof, the entire *mountain* – was falling.

Sif screamed as the Quellstone exploded and she collapsed, her eyes rolling back in her head and dust and flakes of stone falling from her blackened hand. Awed, Brunnhilde scooped her into her arms and Realm-jumped them away.

TWENTY-SIX
ASGARD

A bright, buttery lightness assailed Sif's eyelids, followed a heartbeat later by a wave of adrenaline-fueled terror so strong that she was on her feet and backed into a corner before she could make sense of her surroundings.

Two figures leaped to their feet at her explosion of movement, one advancing while the other jerked away.

"Stay away from me," Sif shrieked, her voice rusty and choked. The advancing figure halted and raised empty palms, then carefully stepped backwards.

The wall was the only thing keeping Sif upright and she let it take her weight without trying to show any weakness. She blinked hard, willing her eyes to focus.

"You are in Asgardia and you are safe. Brunnhilde is safe. The souls are safe." There was a long pause and then a heartfelt sigh. "It's all over, Sif."

Sif's gaze found the speaker with their first words, and though she recognized him, she did not relax. Heimdall – or a deathless warrior or Cul or maybe even Loki wearing his face – gave her a reassuring smile.

She didn't smile back. "Where is my sword?" Her heart beat in a wild, irregular rhythm, adrenaline tingling through her limbs and sparking along and within every injury her body held. There were a lot of them.

The other person began to speak, but Heimdall held up his hand. "You didn't bring it back with you from Jotunheim, but you can have mine until we can forge you a new one." Very carefully and very slowly, her brother unbuckled his sword belt and laid it on the rumpled blankets of her bed.

Sif tensed as he drew nearer and didn't relax even once he had retreated to the other side of the sunlit room, taking the other person with him. She studied them now and thought she recognized the tall, angular man as one of Asgardia's doctors. "Garth?"

The doctor nodded once, though he kept his hands raised. "Yes, Lady Sif. What Lord Heimdall says is true: you are home and safe in Asgardia, Lady Bright-Battle too. The… souls," and he gave Heimdall a quizzical look, "I cannot speak for. I am here to treat you, and that I have done. You had used up all your energy reserves and had several serious wounds. You have been here for four days."

"Four days?" Sif gasped and then fell into a coughing fit that left her weak-kneed and clutching her chest. Garth began to cross to her side, but Heimdall held him back. They watched her in worried silence as she choked and struggled to breathe. "Stay back," she managed as soon as she could form words. "Where's Brunnhilde? And what about Inge, has she been told? Is she here?"

The outburst left her breathless again. She moved cautiously towards the bed and picked up the sword. The hilt, crossguard, and scabbard were painfully familiar. Sif stared into her brother's eyes and searched for the tell-tale glitter of a soul that wasn't his. She couldn't find it.

"Well?" she demanded, and this time she unsheathed the sword and tested its weight in her palm. "Brunnhilde? Inge?"

Heimdall nodded. "Bright-Battle is here, and Inge too. Even Aragorn is in the royal stables," he added with a long-suffering sigh. "Just appeared within an hour of your arrival."

"How?" she managed. "How did we get back?"

"According to Bright-Battle, you jumped to two different locations in Jotunheim, and then to Meadowfall. Valkyrie Eira was stationed there. Brunnhilde gave her the souls you saved and then passed out. When Eira returned from Valhalla, she brought you both here."

They let her digest that in silence. It seemed reasonable. Almost against her will, she relaxed. "Let me see her. I need to see Brunnhilde."

Garth and Heimdall exchanged a wary look. Sif advanced around the bed with the sword up in guard. "Let me rephrase that. I wasn't asking."

"Little sister," Heimdall began, and Sif flinched hard, snapping the blade up until the point grazed the flesh of his throat. Sweat popped out on her brow and slicked her palms and spine, cold and unpleasant.

"Don't you dare call me that," she shouted. "You don't get to call me that. Show me your real face!"

"Hey, hey, easy now, Sif," Heimdall said, alarm writ large in the sudden tension in his shoulders. "It's me, it's Heimdall.

Your brother. I… I only call you 'little sister' when I'm worried about you. Or when I'm really proud of you. Right now, I'm both."

He talked on, recalling the first time he'd used the endearment and what Sif had done to earn it. Of course, Cul could have gleaned that from his manipulations, but even the Heimdall of her hallucinations hadn't been this warm or soothing. This genuine.

Her arms were shaking by the time he finished speaking and she made herself lower the blade. She didn't relinquish it. "Brunnhilde?" she managed.

One side of Heimdall's mouth turned up and he nodded once. "Of course; you and I can talk later. Thor would like to see you both as well, but for now, Bright-Battle is down the corridor, second door on the right."

Sif gestured them out first, and Heimdall dragged the doctor away down the corridor in the opposite direction. She watched until they had turned the corner and then put her back to the wall and slid along it, checking in both directions as she went. She reached the indicated door and heard low voices from inside: Brunnhilde and Inge. Heart in her throat and palms damp, Sif paused. Something about this whole situation felt different, felt as if it might be real, and that frightened her more than if it was a hallucination. She wasn't sure she'd survive if it turned out to be another manipulation.

The warrior took a deep breath. She had faced down gods and monsters in the last week; surely, she could face her friends. Still, her heart was in her throat as she tapped on the door. Silence fell within. And then she heard, very quietly, "It's all right, my heart. I'm here and I will check." Inge, reassuring Brunnhilde that she was safe. It unlocked another knot of tension in Sif's gut.

The door swung open. Inge stood there and she, too, bore a sword. The weapon flashed into guard when she saw Sif's naked steel. Sif jerked backwards, having to force herself not to meet the warrior blade to blade in a shatter of sparks. It was a leap of faith and if she had read this wrong, it would get her killed.

Inge's face creased into a smile so wide it was like the sun coming out, making her eyes crinkle at the edges and a dimple flash in her cheek. "Sif!" she cried with what appeared to be genuine joy. She spun in the doorway to face Brunnhilde, but Sif noted that she didn't gesture her inside, instead using her body to block the gap. If Sif wasn't who she said she was, she could run her through and there was nothing the woman could do about it. By the pinched look on the Valkyrie's face, she was aware of that same fact, but the show of trust from Inge had to be a good sign. Sif moved her sword hand deliberately behind her thigh.

"Brunnhilde my love, look, it's Sif and she's awake. Obviously." Inge gave a happy little laugh. "Are you feeling up to visitors?"

Sif peered over Inge's head and found the Valkyrie standing next to her bed. She was pale and twitchy, a look that Sif knew well. They stared into each other's eyes for a long moment, neither of them speaking.

"My brother – if it is my brother – says you got all the einherjar and we really are home. He also says your stupid winged horse is in the stables."

“Aragorn is a prince among animals, and he deserves the best of care,” Brunnhilde said with an edge to her voice. “My lover – if she is my lover – delivered the first batch of souls to Valhalla and has vowed never to let me do that to her again. Eira took the rest, and then brought us here. She didn’t bring Inge, though, and on that, too, my girlfriend has strong opinions.”

Inge turned back to Sif with an outraged expression. “If I could have, I’d have gone back to Jotunheim just to punch her in the face,” she said in an acid tone. “You have no idea how much it hurt to extricate those souls. They were actually inside me.” She gave a full-body shudder. “And the jump-sickness. Gods alive, Sif, the sickness. But you knew she was going to send me away, didn’t you?”

Bizarrely, her anger was the thing that finally convinced Sif she was home and that this was all real. A smile threatened at the corner of her mouth and Inge squawked, her annoyance intensifying. The black-haired warrior pressed her lips together. “It was for the best. Brunnhilde only had your safety in mind. I support her decision.”

Inge actually stamped her foot. “You would,” she snapped, before her gaze swiveled to Brunnhilde, who was pretending to cough to cover her mirth. “Are you laughing? At me? After all this?” She gesticulated at herself, the room, and then both Brunnhilde and Sif.

“She’s still, ah, touchy from the sickness, which, as I’ve said, my heart, is why Eira didn’t bring you directly here.” Brunnhilde looked over her head at Sif, mirth mingling with the fatigue in her eyes.

Inge wound up to start again and the Valkyrie made a

theatrical pretense at collapsing onto the bed, one hand pressed to her temple. "Let her in if you're going to shout at her, love. If she's anything like me, she'll need to sit down for it."

Sif breathed through the upswell of relief and affection and propped Heimdall's sword against the wall outside the room. Inge pretended to glare at them both, but she stepped away from the open door and retreated to the bed, sliding on to it and dragging Brunnhilde against her side. The Valkyrie was several inches taller than her, but she scrunched down to rest her head on Inge's shoulder. There were dark shadows under her eyes and her skin and lips were pale, but she moved into the embrace readily enough.

Awkwardness consumed Sif. She hovered in the doorway, fidgeting with her cuffs. "I should probably leave the two of you alone," she said abruptly. "I just wanted to see you were safe and, and here. That I'm really here."

"I've been awake since yesterday morning. We've had more than enough time to catch up," Brunnhilde said. She gestured at the chair in the room. "Please have a seat; it really is good to see you."

Something warm and strange blossomed in Sif's chest and she couldn't quite suppress a shaky exhalation. She crossed the room on trembling legs and sank gratefully into the chair. "You did so much more than me," she said as she parsed the words. "How did you wake up earlier?"

"First, that's absolutely not the case," Brunnhilde said with enough snap in her voice that it seemed like she really meant it. "Having seen you wield it, I'm staying far away from Quellstones and their backlash forever. Second, it was my

Realm-jump energy specifically that was drained and that my sisters could transfer to me once I got back to Asgard. It's part of what joins us, like our telepathic communication. That link meant I recovered faster. The rest is just healing," she added, gesturing to her entire body. Sif nodded at that: she was swathed in bandages herself.

Inge was scowling, but not enough to hide the love and relief shining in her face. "By the time I got here from Meadowfall – by the time I'd *borrowed a horse and ridden here* – there were half a dozen Choosers of the Slain just waiting to transfer their Realm-jump energy to her. Apparently once her body had enough of that, it could concentrate on resting and healing. It didn't take long after that for her to wake up."

Brunnhilde laughed and gave her an affectionate squeeze. "How do you know I hadn't been awake for a day and just didn't want to get shouted at?" she asked, ducking when Inge pretended to swipe at her.

Sif was left momentarily despondent; scores of Valkyrior had come to Brunnhilde's aid while she herself had languished unconscious. She tried to hide the thoughts, but it was clear they showed on her face, because Inge tutted and gave a little shake of her head.

"Lord Heimdall sat with you the whole time and I'm pretty sure Doctor Garth will never be the same again. Your brother was not subtle in his threats about what would happen if you did not recover," she said and then couldn't suppress the sly grin that crossed her mouth. "And I believe the God of Thunder himself took an interest in your recovery," she added, winking. "Some lingering guilt at the Quellstone's effect on you, apparently. I heard he was quite concerned."

The black-haired warrior felt a blush heat her face but raised her chin. She met their gazes squarely. "As well he should be," she said in a haughty tone that completely failed to mask her delight. "The number of times I've saved his life and he sends me, quite literally, into the Serpent's lair without giving me all the facts." She ignored their clear amusement and willed her flush to fade.

"But more importantly, how many einherjar?" she asked. "The total from the Record-Keeper. And the ones we killed in Meadowfall and the north, what about them? Are they… lost?"

The Valkyrie sobered. "Almost two hundred soul-snatched, stretching back more than a year," she said softly.

Sif was glad she was sitting down; the number was so much higher than she'd expected, high enough to punch her in the chest and steal her breath.

"But we know how to find the einherjar released when the deathless were killed," the Valkyrie added. "My sisters are performing that duty with the utmost care. We won't lose any of them, I swear."

"I believe you," Sif said as Inge murmured her own agreement. Relief flooded her. Despite everything, they'd won. She could scarcely believe it. She gripped the arms of the chair, feeling the wood digging into her palms. *I'm here. I'm here and it's real. I'm home.*

"So, you Realm-jump now?" Brunnhilde asked abruptly. "Or was that my dying brain playing tricks on me?"

Inge gasped and turned to Sif, almost bouncing the Valkyrie off the bed in her haste. "You do? How? What happened? Also," she added with an emerald glare at

Brunnhilde, "no more mentions of dying. Ever."

Sif rubbed at the back of her neck, flustered but glad of the distraction. "I don't know if I can. It was probably just sheer desperation. Cul dragged me into the between-space and somehow, I got back out. I… did do it again, but I have no idea how. The Quellstone, I thought."

The Valkyrie hummed, tapping her fingers absently on Inge's thigh. "It's more likely the orb unlocked a latent ability. Once we're both fully recovered, I can teach you. Please don't attempt it on your own – it's far too easy to get lost in there if you don't know where you intend to emerge."

Sif shivered. "I won't," she promised. "And… thank you. For everything. I wasn't the most reliable person you could have had at your side in there."

Inge opened her mouth, but Brunnhilde squeezed her leg sharply, and she closed it again. The Valkyrie stood and crossed the room, took Sif's hands and pulled her up to standing. Her grip was weaker than she was used to, but then Sif's own legs trembled for a moment and threatened to dump her back into her seat. They clung, each pretending not to notice the other wobble.

"Lady Sif the Reckless," Brunnhilde murmured with a soft curl to her mouth, "there is no one I'd rather face down gods and giants with than you. Today, tomorrow, whenever."

Sif swallowed the lump in her throat and nodded, unable to speak.

"Well," said a disapproving voice from the bed. "On the basis you both look ready to pass out, maybe not actually today, thank you very much."

The warrior laughed, but then she leaned closer. “Not today – not unless Asgard needs us,” she whispered, too low for Inge to hear.

The Valkyrie nodded and squeezed her hands. “Not unless Asgard needs us,” she promised.

Acknowledgments

Huge thanks to my agent, Harry Illingworth of DHH Literary Agency, for his ongoing support, invaluable advice and regular reminders to take a break. Thanks also to the team at Aconyte Books, particularly editors extraordinaire Lottie and Gwen, for their excellent feedback in helping me craft this tale. And to Caitlin O'Connell at Marvel, and to Max Haematinon Nigro for the gorgeous cover art.

Thanks also to all the authors of the Bunker for their cheerleading as I wrote this book, and to all the readers excited to read about fierce, heroic women accomplishing extraordinary things despite the odds.

Lastly, to my family, my friends and Mark: thank you. I love you.

About the Author

ANNA STEPHENS is the acclaimed British author of the Godblind Trilogy – an epic fantasy series somewhere on the grimdark scale, as well as a selection of novellas and short fiction. She has a second Dan black belt in Shotokan Karate and trains in sword fighting.

anna-stephens.com
twitter.com/annasmithwrites

MARVEL XAVIER'S INSTITUTE

The next generation of the X-Men strive to master their mutant powers and defend the world from evil.

WORLD EXPANDING FICTION

Do you have them all?

MARVEL CRISIS PROTOCOL

- ☐ *Target: Kree* by Stuart Moore

MARVEL HEROINES

- ☐ *Domino: Strays* by Tristan Palmgren
- ☐ *Rogue: Untouched* by Alisa Kwitney
- ☐ *Elsa Bloodstone: Bequest* by Cath Lauria
- ☐ *Outlaw: Relentless* by Tristan Palmgren

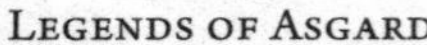

LEGENDS OF ASGARD

- ☐ *The Head of Mimir* by Richard Lee Byers
- ☐ *The Sword of Surtur* by C L Werner
- ☑ *The Serpent and the Dead* by Anna Stephens
- ☐ *The Rebels of Vanaheim* by Richard Lee Byers *(coming soon)*

MARVEL UNTOLD

- ☐ *The Harrowing of Doom* by David Annandale
- ☐ *Dark Avengers: The Patriot List* by David Guymer
- ☐ *Witches Unleashed* by Carrie Harris *(coming soon)*

XAVIER'S INSTITUTE

- ☐ *Liberty & Justice for All* by Carrie Harris
- ☐ *First Team* by Robbie MacNiven
- ☐ *Triptych* by Jaleigh Johnson
- ☐ *School of X* edited by Gwendolyn Nix *(coming soon)*

EXPLORE OUR WORLD EXPANDING FICTION

ACONYTEBOOKS.COM

@ACONYTEBOOKS

ACONYTEBOOKS.COM/NEWSLETTER